Murder Under the Marquee

MURDER UNDER THE MARQUEE

Elmo Simpson Mysteries

J.C. Kenney

TULE
PUBLISHING

Dedication

Murder under the Marquee is dedicated with much gratitude to the late great Elmore Leonard and the alive and kicking and every much as great Carl Hiaasen. Their remarkable storytelling means more to me than I can adequately put into words. Absolute legends!

CHAPTER ONE

I STARED AT the monstrosity before me. My fingers trembled. Sweat broke out on my forehead. From the deepest depths of my soul, there was no doubt it was the embodiment of evil incarnate. The fact that it was lying on a plate, inert, didn't lessen the revulsion. I had to close my eyes. My stomach churned at the horrific thought that somewhere, some insane person thought this abomination could be considered acceptable in a civilized society.

"Don't be such a drama queen, Elmo. Be a big boy and do what you have to do." Goob's words carried the ever-present, kind tone the elderly shopkeeper was known for. They carried an unmistakable touch of impatience, though.

"All right. I'm a man of my word." I opened one eye, then the other. The slice of Hawaiian pizza hadn't magically disappeared. So much for praying for a miracle.

The absolute horror of pineapple combined with ham, marinara, and mozzarella cheese mocked me as I fingered the crust. A defeated sigh escaped me. There was nothing else to be done.

I bit into the pointy end of the slice. And chewed. The thin crust was crispy. The sauce, tangy with a few chunks of tomato to give it texture. The ham was tender and smoky, the result of it being cooked at the Riptide. The pineapple…

I shuddered as my taste buds made contact with the fruit. With an effort, I fought back a gag the pineapple's cloying sweetness elicited. Then I swallowed. And took three more massive bites in rapid succession.

"Done." I hopped away from the counter as if I'd just been shocked by a jolt of electricity from a faulty outlet. Something I'd experienced from time to time. I took a big gulp of my soda pop. The gathering cheered me on my accomplishment.

Except for one. Police Chief Susan Eikenberry shook her head as she slipped her phone in her pocket. "Your debt's been paid, Simpson. However, if you ever insult Hawaiian pizza in my presence again, you will spend a night in a holding cell."

"Fair enough." We shook hands. "Any time you want, I'll be happy to prepare you a genuine Indiana-style tender-loin sandwich. With the pork properly flattened to within an inch of its life, breaded, and then deep-fried. Served on a toasty bun with lettuce, tomato, onions, a dollop of mayo, and pickles on the side."

This time, it was Susan who shuddered. It was common knowledge around the oddball town of Paradise Springs, Florida, that she loved ham and all pork products, except when it was deep fried. Which was a crime in and of itself, in my opinion.

"Let's put a pin in that." Her radio squawked and the dispatcher requested the chief respond to a call from the marina. "Duty calls. No rest for the weary."

Late June was one of the busiest times of the year for the businesses of the Springs. It was the same for the police. The sugar sand beaches and crystal-clear waters of the Gulf Coast community made it a favorite for tourists who wanted the sun and surf but also wanted to avoid the crowds of larger cities like Panama City Beach, Pensacola, and Destin.

That didn't mean the tourists were better behaved than anywhere else. From dustups in restaurants to alcohol-fueled disturbing the peace to general foolishness, the Paradise Springs police force had been running themselves ragged for weeks now.

With no letup until September.

Oh, and it was going to get worse the closer we got to the Independence Day holiday. Around my adopted hometown, July Fourth seemed to last for about ninety-six hours, not the standard twenty-four.

Like the cherry on top of a vanilla shake, the tourist crowds were bigger than ever in this little slice of heaven. A sensational murder case I'd gotten myself involved with earlier in the year had made a splash on the internet. My town was a hidden gem no more. The police, like most everyone else, were struggling to keep up with the increased crowd sizes.

With my debt paid, the dozen or so Paradise Springers who'd witnessed the affair drifted away. I returned to my stool and pushed the uneaten portion of the slice toward Goob.

"Good to see you survived." He deposited the uneaten portion into a to-go box with the grace of someone a fraction of his eighty-plus years. Or ninety-plus. Nobody in town was sure. "I think some of them in the crowd were hoping you'd upchuck. Especially the ones with their phones out. That would have gotten you a lot of looks on social media."

"Thank the stars above for that." I leaned across the counter and lowered my voice so I wouldn't be overheard. "Between you and me, I thought there was no way in the world I would lose that bet. I mean, I'm in good shape."

The man smiled, his eyes sparkling with mirth behind his pink-rimmed glasses.

"That, my friend, is why you never, ever make a bet with Little Suzi. She'll make you pay every time."

I was about to ask the man how he got away with referring to the Springs' top cop so informally when a customer walked in.

"Can you tell me where I can find Craig's Cruises?" The man, who had two teenagers in tow, was wearing a wide-brimmed hat and had a large camera bag slung over one shoulder.

Goob handed the visitor a map of the marina. "When you go back outside, turn left. It's about a ten-minute walk from here. There's a red, white, and blue sign. You can't miss it."

After the tourists left, Goob's smile turned into a frown. "Craig's Cruises. That operation's nothing but trouble. I wish they'd have picked any other place on the Gulf than here."

"You and me both."

Craig's Cruises arrived in Paradise Springs the previous

March with so much fanfare that you would have thought the operation was single-handedly saving the town from financial ruin. With six pontoon-style tour boats and another dozen Jet Skis, the company's owner, Craig Abbott, had promised good-paying jobs, environmentally friendly business practices, and never-before-seen recreational opportunities for the good citizens of and visitors to Paradise Springs.

Seemingly overnight, glossy trifold flyers touting the company's offerings were all over town. Digital billboards, one on each side of town, informed passersby where to find Craig's Cruises. The owner himself had appeared in a puff piece on the front page of the local news weekly, the *Paradise Springs Palladium.*

A lot of people were thrilled with the development, including Mayor Wil Crabtree, who never said no to a business development opportunity. Many others weren't. I, along with Goob and a lot of the group of small and independent businesses, aka the Old Guard, was among the unhappy crowd. There were a lot of reasons why I'd opposed the new venture.

Craig's Cruises was in direct competition with Paradise Springs Charters, the business owned and operated by my on-again, off-again girlfriend, Nicola Beecham. With whom I was happily back in the on-again stage.

"How's your lady friend doing?" Goob wiped down the counter with a dry cloth instead of the normal damp one. Nic's predicament had my old friend worried to distraction. He really was the godfather of the Springs' OG.

The good kind of godfather. Not the scary Marlon Brando kind.

"She doesn't want to admit it, but she's struggling. Losing Desiree was a tough blow. She's been doing the work of two people, maybe three, for months now."

Desiree LaFontaine had worked with Nic for nine years. She started out as deckhand and was promoted to first mate in 2019. Over the years, she'd become like a sister to Nic.

Within two weeks of Craig's Cruises' arrival, Desiree submitted her two-week notice and went to work as Craig's Paradise Springs chief of operations. When Desiree told Nic how much the new position paid, Nic didn't bother countering. It truly had been an offer Desiree couldn't refuse.

Since then, the punches to Nic's livelihood hadn't stopped coming. Staffing shortages and equipment trouble had been constant headaches.

"I'd imagine. Sybil was in this morning. Told me Nicola and Craig got into a row at the Magnificent Marlin last night and almost came to fisticuffs. Is she okay?"

"First I've heard of it. I'll swing by her place later."

"Well, give her my love and tell her the next time she drops by, a grouper sandwich has her name on it. My treat."

"Will do." My phone buzzed, a reminder that I had an appointment for my critter removal business in twenty minutes. It was time to get going.

I gathered my things, but as I moved for the door, Goob draped his arm over my shoulder. "Rumor has it the Sea Breeze has a new owner. Someone local." He winked. "Good luck on the new adventure."

"Um." So much for a witty denial. *Good going, dummy.* I'd been so careful. Or so I thought. Every step I'd taken toward the purchase of the Sea Breeze Resort, the largest private employer in the area, had been made with two thoughts in mind.

First, it needed to stay open. The previous owner was in jail. He was liquidating his assets to pay for his legal fees. I couldn't bear the thought of the Sea Breeze being left rudderless until new ownership took control. I had the cash to make the purchase. So, I did.

Second, I wanted to maintain my low profile. The community didn't need to know I was assuming control. All that mattered was that the new ownership was local and was committed to the resort's long-term prosperity.

"Sorry, Goob. I don't know what you're talking about." It was a better response than nothing.

My friend laughed. "Of course you don't. My lips are sealed."

As I exited the store, a disturbing thought came to me. Goob was a great guy. I'd trust him with my life. Not everybody in Paradise Springs was a kind soul like him, though. That begged the question.

If he knew about the purchase, who else did? And was there anyone among those in the know who wanted to cause trouble?

CHAPTER TWO

ONCE OUTDOORS, I came close to banging my head against the hood of my truck. I'd gone to great lengths to keep the Sea Breeze purchase quiet. Apparently, those efforts had been futile.

The reason I wanted to keep my involvement on the down-low was because I didn't want folks knowing what my financial situation was. If I could afford to buy a resort, I must have gobs of cash, right?

I'm not ashamed of how I made my fortune. It's just that I went through so much pain leaving the tech world. I'd decided long ago to hold off using that money until it could be used to make a difference in the world. I hadn't found what I was looking for until the Sea Breeze became available.

Buying the place meant a lot of people would keep their jobs. Property tax payments would continue to help fund government services. The list of benefits went on. Yes, to me, the deal was the difference maker I'd been looking for.

Despite my frustration with the news leak, I couldn't help but chuckle. We all had secrets in Paradise Springs. The challenge was how to keep them quiet. Or, more to the point, which were the ones people *really* wanted kept under wraps.

I pulled away from Goob's and I shifted my thoughts back to the work of the day. Even though I'd solved a murder here in town recently, I still had to make sure I kept the lights on.

And my good feline buddy, Oscar, fed.

On my way to the appointment, I sent a voice text to Nic asking how she was doing. Sure, it was way safer than typing out a traditional text, but it was cool, too. Like *out of an Avengers movie* cool.

I wouldn't say this in public, but I kind of wish Nic would have knocked out Craig. I never liked the guy from the moment he showed up in town. He seemed too well-dressed, too polished, too perfect, especially for the oddball haven of Paradise Springs, Florida.

A few minutes later, I arrived at the job site. A young Black man pulled up next to me on a neon pink cruiser bicycle.

"What up, boss?" Jordan Selassie dismounted, giving the bell on his handlebars a ring.

In the weeks after I figured out who murdered long-time resident Fran Cohen, service calls to my critter removal business quadrupled. Apparently, folks in the area thought it was cool to have a real-life crime fighter of sorts removing their pests.

Who was I to argue?

All the interest made it clear I was going to need help. That's where Jordan came in. The kid was smart, hardworking, and creative. He also happened to be looking for a job when I needed someone.

We crossed paths one evening at the Paradise Springs Pier, a thousand-foot-long structure to the west of town that juts from the beach out over the water into the Gulf of Mexico. He was performing a contortionist act. I dropped a couple of bills into his black top hat and raved about his act when he gave me an embarrassed smile.

"Thanks, dude. It's fun. It's not going to make me rich, but I have a good time."

His honesty made an impression. I introduced myself and asked him what his name was.

"Jordan, like the basketball player. My parents named me after him. They were huge Chicago Bulls fans back when M.J. was ruling the court. They hoped I'd grow up with some of the same mad skills he had." He let out a little laugh. "I tried my best to make them happy. But about the only athletic skill I have is my ability to turn myself into practically anything I want."

To drive home the point, he put his right arm behind his back, then lifted the left leg behind him until he grasped it with his right hand. With only his right leg for support, he lowered himself to the surface of the pier, then folded the other arm and leg in, and collapsed into the shape of a box.

I didn't know what to say at the freakish display of flexibility, so I gave him a round of applause. And dropped a five-dollar bill in the top hat. All at once, he sprung right back up to a standing position, like a jack-in-the-box, to his full height of six feet and change. With a big grin, he bowed straight from the waist all the way down until his nose touched his knees.

"Amazing. You know, I could put your unique skillset to work. If you're interested in supplementing your income, I have something in mind." I handed him one of my business cards. I kept some on me at all times because I never knew when I was going to meet somebody who needed my services. Or when I might meet somebody who'd make a good addition to Elmo's Critter Removal.

He'd called the following day and was working with me a week later. I still couldn't believe my good fortune at meeting this one-of-a-kind young man.

"What do we got going on, boss?"

"Nothing too complicated. Just need to check the traps and see if there are signs of critters trying to move in." I hauled my toolbox out of the truck and led Jordan up the concrete drive to the house.

Twenty minutes later, we'd completed a check of the building's exterior and found no sign of burrowing rodents or any other potential problems. Thanks to Jordan's eyepopping flexibility, while I was checking the outside, he conducted a thorough exam of the crawl space. It was a cramped area that would have taken me an hour to get through due to my size. With his inexplicable ability to bend in ways that deemed inhuman, Jordan squeezed through the crawl space entrance, got a look at every nook and cranny, and slithered back through the opening without breaking a sweat.

With the inspection complete, I wrote up a report while Jordan took a few minutes to chat with the homeowner. Not only did he have the ability to maneuver his arms, legs, and other parts of his body into unique positions, he was also extremely friendly. He had an easy smile and a natural gift for putting our customers at ease.

I didn't regret hiring him for a split second. Even on his first day, when he got spooked by a chipmunk who ran out of a hole. Caught completely off his guard, Jordan sprinted off into the bushes, screaming at the top of his lungs about seeing a striped panther.

I didn't tease him much about the incident, which came to be known as the Monster Squirrel from the Depths of the Earth Affair. It made for an entertaining story for him to share, though.

"What's next on the agenda, boss?" Jordan took a look at his phone. I'd ordered him a tablet for business use, but it hadn't arrived yet.

The only work we had for the rest of the day were three routine inspections. I asked Jordan to take care of them because I had other things on my plate.

"Like what?" He put a bag that contained the supplies that he'd need into a basket attached to his bike's handlebars and secured it with a couple of bungee cords.

"I want to swing by the marina. I heard there was a dustup last night at the Magnificent Marlin."

Jordan bounced up and down on his toes. "Yeah. Word is your Miss Nicola was involved."

"I heard the same thing. Figured I'd see if I can find out what happened." I shook my head as I looked at my phone. Nic hadn't responded to my text message. I'd known her for a long time. It wasn't like her losing her cool in public. I figured I'd check it out. Talk to a couple of folks. And if needed, see if I could smooth over any ruffled feathers on her behalf.

"Well, good luck to you, my dude. The Merrell sisters aren't the nicest folks if you get on their wrong side. Believe me. They were more than happy having me do my act in front of their club as long as people didn't spend too much time watching me. Once the crowds got a little too big for their liking, they turned on me. Let me know that the Stupendous Selassie was no longer welcome near their establishment."

He mounted his bicycle. "Their loss. I'm making more out on the pier, anyway."

We exchanged a fist bump and then I got into the truck. As I backed out of the driveway. I speed-dialed Nic's number. There was no answer, so I left a message. I wasn't trying to be an overly protective boyfriend. That would never fly with Nicola Beecham. I was worried about her, though.

Normally, she responded to text messages super quick since she used her phone for both business and personal use. Well, at least messages she received between the hours of seven in the morning and midnight. If you texted her outside of those hours, she might get back to you, or she might not. She told everybody never to bug her when it was past bedtime. I made that mistake once. I never tried to contact her at a late hour again.

Today was Tuesday. It was her day off. That meant she wasn't out on a cruise. I decided to pay her a visit on my way to the Magnificent Marlin. I'd be passing Nic's berth anyway, so I could stop and see if I could do anything for her.

As was typical for a Tuesday afternoon in late June, the Paradise Springs Marina was bustling with activity. All kinds of folks coming and going, especially the fishing boats. It was good to see. In recent weeks, there'd been an uptick in vandalism in and around the marina. It hadn't been anything over-the-top horrible like a ship getting blown up. Instead, there had been a lot of little things.

One boat had had their fishing nets cut. That led to a booking being canceled. Another boat had a spark plug wire unhooked. By the time the owner diagnosed the problem, the customer changed their plans and asked for a refund.

I felt bad for the victims. Like me, Nic, Goob, and my gator rancher buddy Rambo, they were small businesses. They depended on their vessels for their survival. When something happened to one of their boats, they lost money. That was bad for them. It was bad for the rest of us in the Springs, too.

When one company was hurting, we all felt it. In our hearts as well as in our pocketbooks.

I parked in the gravel lot and walked down the dock to Nic's berth. Her large charter boat bobbed up and down in the water as the waves gently rocked it. The ship was a gorgeous craft. Large enough to accommodate twenty passengers in comfort.

"Craig's operation will never be as classy as yours, Nic."

"Pardon me?" A tall, gray-haired man with round glasses stopped. He had a lyrical Irish accent that made me think of a dinner of shepherd's pie with a pint of Guinness in a cozy pub that featured a warm fireplace and music from the Chieftains. Apparently, he thought I was talking to him.

"Sorry about that, friend." I chuckled. "Just thinking out loud."

He tipped his Tilly-style cap to me and went on his way.

The next berth was where Nic's personal craft was found. Well, usually because currently it was nowhere to be seen. A little odd, but not unheard of. Its absence usually meant one of two things. That she had taken the boat to go visit her parents in Alabama. Or, she had taken it out into the Gulf, dropped anchor, and left the world behind for a bit.

I was ready to bet my lunch money on the second option. One of the things she often did when out on the water was turn off all of her communication devices except for emergency ones. She was independent, but she wasn't foolish. If she was in trouble, the maritime authorities would know. The rest of us would have to wait until she contacted us.

With that mystery solved, I made my way to the Magnificent Marlin.

As the three-story entertainment center came into view, I was thrown for a loop. Two Paradise Springs police vehicles were parked by the entrance. One was a police cruiser the uniformed officers used. The second was the SUV the police chief used. The call she received at Goob's must have brought her there. Hopefully, the police presence didn't have any connection to Nic and Craig's argument the night before.

Elmo Simpson getting paranoid again. Even if nobody was out to get me. That I knew of.

It was a little after two in the afternoon. Yet the crowd that had assembled around the entertainment center was easily ten times bigger than normal.

The reason for the crowd became clear when I got closer. There was yellow police tape strung between light poles that surrounded the establishment.

The onlookers were congregated three deep against the tape that featured the all too well-known black lettering. CRIME SCENE DO NOT CROSS. I quickened my pace to find out what had happened.

The police must have been on the scene for a while. In addition to the onlookers, Mike the Magician, Ulysses the Unicyclist, and Jerry the Juggler were on the scene. They were entertaining the crowd with their usual antics. Jerry had really stepped up his game. While he was juggling flaming torches, he was also singing opera. In Italian.

I took a good look at the building. It was a new addition to the Paradise Springs scene, having opened in May. The top floor featured a dance club full of neon lights that featured different nightly drink specials. The main bar and restaurant were located on the ground, or main, floor. There was a third floor, which was really a basement. It served as a beach bar that opened directly to the beach. A set of wooden stairs was located on one side of the building. It ran from the top floor all the way to the bottom floor, providing access right to the beach. A few feet of seagrass provided some protection from rising water levels that were the product of extreme weather.

The building was located at the eastern edge of the marina and served as kind of a dividing line between the open beach and the marina itself. On the side of the building opposite the water, a parking lot was level with the second floor of the building. The last time I visited the place, it had been running a special on beef po' boys. They had tasted pretty darn good, though not on par with the cuisine at my favorite hangout spot, the Riptide.

On the other side of the police tape, not far from me, I spotted Officer Thomas Nimoy, better known, unofficially of course, as Spock. I raised my arm and shouted hello. At my greeting, he looked up, did a double take, and then headed directly toward me.

I wasn't used to the Paradise Springs Police Department treating me like a bigwig. Then again, I had been very kind and patient with Spock while I searched for Fran Cohen's murderer. Maybe that had bought me some goodwill with him, since a lot of folks in town didn't take him seriously.

"What's going on, man?"

"Official police business, Mr. Simpson." He squared his shoulders and placed his fingers through the belt loops of his pants in an attempt to give himself the look of authority. The problem at this particular time was that his baseball cap was sitting askew on his head. It made him look more like a six-year-old kid playing Little League ball for the first time than a cop.

I gestured with my hand like I was holding the bill of a baseball cap. He must have gotten the message because he straightened his hat a moment later. Now we would get down to business.

"Yep." I kept my response short. The yellow tape was a bit of a giveaway, after all.

"Indeed." He leaned close to me and put his hand to one side of his mouth. "We have a homicide on the premises. Please don't say anything to anybody else. We don't want to cause a panic with a crowd this size."

"Is there anything I can do?" There really wasn't, but having grown up in the Midwest, I always tried to be polite and offer assistance whenever possible.

Spock gave me a long look, then scratched his chin. He flipped through a few pages in his notebook. After a couple of seconds, he put his index finger up and told me not to go anywhere. Then he walked away and disappeared from my sight around the other side of the building.

"Any info from the copper?" Ulysses pedaled by with her top hat out to collect donations. She asked the question without breaking stride. There was a QR code taped to the hat. Street performance had gone hi-tech in the Springs.

With Spock's admonition echoing in my ears, I shook my head. "No. He was just coming up to say hi. Why is beyond me. But, you know, whatever."

Ulysses let out a laugh, then spun on her unicycle and headed toward the other end of the crowd, resuming a poem she was reciting. The Paradise Springs street performers gave their audiences their money's worth. And then some.

I took a moment to check my phone. Still no word from Nic. I was becoming a little worried with her lack of response. I was certain she was out on the water, and that all was well. That didn't change the fact that a murder had been committed. At a place she'd been at the night before.

If that wasn't cause for concern, I didn't know what was. I had to put my worries aside, though, as a second later, Spock came around from behind the building. This time, the police chief was at his side.

When they got about ten feet from me, the chief gestured for me to cross under the tape. Evidently, she wanted information from me.

"Long time no see, Simpson." She gave me a quick nod. "Glad to see you're still ambulatory. I take it Officer Nimoy told you what's going on here?"

I thought the world of our police chief. I liked to think that we were friends. However, at the moment, she was all business, despite the dig. Now was not the time for a pithy retort.

I couldn't think of one, anyway. Oh, well. It was for the best.

"Yes, he did, Chief." I looked at the building and shook my head. "I'm sorry to hear what happened. How can I help?"

"You can tell me where you were last night around two A.M."

I scratched my head. The question seemed odd. Then again, it was probably a routine query for anybody the police were talking to regarding the murder.

"I was at home, asleep. Oscar and I had dinner around nine. After that, it was lights out. Around eleven, I'd say."

"Were you with anybody else?" Spock asked. "Besides your cat, that is."

"No. Nic told me she had a business dinner. I was wiped out after dealing with a call to remove a raccoon. It was a stubborn little fella. The average citizen has no idea how strong they are, I'll have you know."

"Uh-huh." The chief shook her head. "Can anybody verify your whereabouts during this time?" With her eyes hidden behind reflective sunglasses I couldn't tell what she was thinking. She didn't expect me to be the murderer, did she?

"I could give you my client's contact info. They can tell you when I left. Beyond that? I might be able to show you the time I logged on to watch TV after dinner. But you know Oscar. He doesn't have much to say when you question him."

My attempt at levity failed because the chief just pressed her lips together. She nodded toward the building. "Come with me."

Once we were alone, she took her sunglasses off. Her blue eyes stared straight into my soul. It was the kind of look that made criminals confess within seconds. I'd been on the receiving end of the look only once or twice. At times like these, you did not mess with Chief Susan Eikenberry.

"Okay, Simpson, level with me. Do you know where your girlfriend was last night between the hours of eleven and three?"

I scratched my head. "No. I already told you I was asleep. Why?"

"Desiree LaFontaine was murdered last night. A whaling harpoon was sticking out of her chest."

Yikes. That sounded gruesome.

The chief's shoulders sagged, as if the weight of the entire Florida Panhandle had fallen on her shoulders. "Evidence suggests Nicola may be involved with the murder."

CHAPTER THREE

N IC? A MURDERER? That was insane.

"What do you mean by *involved*?"

The chief removed her ball cap and wiped a line of sweat from her forehead. She looked to the left, then to the right, then bit her lip. She seemed to reach a decision after carrying on an internal debate.

"Here's the deal. Last night, at around ten, Nicola was witnessed arguing with the victim, Desiree LaFontaine, and her boss, Craig Abbott."

"Yeah, I heard about that."

"Who from?"

"Goob. He said he heard it from Sybil. From what he said, it sounded like a shouting match. Nothing more."

"Yes, it was a shouting match. But it was more than that. She threw a drink at Mr. Abbott and said some things that could be construed as threatening."

I shoved my hands in my pockets. Nic had hired Desiree when the deceased graduated from high school. Nic saw in the younger woman someone who was a kindred spirit, who shared a deep love of the sea.

Desiree had started out as a deck hand, and quickly caught on. It had been a big moment when, a few years back,

Nic promoted her to first mate. Nic even threw a party at the Riptide to celebrate the occasion.

As part of the fun, I gave them matching Leatherman multitools. When they opened the presents, they both laughed. I asked them what was so funny.

"We were actually talking about getting multitools with the company logo printed on them." Nic put her arm around Desiree. "I guess we don't have to do that now. Do we, First Mate LaFontaine?"

Desiree grinned. "Nope. We sure don't. Thanks, Elmo. This is really cool. You're a pretty decent dude, do you know that?"

Now, Desiree was dead and Nic was nowhere to be found.

A lump formed in my throat when I thought about how things had changed so drastically, and suddenly, a few months ago. Shortly after he arrived, Craig offered Desiree a position as the company's point person here in Paradise Springs. He told her he already had operations in Galveston, Texas, and Gulf Shores, Mississippi. Because of that, he couldn't spend all his time here. Which meant that she could run things the way she wanted.

He had also offered her an insane amount of money. So much, in fact, that Nic was unable to match his offer. Heck, she couldn't even come within shouting distance of it.

Nic's company was a one-boat operation. Until recently, there simply hadn't been the demand for anything more. Nic paid Desiree lots of overtime during the busy months of March through October. The rest of the year, demand dropped off. It wasn't unusual for Nic to book as few as two cruises or three per week during January. That's when Desiree would go work for Rambo. It was a shame the young woman had needed to work two jobs to get by. Such was often the case for folks who worked in towns like the Springs.

"Sorry, Chief. I understand you have a job to do. But wanting Nic for murder? Come on. Seriously?"

"I didn't want to have to do this, Simpson, but you leave me no choice." The chief pulled out her phone. She tapped on it, then turned the screen to me. It was a photograph. "Does this look familiar to you?"

The hairs on the back of my neck rose to attention. It couldn't be. But I couldn't deny what was on the screen.

"It's a multitool." I bit my tongue to keep from saying any more.

"Obviously, it's a multitool. Do you recognize it?" The chief began tapping her fingers against her thigh. It wasn't a good thing when she did that.

We both knew the multitool was familiar to me. While I couldn't be 100 percent certain, since I was looking at a photograph, it sure looked like one of the devices that I'd given to Nic and Desiree.

Was the chief implying that the multitool was the murder weapon?

"It looks like Desiree's Leatherman."

"Close. We believe this multitool may be the murder weapon. It was found in Desiree's hand."

"Didn't you say that she was found with a harpoon run

through her? How could that little thing be the murder weapon?"

"Very clever, Simpson. Just answer the question." The chief showed me another picture. "If you look closely, you can see initials etched into the tool. Can you tell me what those initials are?"

I didn't want to look. Nicola Beecham could lose her temper. And when she did, you didn't want to be the cause of her wrath. But a murderer? No way. There wasn't much choice in the matter, though. I took a close look at the picture.

"The initials are a *B* and an *N*? Or, I guess, an *N* and a *B*."

The chief put her phone back in her pocket. "I hope now you can see why we want to talk to Nicola. I'm not saying that she's guilty. I'm not saying that she's innocent."

"Then what are you saying?"

"That a woman's been murdered in my town. And it's up to me to bring the murderer to justice. Now, are you going to do your part and tell me how I can get reach Nicola?"

"This is insane. There is no way under the sun Nic had anything to do with this." I turned on my heel and started to walk away when my phone buzzed. It was a text from Nic. She was returning to the marina and wanted to know what had me so bothered.

I told her to stay on the boat. There was something important we needed to talk about.

"Okay, Chief. Nic will be docked in a few minutes." At that moment, her craft appeared from around a bend. It motored toward its berth at a leisurely pace like its captain hadn't a care in the world. Inside, I cringed. My girlfriend had no idea what she was getting into.

"There she is." I pointed to her craft. "She wouldn't be coming back if she had anything to hide. I bet my lunch money that if she had anything to do with the murder, she would have taken off and none of us would never see her again."

"Being a little dramatic, aren't we, Simpson?" Susan flipped her notebook shut and began walking toward her SUV. There was no doubt where she was headed.

I quickened my pace to catch up with her. "I'm coming with you. There's no way I'm letting you ambush Nic like this."

"Suit yourself." The chief gestured for me to get in. "You're welcome to observe. But if you say or do anything to interfere with this investigation, I'll throw your skinny Indiana backside in jail. And throw away the key."

I smiled at getting to tag along for the interview. After a moment, though, the smile faded. Susan would, in fact, lock me up if I got out of line. She hadn't done it yet, but one of these days she might make good on the threat.

A few minutes later we met Nic on the deck of her boat. She was sporting a new flame-red hair color. She'd mentioned not long ago she wanted to try something new, but I hadn't really believed she would change from her neon yellow color. She'd been rocking that shade with total style for the past three years. At least it gave me a way to break the ice without putting her right on the defensive.

"Love the color. Who did it for you?"

"Did it myself." Nic patted the back of her head with one hand and struck a pose evocative of a model from New York City. "Hiya, Susan. How's things at the good old Paradise Springs Police Department?"

"You know how it is this time of year. More people getting into trouble than me and my team can handle. Detective Jenkins, poor guy, is drowning from all the vandalism cases."

"I hear you. I've been running myself ragged these past few weeks. Trying to do the job of two since Desiree abandoned me has been tough. To what do I owe the honor of this greeting?"

I glanced at the chief. For the moment, I let discretion be the better part of valor and kept my mouth shut.

"It's about Desiree. Is there someplace we can go where we can be undisturbed?"

"Um." Nic rubbed her hands together while she took a look around the deck. Since this was her private craft, there wasn't a lot of room. One could fit a half dozen people comfortably on the main deck, but inside, the quarters were pretty cramped.

"How about we talk right here?" I opened a storage bin and removed a couple of folding chairs.

Once we were all seated, Susan opened her notebook. She cleared her throat while she clicked her pen open and closed, open and closed three or four times. The normally inscrutable Chief Susan Eikenberry seemed as nervous as somebody from the Great Plains going on their first trip out onto the Gulf of Mexico waters. A pregnant silence continued until I couldn't take it anymore.

"I've got bad news, Nic. Desiree LaFontaine. She's, well, she's dead." So much for keeping my big trap shut.

Nic covered her mouth with her hand for a moment. "Great Goddess of the Sea." Then she squeezed her eyes shut. A tear ran down her cheek.

Susan stared at me. If she hadn't been wearing her sunglasses, I was pretty sure her glare would have left me dead right there on the deck of Nic's boat. It would have been justifiable homicide. I'd made her a promise, after all.

"She was stabbed to death." The chief showed Nic the same picture she'd shown me. "Do you recognize this?"

Nic looked at the picture, then tilted her head to the side. It was a look that Oscar gave me when I told him it was too early for his dinner.

"That's my Leatherman." She dragged the response out like she was in slow motion. "Are you saying this was used to murder Desiree?"

"It was found at the scene. In the victim's hand." Susan opened her little notebook again. "Can you tell me where you were last night between midnight and three A.M.?"

"Sure." Nic blew out a long breath. "I was out on the old girl here. It had been a rough day and I needed to get away for a while. I was anchored about ten miles out into the Gulf."

"Is there anyone who can verify that?"

Nic shook her head. "I don't know if anyone saw me heading it out. Maybe I was caught on CCTV. I can check my GPS. That will show you where I was and when."

"Well, alrighty then." I rubbed my hands together, confident that Nic had answered any questions that she needed to. "I take it our business here is completed. Nic, how about I take you out to get a bite to eat? You've got to be famished after spending all night out on the water."

"Uh, not quite so fast, I'm afraid." Susan looked at the deck. "Do you have any explanation for how your multitool ended up in Desiree's hands?"

"I have no idea. A few weeks ago, someone on one of my tours asked to borrow it. I never got it back, and I've been so busy that I haven't had time to look for it."

"That's what you're going with? You let somebody borrow it. Somebody without a name."

Nic crossed her arms. I didn't blame her for getting defensive. "That's what I'm going, because it's the truth." Nic turned to me. "Elmo, I'm sure I mentioned that it was missing, didn't I?"

"I remember you asking if I'd seen it, but that was it." I averted my eyes from Nic's gaze. A sinking sensation in my gut made me feel like I just betrayed her. That was the last thing I would ever do.

I had to tell the truth, though. The past had taught me a lot of things. One of the most important ones was don't lie to the authorities. No matter how smart you think you are, eventually those lies catch up to you.

"Look, Chief, I've got to get supplies for my cruises tomorrow. Is there any way we can continue this conversation later?"

"According to witnesses, you got into an argument with Craig Abbott and the victim last night at the Magnificent Marlin. Is that true?"

"Yes. I got into a shouting match with them. That snake is doing everything he can to drive me out of business. Including stealing Desiree from me. Can you blame me for getting a little heated when they tried to pressure me into selling out to them?"

Sell her business to them? That was bombshell of massive proportions. And news to me.

"I hear you," Susan said. "The witnesses also said that you made some rather pointed comments. Threatening the lives of both Desiree and Craig. Is that true?"

Nic scratched her forehead. "I may have said some things. But it doesn't mean I was angry enough to kill either of them. I mean, come on. Desiree and I were friends."

"A minute ago, you told me that you felt that Desiree abandoned you. So how could you still be friends with her after she'd done something like that?"

I squirmed in my chair. I respected Susan. She was smart and was an excellent police officer. But to witness her giving Nic such a tough cross-examination was soul crushing.

"You know what? I'm done here." Nic opened the boarding gate and gestured for Susan and me to go through.

"Are you refusing to answer my questions?"

"I told you, Chief. I have a million and one things to do. I'm more than happy to talk to you, but I have my livelihood to think about. How about we get together and talk more tomorrow? I can meet you when I get back from the sunrise cruise."

"I'm afraid that doesn't work for me, Nicola. I'd like you to come with me to the station for some more questions. Now."

I put my hands up in a pleading fashion. "Chief— Susan—is this really necessary? You and I both know Nic is innocent. About the only thing she's guilty of is making stuffed poblano peppers that are hotter than the sidewalk in July."

The chief shrugged, unimpressed with my argument. "Help me out here, Nicola. We can do this the easy way, or we can do this the hard way. The hard way means I have to arrest you. I don't want to do that. How about you do this the easy way and come with me? In return, I'll tell everybody that you're a cooperating witness. Nothing more, nothing less."

Nic dropped her chin to her chest. It was a defeated look that I rarely saw from her. She would come back later as victor in this match, though.

"Have it your way. Elmo, meet me at the station in ninety minutes. That's all the time I can give you today, Chief."

Susan pulled a key fob from her pocket. "That works. After you."

All I could was watch, as helpless as an abandoned baby bunny I'd removed the week before, as my girlfriend was assisted into the police vehicle.

On second thought, there was one thing I could do. I made a promise.

"I'll get you out of this, Nic." Then I doubled down, like

a Las Vegas gambler, which I most definitely was *not*. This was no time to be timid, though.

"And I'm going to find out who murdered Desiree."

CHAPTER FOUR

WHAT DO YOU do when your girlfriend has been taken to the police station? Panic came to mind. As much as I wanted to, I wouldn't do that. Nor would I go to the Riptide in an ill-advised attempt to drown my nonpanicking sorrows.

Once Nic had a chance to talk to the chief about her whereabouts, she'd be cleared. The thing was, we were only days from the July Fourth holiday. The crowds around town would continue to get bigger. That meant businesses were getting busier.

Circumstances like that were normally excellent news for Nic, whose job was dependent on tourism. Maybe I was just being a Negative Norton, but being taken to the police station for questioning, and the rumors that would start circling about said trip wouldn't do her bottom line any favors. For the moment, it wasn't so much a matter of me doing what I could to prove Nic's innocence. That would eventually work itself out. What I needed to do was figure out a way to limit the damage to Nic's reputation.

I hadn't seen anybody taking photos of Nic getting into the chief's cruiser. That didn't mean they hadn't been taken, though. I couldn't discount the possibility that photos of her being accused of murdering her former coworker would start popping up all over the internet. As much as I love living in the Springs, one of the things that I didn't care for at all was its energetic rumor mill, known by locals as the Springs Signal. All I had to do was take a moment and go back to when I had first moved to town. While most of the locals were fine with me not talking about my past, a few Nosy Nathans tried to find out why I clammed up when the topic came up.

That included the reporter for the *Paradise Springs Palladium*. She paid me a visit to do a profile about the town's new resident and his unique critter removal job. It was when the conversation turned to my past that I changed the subject.

Those concerns proved to be legit the next edition of the newspaper came out. I was referred to as PARADISE SPRINGS' NEW MYSTERY MAN/WILDLIFE HERO. The *Wildlife Hero* part gave my business a lot of free publicity. That was good. The *Mystery Man* part led to lots of people coming up to me and introducing themselves at all times and places. Some of those greetings were friendly. Some were nosy. In the three days following the article's publication, I received at least seven offers to go out on dates. All the attention was unnerving. Which wasn't so good.

It took a few weeks, but eventually the interest in me waned. It helped when a paraglider crashed onto the beach. He turned out to be a drug runner carrying two kilos of narcotics. All of a sudden, nobody cared about the mundane critter removal specialist.

At the end of the day, the attention had been mostly positive. It wouldn't be the same for Nic. She couldn't afford bad publicity.

Nic had helped me out of tight spots too many times to count. It was my turn to return the favor. The quicker I got her back home and got word out that she had nothing to do with the murder, the less likely it became that she'd have bookings canceled. Or worse, have her summer helpers quitting for fear of being associated with her.

I was almost at my truck when someone shouted my name.

"Elmo, my dude." It was Clarice from the *Paradise Springs Palladium*. She pushed her pink cat-eye glasses higher up on her nose, then jogged toward me. A camera was draped around her neck, bouncing with each step she took.

"I see that you were just with Chief Eikenberry and Nicola Beecham. Do you know why Nicola got in the chief's car?"

"They're old friends. I think they just wanted to go get a coffee to get out of the heat." I glanced up at the sky. Clouds were beginning to form to the west. In another couple of hours, we'd be doused with our Florida Panhandle daily thundershower.

The ominous thunderheads seemed fitting for the situation. Especially because the last thing Nic needed was having her name splashed all over the home page of the *Palladium*'s website.

"Now, now. You wouldn't want to be accused of concealing anything and hampering my job of reporting the news, now, would you?" She clicked a pen in her hand. It was a shade of lavender that matched her polo shirt.

"Come on, Clarice." I massaged my head. A migraine was beginning to bore its way into my skull. "I know you have a job to do. And I know you're here about the murder."

"Very good. I'm glad we're on the same page. What can you tell me about the conversation the chief and Ms. Beecham just had?"

Clarice Sterling wasn't a friend, but she seemed decent enough. Plus, she'd never blindsided me like her predecessor had.

She'd spent her entire forty-career career working for a newspaper on the West Coast. She'd even won awards for her investigative reporting. Like so many people in the traditional news-gathering industry, though, a few years ago, she lost her job due to cutbacks.

With no prospects, she bought the site and moved to the Springs when the *Palladium*'s previous owner decided to retire and put it up for sale. Clarice covered the news. Her husband ran the business end of the operation, which included advertising and maintaining their website. The third member of their operation was high school student who gathered information on local sports, performing arts, and other activities of interest to younger folks in the area.

The Old Guard crowd of folks like me, Nic, and other independent businesspeople and long-term residents didn't pay much attention to the *Palladium*. The Springs Signal, was a reliable enough source of information.

The roots of the Springs Signal went all the way back to

1858, when a traveling salesperson came to town with a harebrained scheme to provide communication services via smoke signal. He built three twenty-foot-tall wooden towers. All went well with the venture for a week. Then one tower's signal operator managed to catch the structure on fire by using too much grass to start his signal blaze.

Things went from bad to worse when a few weeks later, when one of the other towers was struck by lightning and burned to the ground. With only one tower left, thus nobody to communicate with, the entrepreneur packed his things and headed west swearing he'd never set foot in Florida again. The remaining structure collapsed into a pile of rubble one night. Legend said that four hooded figures were seen near the scene around the time of the disintegration. One of the figures was dressed in all green, another in red, the third in blue, and the final one in yellow. Their identities were a mystery to this day.

Tourists, on the other hand, loved the *Palladium*. It was a great way for businesses to advertise dining, nightclubbing, excursions, and all the other typical vacation fare.

I didn't need to advertise in the *Palladium* since Elmo's Critter Removal kept me as busy as I wanted. Out of a sense of civic duty, and at the urging of Wendell Banderas and Rambo, I started putting an ad in the *Palladium* twice a year. It was good PR, didn't cost an arm and a leg, and it kept me on Clarice's good side.

The woman did have influence in the area, after all.

After giving the issue some thought, I decided cooperating was better than blowing her off. She'd find out what was going on soon enough. I might as well put a Nic-friendly spin on the situation.

"Here's what I know. Nic got into an argument with Desiree and Craig last night. Afterward, she spent the night out on the water. Her GPS will confirm that, by the way. The chief wanted to talk to her about the argument."

Clarice scribbled away furiously in a notebook. "Did you participate in that conversation?"

"A little. The chief asked me if I knew where Nic was. That got the whole thing started."

"Do you know if Nicola Beecham is a suspect in the murder of Desiree LaFontaine?"

"I know for a fact that she isn't. The reason she and the chief took off together was because they didn't want to be out in the sun while they talked."

She tapped on her notebook. "Some people have suggested that the police possess evidence that links Nicola directly to the murder victim. Would you care to comment on that?"

I shook my head. Clarice was just trying to do her job. I had a job to do, too, though. And that was to help my girlfriend.

"I'd rather not comment on what other people may have told you. Nic is giving the chief key information that will help with the investigation and she'll be at work early tomorrow morning, ready to give folks cruises of the lovely Florida Gulf Coast."

"Is there anything else you'd like to say? Anything off the record, perhaps?" She closed her notebook and winked at me. Nobody had winked at me since Daisy Fletcher when we were first-year students in college. She later claimed she hadn't winked. She'd gotten dust in her eye. "You know, just between you and me."

There was no way I was going to fall into the trap of giving an off-the-record quote. I shook my head once again. "Sorry, my friend. That is truly all I know about the situation. I hope the murderer is caught quickly. And I hope Desiree's family gets the justice they deserve."

Clarice pushed her glasses up her nose, then thanked me for my time. I told her if I heard anything from Nic about the case, I'd let her know.

She gave me a little smile, then went on her way. I headed toward the crowd. I wanted to see what I could find out before picking up Nic.

Nicola Beecham could wield a sharp tongue. But she had a heart of gold. It made no sense that she'd murder her old friend and crewmate.

That was the crux of my conundrum. In Paradise Springs, Florida, things that didn't make sense were every bit as common as things that did.

CHAPTER FIVE

I HAD ABOUT an hour before I needed to head for the police station. The legendary Jim Rockford from *The Rockford Files* could probably solve this mystery by dinnertime. He was a real private investigator, though. Well, at least as far as fictional characters go. His gold Pontiac Firebird was a million times cooler than my truck, too. I preferred a more methodical approach to my sleuthing. One that involved fewer car chases and punches to the jaw.

Rambo and Nic both called it being a slowpoke.

Whatever. Despite their friendly ribbing, I had no interest in abandoning my measure-twice-cut-once approach to completing tasks. Even under my current time crunch.

So, I did a little compromising.

On my stroll back to the Magnificent Marlin, I put together a to-do list in my head. First thing, I let Jordan know I was delayed and needed him to cover anything that came up in the next few hours and to use a rideshare if there was something that took him someplace outside reasonable bicycling distance. He responded with two thumbs-up emojis.

And no questions.

He was either oblivious to the Springs Signal or he knew

how to exercise discretion. Which was about the only exercise the kid needed. He had the metabolism of a Tour de France bike racer. One time, we stopped at the Riptide for lunch. He ate a whole chicken and a rack of ribs, plus the sides, and was complaining two hours later that he was hungry. Oh, to be young again.

With work taken care of, I waded back into the crowd outside the Marlin. A white SUV was pulling away from the building. The words MEDICAL EXAMINER were spelled out in blue lettering on the vehicle's doors. It didn't take a genius to figure out who the passenger was.

A tiny woman sitting on a Vespa scooter caught my attention. She was wearing a rainbow print sundress and sporting wraparound sunglasses that hid half of her face. With my hands in my pockets, I sidled up to her.

"Hey there, Sybil. Awful news, huh?"

"Two days ago, I had a vision of Miss Desiree's untimely passing. I didn't want to believe it, so I ignored it. When I heard the news, I had to come see it for myself."

"Ah, seeing is believing, eh?" I stifled a chuckle at the joke. Sybil the Seer was Paradise Springs' preeminent fortune teller, medium, and psychic. It said so on her website. She was also the Springs' only fortune teller, medium, and psychic, but it was best not to quibble with the woman about such things.

Especially when she was astride her scooter. The vehicle not only got Sybil around town, but it also served as a weapon. When she became angry with someone, she tried to run them over with it. I'd been on the receiving end of one of those confrontations and still had a tiny lump on the back of my head from it.

The laughter died on my lips when Sybil turned the scooter's engine on. Message received.

"I don't suppose the spirits told you who the murderer is?" I kept my tone respectful this time.

"No. Which is frustrating." She pushed her shades farther up her nose. "Such is the way of those beyond the veil. I hope you're as successful with this investigation as you were last time around. If you need guidance, feel free to schedule an appointment. I'll give you a 5 percent discount."

She donned her helmet, which featured a hot pink mohawk on the crown, and puttered away. Before she got too far away, she put up her hand. Whether it was to wave goodbye or flip me the bird, I wasn't sure. With Sybil the Seer, it could have been either.

I took a step, then stopped. How did she know I was going to conduct my own investigation? It had to be a guess. Nothing more. There was no way for her to know my thoughts.

Was there?

Following that train of thought led to one place. Madness. My life was complicated enough at the moment. No need to invite lunacy into the conversation. Instead, I shook my head and made a beeline for Spock, who was standing by his cruiser.

"Hey, Officer Nimoy." With as much casual effort as I could muster, I leaned against the driver's-side door of his vehicle. "I'm about to head out. Thought I'd check in with you before I left. In case, you know, there's anything you need from me. Spare you the hassle of having to track me down."

Holy cow, I'm rambling. Get it together, Simpson. I clamped my mouth shut and smiled. And crossed my fingers that my facial features looked more like a friendly gesture than someone who was experiencing intestinal distress.

"Not at this time, Elmo." Apparently, we were back on a first-name basis without anyone else within earshot. "I assume you were there when the chief interrogated Ms. Beecham?"

My hands balled into fists. I closed my eyes for a moment and uncurled them. The intense reaction surprised me. I was going to have to be on my guard. Apparently, I was sensitive about Nic being associated with a murder. Shocker.

Someday, I'll tell her about this. In my mind, I envisioned her putting her arms around me and giving me a big kiss to show appreciation for my intense desire to defend her. It was like I was Ralphie from *A Christmas Story* daydreaming about life with his precious Daisy Red Rider BB gun.

A guy could dream, right?

Then reality returned. I rubbed the sleeves of my shirt.

"It wasn't an interrogation, man. It was a conversation. The chief asked Nic a few questions and Nic answered them. They agreed to finish the chat at the station, out of sight of prying eyes and ears."

He took a notebook from his pocket and dropped it twice before finally wrangling it open. It was like sometimes the guy's brain didn't communicate well with his hands.

"That's very interesting." He scribbled something down. "Why did the chief want to talk to her at the station?"

"You'd have to ask her." I wasn't going to take the bait Spock was dangling in front me. And I sure as heck wasn't going to say something that could come back on Nic. All too often, I'd say something seemingly innocuous and then have it taken completely out of context.

It wasn't going to happen here.

Instead, I went on offense. "Are y'all sure the multitool's the murder weapon?"

"It was found in the victim's hand. There was a stab wound to her armpit. She bled out from there. It appears an artery was severed. The harpoon was probably an attempt to throw us off."

"So, you're not sure."

Spock furrowed his eyebrows. "No. Wait, yes. Well, it seems pretty obvious. A weapon with blood on it was found at the scene of the crime. One that may have cut the artery."

Credit where credit was due, the man had made strides in his career. Not so long ago, he would have crumbled after a question or two, gotten in his cruiser, and left. Now, he was defending himself.

I was proud of him. He might be easy to make fun of, but he was trying to do a tough job to the best of his somewhat limited ability. There was hope for Spock, after all. I wasn't going to let him off the hook just yet, though.

"Sounds like you're going to have to wait for the medical examiner to make an official call. I mean, at this point, who knows? Maybe someone slipped rat poison into her drink or injected her with something and the cut to the arm is a cover."

"Sure, those are all possibilities." Spock tugged at the collar of his shirt. The humidity was getting so oppressive his shirt was sticking to his skin.

"Which means you shouldn't jump to any conclusions. That's what a good detective would say and do, right?"

"I guess so." He dropped his chin to his chest. "Shouldn't be a surprise you're telling me I won't be a good detective. Everyone else is saying the same thing. My ears work, you know."

My heart went out to the guy. All he wanted to do was be a cop. Granted, he wasn't very good at it, but he knew the law and he wanted to help people. And he was getting better at his job.

Even if it was at a snail's pace.

"I never said that. Just be careful of what you say. You want to make sure you can back up everything with evidence. That way, you won't have to correct yourself down the road. That'll save the chief headaches. We all want that, right?"

"Yeah, I guess." He gave me a half smile.

"That's the lad." I gave him a friendly punch to the shoulder. "Oops. Sorry about that. I know people aren't supposed to touch you when you're on duty."

"I'll let it slide. This time." A smile grew from one ear to the other. I got the feeling he hadn't been treated with respect while on duty very often. If ever. It was good to see him happy. Even if it did reveal a number of teeth in serious need of a visit with an orthodontist.

"Great. Thank you. See you around." I gave him a little salute.

"Remember, if you see something, say something. You know how to reach me." He tipped his hat before he drove off.

As I made my way to the truck, I kept my eyes peeled. The crowd around the Magnificent Marlin had dwindled to a mere dozen or so hangers-on. One of those was Drunk Paul, who was probably just waiting for the bar to open.

I approached him. He stood astride his battered bicycle with his arms crossed and eyes closed, humming a tune. He had quite the melodic voice and often took in a decent amount of cash on karaoke night at the Shark's Fin, a popular hangout among the local crowd.

"Hey, Paul. How's it going?"

He turned to me. His eyes were as clear as a Gulf Coast sunrise. Despite the unkind nickname given to him, the man didn't have a problem with alcohol. Yes, the guy could drink. A lot. His real problem was being stuck on disability due to back and head injuries suffered while working at a construction site.

"Could be better. Could be worse. You know how it is."

"That I do. You wouldn't have happened to be here last night, would you?"

"What do you mean?" He stiffened, whether it was due to a perceived insinuation about his drinking or something about the murder, it was impossible to tell. "I don't know anything about Desiree's murder, if that's what you're asking."

"Relax, dude. I just thought—"

"That's what you get for thinking, Elmo." He slipped a pair of Wayfarers on. "I gotta go."

He pedaled away so fast, you'd have thought he was being chased by a ghost. I didn't know Paul well. I did know one thing, though. People with nothing to hide didn't get defensive when asked where they were the night someone was murdered.

That made Drunk Paul murder suspect number one.

CHAPTER SIX

I WAS HANGING out in the lobby of the police station, waiting for Nic, when my phone buzzed. It was a text from Gretchen Cooper, the concierge at the Sea Breeze Resort. She was also a buddy.

"Not an emergency, I hope." It was Nic. I'd been so busy reading and then responding to the message, I hadn't heard her approach.

"Nope." I stood. "Just Gretchen, confirming our appointment later today."

"Well, I hope your chat goes better than the one I just had." Nic filled me in on her conversation with the chief while we walked to my truck. The interview hadn't been combative. It hadn't been friendly, either.

"Susan can't seriously think you murdered Desiree, can she?" I held the passenger-side door open for Nic. Chivalry wasn't dead with Elmo Simpson on the scene. "What could you possibly have to gain from taking her life?"

"Revenge." Nic closed the door. With a reply like that, I practically sprinted to the other side of the truck to continue the conversation as quickly as possible.

"Oh, come on. Yes, quitting without giving you notice was a total jerk move. And, yes, you've been shorthanded ever since because she kept poaching your employees. And, yes, since you're shorthanded, you've been running yourself ragged. And at the same time, you can't schedule more cruises to meet the demand."

She leaned back against the head rest and blew out a long breath. It was the most defeated sound my girlfriend had ever made in my presence. And I'd annoyed and disappointed her plenty of times in the past.

"Anything else? With a list that long, I might as well go back in and sign up for the firing squad."

That stopped me cold. "Do they really do that here?"

"No, you blockhead." She slapped me on the arm. "It was a metaphor."

"Good. I mean, I'm glad you weren't being serious. And that they don't do that here."

She gave me a narrowed-eyed look that seemed to say if she had a gun, she'd use it to shut me up.

"Can we go now?"

I kept quiet until we were out of the parking lot. A while lasted two minutes. Sometimes, I couldn't help myself.

"My point back there was, bumping off Desiree wouldn't make any of those things better. If you were going to murder someone out of revenge, Craig would make more sense." I took a breath. "Though, if you wanted Craig gone, I bet Rambo and Seven could make sure his body's never found."

Nic stared out the passenger-side window. After a few moments, her shoulders began to shake, followed by a laugh. "God, you can be such a goober at times. You're right, though."

"If inarticulate."

"True. This whole thing is blowing my mind. Desiree and I were friends. To have her life taken is horrifying. That's bad enough. But to have Susan put me under a cloud of suspicion really takes the wind out of my sails, you know?"

"I'm sorry." I gave her hand a reassuring squeeze.

"Thank you. And to have this go down right now, at the height of the busy season, makes everything worse." Her text alert tone went off. "Great Goddess of the Sea. Just had a party of four cancel for tomorrow. Flipping fabulous."

"How can I help?"

"Are you being serious now?" Nick looked at me with tears in her eyes. It made my heart break.

"Totally." To drive home the point, pardon the pun, I made a quick lane change and drove us to the store where Nic got her cruise supplies. "Give me a list of what you need, and I'll get it. You can hang out here in the truck or go for a walk or even come in with me if you want. When we're done here I'll drop you off at your boat and load the supplies on the cruise ship."

"In that case." She grabbed a pen and a piece of paper from my glove box and jotted down a list of things she needed. The final item was a bottle of rum. "Here you go. That last one is for me. For tonight."

For a moment I thought she was kidding. After all, she didn't mention how I was supposed to pay for the materials. But, being the good boyfriend, I took the list with a smile and got out.

Nic hollered at me to stop when I'd only gotten fifteen

MURDER UNDER THE MARQUEE

feet from the truck. She jogged toward me with something in her hand. It was a credit card.

"Can't in good conscience ask you to pay for my supplies, can I?" She slipped the card into my back pocket. "I'll be honest. I thought you were going to suggest something crazy like trying to figure out who murdered Desiree. This is much more practical and, if I may say so, useful."

"Yeah." I gave her a slow nod. "That's totally what I was talking about. Absolutely. Nothing more. I'm sure the police will get this solved in no time."

I hated fibbing to Nic. It was totally uncool and would probably undermine her trust in me. Or, to be more accurate, undermine her trust in my judgment. I could live with that, though. What mattered most was for me to do all I could to get her out of the pickle she was in.

An hour later, I emerged from the store with a shopping cart full of groceries. Nic was nowhere to be seen, so I loaded up the truck and sent her a text that I was finished. Two seconds later, she appeared from behind a Sabal Palm.

"Operation resupply Nic's boat is complete." I gave her the credit card and the receipt. "Any place else we need to go before I drop you off at your place?"

"Nope." She batted her long eyelashes at me as she got in the truck. "There's something you can do for me when we get to my boat, though. Something that will be super helpful and for which I will be eternally grateful."

I will freely admit that I'm not the suavest dude on Earth. But when I was on the receiving end of a line like Nic had just served up, there was no way I was saying no. With a grin, I started the engine.

"My pleasure."

Little did I know that what Nic wanted me for and what I was *hoping* Nic wanted me for were two completely different things. After dropping off the supplies on the cruise ship, I returned to her personal craft. I'd just put a case of bottled water in a cooler when she told me what she wanted.

"Really?" I wiped a bead of sweat from my forehead. "That's it? That'll take me, like, ten minutes, tops."

"Good. This is one time when I'm happy to have you finish early." She kissed me on the cheek. "Here's a chance to impress me with your big tech brain. I'll be in the galley making dinner."

I sulked all the way to the bridge, grumbling under my breath so Nic wouldn't hear my complaints. She wanted me to download the ship's GPS records for the last twenty-four hours. Nothing more.

My overactive imagination had let me down again.

I turned on the ship's navigation controls. While the system booted up, I rummaged through my tool bag. Out of habit from my days working in the tech world, I always carried a blank SD card and an empty flash drive. I inserted the card into a port on the side of the ship's GPS unit.

After keying in a few commands, a copy of all navigation information from the previous day was ready for download. I took a seat in the command chair and looked at the ocean while the data transferred. It was a breathtaking view, with impossibly tall thunderheads intermingling with a sky so blue a lump formed in my throat. No wonder Nic insisted that she'd never trade her life on the water for a home on land.

At the moment, I couldn't blame her.

In the galley, Nic was putting the finishing touches on BLT sandwiches.

"Here you go." I gave her the card.

"You are the best." She gave me a long kiss on the lips that left my heart racing. Her kisses tended to do that to me. "Susan's going pick this up tonight. She said it'll help prove my innocence. How about that?"

It had been silly of me to be annoyed at Nic for playing games with me. All that should have mattered to me was how to help her prove her innocence, not anything...else. Evidently, I'd helped do just that. I was missing something, though.

"All this proves is that the boat was out on the water. It doesn't confirm whether you were on it or not. No offense."

"None taken." She grabbed a bag of barbeque potato chips and pointed at the sandwiches. "I offered to give the data to Susan. After all, with nothing to hide, might as well be cooperative, right? As to your issue, I put her in contact with the marina's head of security to get CCTV footage from last night. The video will show when I left the marina and when I returned."

"Which is great." We got seated at the little foldout table in the galley. "What if someone claims you parked the boat, came back to shore to commit the deed, then returned here?"

"You have a devious mind." She bit into her sandwich. Her brown eyes sparkled. Now that she was home, apparently things weren't so bleak. "The GPS will show I was anchored too far out to swim to shore. And my lifeboat is still in storage. Uninflated. Go ahead. Check if you want."

There was no need. If Nic said the lifeboat was rolled up in its storage compartment, that was good enough for me.

"This is great. Where do you go from here?"

"Susan will look at the lifeboat when she's here. The marina won't make the video available until they get a subpoena. Covering their backsides, I guess."

"That's not so bad." I lifted my water bottle to her. "Then you're home free, right?"

She rolled her eyes. "I wish. There's still the question of how my multitool ended up in Desiree's hands. To that, I have no answer."

"Which is why I'm going to find out what happened to it. And that, my lady, will put you in the clear once and for all."

"And after that?" She raised her eyebrows. The woman could see right through me.

"Well." I cleared my throat. "I'm 100 percent confident the Paradise Springs PD will put every effort into finding Desiree's murderer."

"As am I. A murder investigation can take time, though."

"And the longer it takes, the longer a proverbial black cloud will hang over you. Even after you've been cleared."

"I'm glad we're on the same page." She rubbed her hands on her shorts as she let out a long breath. "You have thoughts on how to catch the murderer quicker?"

"As a matter of fact, I do." I rubbed my chin with my

thumb and forefinger, enjoying our back and forth. Especially since we were in agreement on the issue. "I know a guy. Simpson's his name. Rumor has it that he'd do almost anything for you. He's got a little experience investigating murders. He'll be happy to do some snooping."

"Sounds like my kind of guy. Does he know it could be dangerous?"

"Some people would say that danger is his middle name."

She snorted. "Those people need to have their heads examined. Nonetheless, does Danger Guy Simpson understand I won't be able to work with him like last time?"

"All the more reason for him to get to work ASAP."

"I can't argue with that." She took my hand. "Seriously, though. Promise me you'll be careful. You getting yourself killed won't help things."

"Deal. Getting killed is not on my agenda anytime soon."

We finished our meal with a sense of shared relief. Nic thanked me for all my help so far. I responded that it was my absolute pleasure. We were a team, after all. Maybe even a real-life version of Shawn Spencer and Burton Guster from *Psych*.

It didn't take a private eye to figure out who was the goofball Shawn and who was the grown-up Gus in this arrangement. Nic would always be the more responsible one. If I was the flaky one, so be it. It seemed to work for Shawn. Maybe it could work for me, too.

So, it was time to get to work.

The question was where to start. As I disembarked from Nic's ship, I snapped my fingers. I knew the perfect place to begin my search.

CHAPTER SEVEN

ONE OF THE problems I faced as an amateur sleuth was that I still had day job to deal with. That included research for my super-secret purchase of the Sea Breeze.

Which, based on Goob's comments, was not so super-secret, after all.

Still, the deal wasn't done until I signed on the dotted line. That hadn't happened yet. I wasn't going to turn my back on my town. I needed the inside scoop on the resort, though.

That's where my old friend Gretchen came into the picture.

"Tickle Me Elmo, what is up?" She came from around her desk stationed at the edge of the Sea Breeze's lobby and gave me a high five. "Does Nicola know we're seeing each other?"

Her high-pitched laugh grated on my nerves. It was one of the reasons I broke up with her. We'd only gone out a few times, though, and went our separate ways on friendly terms. The good old *It's not you, it's me* excuse had worked.

"She does. Nic was the one who suggested it."

"In that case." Gretchen wrapped her arms around me and squeezed as tightly as she could. "I can't thank you enough for what you're doing. You're a prince."

I stepped back from the hug, needing a moment to recover from the viselike squeeze she'd put on me.

"Nothing's finalized yet, so hold off on the compliments for now. Is there someplace we can talk?"

"I've got a conference room that the sales team uses reserved." She grabbed me by the hand and practically pulled me down a hall. "Come on. I can't wait to get you alone."

She laughed again. Her bubbly mood was a welcome change from the negativity and stress I'd been dealing with throughout the day. That was one of the things about her. She was one of those folks who was always in a good mood. I had no idea how she managed it, but it was genuine. I had to tip my hat to her.

In the conference room, she poured a glass of water for each of us and raised hers. "To the new owner of the Sea Breeze Resort."

We clinked glasses. If the warm welcome had come from anyone else, I would have been on my guard. Gretchen didn't have anything up her sleeve. Her only motivation for agreeing to meet with me was to do her part to keep the resort open for business.

"So, what do you want to know?" She opened an app on her phone. "I jotted down a few things. Occupancy rates, vacant positions, customer complaints, and some others."

She was like a student on the first day of school eager to impress her teacher. I appreciated her preparation. The woman was the consummate professional. That's not what I was after, though. I wanted more esoteric information.

"Gretchen, I don't want numbers. I want to know what you think about this place. What's good? What's bad? If you were in charge, what would you keep? What would you change? Stuff like that."

She blinked. "Um, okay, let me think. Mr. Raines was nice enough but only ever cared about the bottom line."

If the purchase went through, I planned on taking a completely different approach. Paradise Springs was my hometown. The people who worked and lived here were my neighbors. The last thing I wanted to do was screw anybody over.

I wanted to make the situation better. Kind of like how I wanted to fix the predicament Nic was in. First things first, though.

After a few moments of silence, Gretchen tapped the tabletop with her fingertip. "You know what? It would be nice if the next owner was more transparent about the resort's financial condition. Whenever someone asked if we were doing okay financially, or if there were things we could do to make sure we stayed competitive with other resorts, Mr. Raines always said that information was confidential. All we needed to do was keep doing our jobs and everything would be fine."

I barked out a laugh. "Sorry, Gretchen. I'm not laughing at you. Of course he wanted the financials kept under wraps. I've seen them. They're a mess. We're probably going to find out this place is losing cash on aboveboard operations. It appears Roger was using the resort to launder money."

She put her hand over her heart. I think I scared the poor

woman out of her wits.

"Whenever someone says things like that, it's always followed by cutting services and announcing layoffs. Are you going to do that?"

"Not by a long shot. I'm not doing this to make any money."

"That's a relief." She sat back in her chair. "Mr. Raines kept the resort's financials under pretty tight wraps. He always said that it was his responsibility. Are you going to do the same thing? You know, with your critter removal business?"

I had to give Gretchen credit. She knew how to get to the crux of an issue. People around town often saw the bubbly woman at the concierge desk and failed to give her any more thought. That was their mistake. She was smart. She also loved her job. As a Paradise Springs native, she was proud of our little slice of the Emerald Coast and wanted others to enjoy it as much as she did.

Her brains and enthusiasm made her a perfect candidate for a task I had in mind.

Before making my proposition, we talked about the resort for a while. Gretchen knew the customer service part of the operation inside and out. Not surprising, since she'd worked at the resort for as long as I'd known her. She also had a solid grasp of the operations end of things, even recommending we provide higher quality toilet paper in the rental units and start using LED light bulbs.

When I'd heard enough, gave her two thumbs-up. "This is exactly what I needed. I appreciate it. Now, I need to be straight with you. I'm hoping to be pretty hands-off and leave the operations to folks who know this place a lot better than me. That means I'm going to need someone to oversee day-to-day things as chief of operations. I want you to be that person. What do you say?"

"Really?" She clicked her tongue a few times, then pushed a few strands of her brown hair behind an ear. "I'm in. On one condition."

I didn't want to get into a negotiation, but I'd brought it up. It was time to reap what I'd sown. "Name it."

"We always had a fireworks show on July Fourth. With things up in the air, there are no plans for it. You give us the go-ahead on that, and I'll do it."

That's all? No mention of salary or time off? I'd been right about Gretchen. She wanted the resort to succeed as much as I did. I extended my hand.

"Do it. Send me the bill."

We shook hands, then Gretchen gave me another hug. The woman was a hugger. I wasn't. With the exception of Nic and my mom. It was something I was going to have to get used to. There were worse things I'd have to adjust to.

I put my index finger up. "By the way, I was chatting with Goob earlier. He knows I'm buying the resort. I really want to keep that under wraps for as long as possible *Especially with a murderer to catch.* Any idea how he found out?"

"No." Her cheeks pinked up. "I can do some tactful asking around if you want."

She was lying to me. My heart sank. Gretchen had always been honest and forthright. That was a rarity in the

Springs. The question was why? If she'd accidentally let something slip, it wasn't the end of the world. My request for anonymity was just that, a request.

What was done was done. I told her to go ahead and ask around. Since I was her boss now, it couldn't hurt to see how she responded to a problem.

Her denial raised another issue, though. Had she lied to me about anything else? Sure, I wasn't in a trusting mood, given my promise to Nic. I couldn't help wonder, though.

Could I trust Gretchen? Were there other secrets she was hiding from me? I'd have to give the questions some serious thought. In the meantime, I'd act normal. Or as normal as I was capable of acting.

She walked me out of the resort. The storm had blown through during our meeting. Like most summer rains in my neck of the woods, it had moved on at a breakneck pace. Everything in sight was dripping wet. A noticeable stream of water ran down a drain in the resort's parking lot. The clouds had moved on, too, though. Once again, the sun was out amid a clear blue sky.

The humidity was at about a thousand percent, but what could I do? Such was the life in my hometown.

Gretchen and I agreed to keep the details of our conversation between us. If anyone asked, we'd tell them it was a discussion about the fireworks show. Feeling pretty good with myself, I was about to head for my truck when she put a hand on my elbow.

"Are you going to look into Desiree's murder? You know, like you did back in February? If you are, be sure to check out Bobby Darrin."

My mom was a fan of the singer Bobby Darrin. But he'd been dead since before I was born. Gretchen couldn't be referring to him. Then again, this was Paradise Springs.

She must have seen the confused look on my face because she laughed. "Not the teen idol, you goombah. Bobby Darrin was Desiree's ex-boyfriend. Their relationship put the storm in stormy."

"I'll check him out. Thanks for the tip."

"No problem. Just be careful. He knows some rough people. I don't want to see you get hurt, boss-to-be."

"That makes two of us."

On my way home, I made a note to ask around about this Bobby Darrin fellow. Someone had used a knife to murder Desiree. One of singer Bobby Darrin's biggest hits was "Mack the Knife."

It had to be a coincidence. Didn't it?

CHAPTER EIGHT

T HE DAY HAD been one for the ages. I don't think I was ready to write an epic poem about it, though. A late dinner was enough. I gave Oscar a report while I grilled chicken on the patio. I finished my recount wondering aloud who, besides this Bobby Darrin character and Drunk Paul, would want Desiree dead.

Oscar ignored the question and attacked his shredded chicken with the gusto of an animal who hadn't seen food in weeks. I was pretty sure if I asked him how long it had been since he'd eaten, he would have meowed, *Not a single morsel of food has passed my tongue since the last full moon. I barely have the strength to eat this meal. Give me more. Right now.*

In reality, it had been a few hours.

Such was the mind of my cat. Though what he did all day to create such an appetite was beyond me. It seemed that he spent most of his time lounging in the sun on the front step or napping in one of the chairs on the patio.

A tough gig, indeed, for my twelve-year-old buddy.

"In other news, looks like I've got another side gig. I mean, on top of the Sea Breeze one. Does that mean it's the side gig of my side gig?"

Oscar lifted his head long enough to pin his ears back.

"Got it. Focus, Elmo. Nic's old first mate, Desiree, was found murdered today. You met her a few times and liked her. I liked her, too. Anyway, at first the cops thought Nic did it."

He stopped on his way to his water fountain and let out a low growl. While he liked me, he adored Nic. I couldn't blame him.

"My thoughts exactly. And, yes, I know the chief's your buddy, too, and she can handle the case without my help, but I'm gonna investigate anyway. I promised Nic I would. Sort of."

Sort of was the key phrase.

One of the challenges in my relationship with Nic had been her frustration with my unwillingness or inability to see something difficult all the way through to the end. I totally got it. After my tech career fell apart, I decided I wanted as few complications in my life as possible. That was one of the reasons Paradise Springs became my new home. There was an unwritten rule in the community that someone's past was that person's story to tell. And nobody else's. Prying was frowned upon. Here, I was able to leave my former life in the past and spend my days removing critters from spots they didn't need to be and my nights hanging out with Oscar.

Things changed a few months ago when a resident of the Sea Breeze was murdered. When a friend told me it was time to pay up for a series of favors, I got involved. Despite a few hair-raising moments, I managed to crack the case.

My dogged determination to see the murderer brought to justice impressed Nic. It was a side of me she'd never seen before. A side that, I think, proved to her that I could be the kind of guy who didn't head for the door when things got tough. In the process, I proved it to myself, too.

Was I becoming the guy my mom had always told me was there inside me? A man who could commit to a relationship that was more consequential than living with a cat? I sure hoped so. Provided Oscar never got word that I considered my relationship with another human more important than my relationship with him.

Removing the cloud of doubt about her involvement in Desiree's demise that still hung over Nic, thanks to the multitool, would do one thing: Restore her reputation to the sterling status it had been before this awful thing.

And if it earned me some points in the scorecard of *Whether Elmo Is a Good Long-Term Catch or Not?* Well, that was a bonus.

After dinner, I let Oscar out for his evening prowl. A laugh escaped me as he wobbled around the corner of my trailer. There was no slinking around for my buddy. While he still had all of his claws, and some of his teeth, his hunting days were behind him. These days, instead of being out half the night and returning home with a bird or small mammal in his mouth, his outdoor trips lasted an hour, maybe.

I think it was a matter of pride as much as anything for Oscar. The piece of property we lived on was his domain. He wanted to keep an eye on things. Make sure I was safe. That was my cat, all heart. And belly. Don't tell him I said that.

The sun didn't set until nine o'clock or so this time of year. I took advantage of the daylight and carried my copy of

Following the Equator to the patio for a bit of relaxation while I waited for Oscar to return from patrol.

When I found myself rereading the same page three times, I had to admit that my mind was preoccupied with other things. Other things being Desiree's murder, of course. What incredible powers of self-awareness, right?

"How about a quick walk while I mull things over? Let the mind wander while I check out HQ." I made my way into the backyard, otherwise known as International Headquarters for Elmo's Critter Removal. While I pondered the case, what little I knew of it, I inspected supplies and equipment. Jordan had started cleaning and putting things away at the end of the day. This would be a good chance to double-check his work.

I left the book behind but brought the drink with me. There was no way I was going to leave fine Irish whiskey defenseless against consumption by who knew what.

Sometimes, a man had to have his priorities in order.

My first stop was the shed. It housed critter removal equipment and a sink for cleaning said supplies. I made sure the tools were clean and in their correct spots while I pondered suspects.

There was Nic. To be clear, she was only a suspect because Chief Eikenberry said she was one for the time being. The only person I could ever see Nicola Beecham murdering was me. And if that were to come to pass, I was most likely to blame. So, Nic was only included in the interests of being thorough.

Next was Bobby Darrin. If Gretchen thought he was

shady, that was good enough for me. I'd have to ask around to learn what I could about him.

Then there was Drunk Paul. What would drive him to take someone else's life? I had no idea. His sketchy response to my question earlier in the day had piqued my curiosity, though.

I took a drink. The shed was tidy, the tools were clean, and I had two suspects worth investigating. It was a start.

After locking the shed, I checked out the shelters where I kept critters until I could release them someplace where they'd be safe. If an animal I removed was sick or injured, I'd keep it out of danger until a vet friend, Dr. Sahara Vaughan, could examine it. Once I got the green light from the good doctor, I returned it to the wild.

The shelters were currently empty. Since Jordan had started, the number of animals needing time to recover from the removal process had dropped by half. I didn't know what the reason was, so I chalked it up to the man's unique gifts. It was another way he was proving to be worth his weight in gold.

The thought of gold brought me to a standstill. I took another sip. As the sweet whiskey flowed over my taste buds, I wondered who gained from Desiree's murder.

My true crime–loving mother had shared with me numerous times that there were the four L's that compelled one to commit murder—lust, love, loathing, and loot. The fact that my mother, who spent her days caring for others as a nurse, was so well-versed in the nuances of murder always left me with a touch of anxiety. That's what I got for watching too much *Dateline* and other true crime shows.

I didn't want to give her a reason to put *loathing* to work on me.

So, for the first L, in no particular order—loot, or money. The love of money was the *root of all evil*, after all, if you went in for that kind of thinking. Second was loathing, hating someone so much you wanted them removed from the land of the living. Revenge, the dish that Antonio Scarpacci from the sitcom *Wings* said was like calamari, best served cold, fit into that category. Both revenge and loathing gave me the heebie-jeebies.

The third L was lust. The good old *I want you so much, I'm going to kill your partner* kind of thing. According to Mom, there were lots of permutations to this one. They all ended badly, though. I mean, had anyone ever gotten away with offing the rich husband or wife so they could run away with the surviving spouse? They never seemed to in the movies.

Then there was love. Sometimes, I could get this one. My grandma spent the final weeks of her life in hospice. There were times late at night when I couldn't help wondering if it would have been better to help her end her suffering rather than let nature take its course. That was a debate for philosophers and scholars, people way smarter than me.

I returned to the trailer to find Oscar waiting on the stoop. "Mind if I hang out here to ponder and finish my drink?"

The cat turned and pawed at the door. Clearly, there was no reason for my problems to delay his return to the air-conditioned environs inside the trailer.

"Whatever, dude." I opened the door. "No bedtime snacks for you tonight."

With half of my drink left, I eased into the chair I'd vacated earlier and put my feet up on another one. I put my hands behind my head and looked upward to the heavens. There were too many stars to count. Those tiny pricks of light always left me with the same thought.

Whether we were alone in the universe or not was immaterial. The fact that we existed at all was incredible. At the same time, it was heartbreaking that so often, life carried little meaning on our little planet. We needed to do better. To treat each other with more love and less hate. Like the immortal Bob Marley sang about, one love.

A frog's croak brought me out of my musings.

"Enough philosophy, dude. Back to the case. What about Mom's four L's?"

Stabbing a woman to death didn't seem to fit into the love category, regardless of how I studied it. Desiree wasn't married and wasn't rich. As far as I knew, she wasn't terminally ill, either. Leaving her wound-riddled corpse for some pour soul to find didn't strike me as a compassion-driven act.

That left me with lust, loathing, and loot. She didn't have a lot to her name, I didn't see someone coming into a big inheritance as a result of her murder. Nic was the most logical person to fit into the loathing category and she didn't do it.

That left me with lust. Did some emotion-fueled individual want her out of the way to pursue the love of their life? That's where Bobby Darrin came in. But if they were split up, why would someone need to kill her to get to him?

Then an idea bubbled to the surface. It fit into the loathing category with the same ease as when I slipped into my favorite pair of old jeans. What if the murder really was trying to frame Nic? Who benefited if she was convicted of murder? Obviously, someone would have to take over her charter boat business.

The hairs on the back of my neck rose to attention as another scenario came to me. What if Gretchen murdered Desiree and set up Nic to take the fall? She knew enough about the resort purchase to have an idea how much money I had. Maybe our breakup back in the day hadn't been as amicable as I thought.

I wasn't so arrogant to think that Gretchen wanted Nic out of the picture so she could get to me. I *was* willing to consider the notion that she wanted Nic out of the picture so she could get to my money. A disturbing thought, indeed. Especially since it wasn't any more outlandish than any other ideas I'd come up with.

My thoughts began to run in circles. It was time to call it a night. I finished off my drink and headed inside. With a lot more questions than answers, my next step was clear.

Would it be dangerous? Absolutely. Could it be avoided? No. Would it be worth it? If it helped catch a killer, it was. Those, at least, were a few things I was certain about.

CHAPTER NINE

THE SCARY THING about the Riptide Barbeque Shack wasn't the menu. Yes, there were things like smoked gator and fried calamari that gave this Indiana kid the shivers just thinking about them. There were the finest smoked meats from land-dwelling creatures on the Florida Gulf Coast, too. And their sides, especially the cornbread, were life-changing.

It wasn't the drink prices, either. Some of the local watering holes charged premiums for popular spirits and trendy beers. Not my buddy Wendell Banderas, owner of the joint. Sure, a pint of something from a local brewery might cost more than a twelve-ounce can of a mass-produced beer. That was to be expected. The same for spirits and nonalcoholic drinks. That's why I didn't complain when a Redbreast on the rocks was fifty cents more than a routine Irish whiskey on the rocks.

No, what really made me quake in my work boots from fear were the people. More specifically, my friends when I asked them for advice. As a group, they were quite opinionated and could get downright intimidating when they disagreed about the advice I was seeking. Especially because each one of them wanted to help.

And were certain their way was the best way.

That's why I slipped into the restaurant a little before noon, hoping for a quiet lunch at the bar. That's where I could hash out the case with Wendell. He was a reliable source of solid advice developed through decades of listening to goobers like me asking what to do about the mundane things in life.

Murder was not a mundane thing. Obviously.

It didn't change the fact that Wendell would be a good place to start my information gathering. I waved to him as I got settled at the bar.

"Good to see you, Elmo." He placed a clear plastic cup filled with ice water on the bar top in front of me. "Awful news about poor Desiree. Nice girl. She and Seven were friends."

"I'm so sorry. How's Seven doing?"

"I'm heartbroken and angry and I want whoever did this to my friend caught, like yesterday." Amelia Banderas, Wendell's daughter and business partner, took a seat on the stool next to me. She was known to one and all as *Seven* because of her resemblance to the actress Jeri Ryan's character Seven of Nine. Her eyes were puffy and her blond hair, which usually looked like strands of spun gold, had lost its sheen. "You're investigating. I heard it on the Springs Signal."

So much for keeping things under the radar.

"I am. That's one of the reasons I stopped by. Wanted to bend your dad's ear about a few things."

"What things?" a deep, gruff voice coming from behind

me asked.

The voice belonged to Waldo Quigley, known to one and all as Rambo. The mountain of a man was normally found at his gator farm at this time of day. To cross paths with him here meant something was going on.

Especially when he settled his three-hundred-pound frame onto the stool to my left. And also had red-rimmed eyes.

With the tall, intense blonde on one side of me and the equally intimidating human mountain on the other, there was no point in wasting time on small talk.

I had two of the toughest and scariest on the Florida Panhandle flanking me.

They were also great friends. And the type of people who could help with my sleuthing.

"Suspects in Desiree's murder." I told them about Nic's involvement, my initial desire to clear her name, and how that goal dovetailed with figuring out who took the woman's life.

"That's my dude." Rambo gave me a slap on the back that may have separated a couple of ribs from their attached cartilage. "I told you Elmo would answer the call."

Seven gave me a quick hug while Wendell brought me a double serving of mac and cheese.

"Lunch is on the house today, buddy." Wendell handed me a menu. "We were trying to figure out a way to talk you into investigating. And here you are. Like the answer to our prayers."

"It's not that we don't trust the police," Seven said.

"I don't," Rambo shot back. "Not after what happened back in February."

"Let me rephrase." Seven closed her eyes and took a breath. "With the exception of Rambo—"

"That's better."

"We know Chief Eikenberry will do all she can to catch the killer. We worry how long it will take with everything else that's going on."

"More like they'll dink around chasing their tails long until the trail grows cold and another crime in our fair city will go unsolved," Rambo said as he clenched his fists.

"That's enough, you two." Wendell put his hands up as a small group entered the restaurant. "Let's take things down a notch. How can we help, Elmo?"

"What can you tell me about Bobby Darrin?"

"The singer?"

"No, Dad." Seven leaned her head back and sighed. "We're talking about Desiree, not music. Bobby Darrin, her ex-boyfriend. Please try to keep up, old man."

"Of course. Sometimes, my fifty-something-year-old brain runs a little slow. Please accept my apologies, my dear whip-smart daughter." Wendell winked at her, then turned his focus to me. "I don't know a lot about the guy beyond the fact that he's bad news."

"Yep. Real con artist. A while back, he tried to talk me into turning part of the gator farm into a reptile zoo," Rambo said. "He wouldn't take no for an answer until I threatened to sic one of my gators on him."

At Wendell's insistence, we took a moment to order

lunch. While we did so, Seven slipped behind the bar to fill drink orders a server turned in. I couldn't help wondering if she truly felt the need to pour the beers or if it was a way to distract herself for a moment. I wouldn't blame her one bit if it was the latter.

"Bobby Darrin's a bad dude." Seven placed the filled pint glasses on the server's tray. "I never understood what Desiree saw in him. It wasn't until he sold her car that she finally wised up and told him to get lost for good."

"He sold her car?" I'd made my fair share of poor decisions in my life. The time I decided to explore the swampland by Rambo's place without bringing any bug repellent came to mind. I'd never pulled a stunt like stealing someone's car, though.

"Yep. Last December. Without telling her." For the past few years, Desiree had worked for Rambo during the winter months when Nic didn't need her. "I told her to go straight to the cops, but she said she wanted to give Bobby a chance to explain. By the time she got an answer out of him, the car was long gone.

"She spent one night crying on my shoulder about it. She was so mad that he'd do such an awful thing and felt stupid for letting it happen," Seven said. "I told her she wasn't stupid. That he'd taken advantage of her. It was on him, not her."

While the information didn't point to murder, it sure painted an unflattering portrait of the guy.

"Any idea where I can find him? What if he tried to win her back, she said no, and he lost it? One of those *If I can't have you, nobody can have you* scenarios."

"All I know is she kicked him out after he sold the car. Served him right," Rambo said.

"You need to talk to the Farrell sisters. They're his aunts." Wendell placed our lunch orders in front of us. "His dad took off when he was in diapers, allegedly on the run from the feds for something or other. His mom died when he was ten. They took him in after that. If anyone knows where to find him, it's them."

The Farrell sisters were life-long residents of Paradise Springs. Cheryl, Beryl, and Meryl were triplets who had done everything together for as long as anyone could remember. Bobby's mom, Carol Farrell-Darrin, was their younger sister. At various times, the trio been referred to as witches, sorcerers, and the Fates because of their uncanny ability to take any situation and turn it to their advantage.

Among their business holdings was the Magnificent Marlin. A while back, I offered Elmo's Critter Removal services to the facility. Meryl, who preferred to remain in the shadows of the business empire but was widely known as the brains of the operation, declined, saying they had other means for dealing with pests.

When I asked her if she'd be willing to share what product or service they used, she gave me a smile that made my blood run cold. Then she let out a light laugh and said something that still made me wake up in the middle of the night in a cold sweat.

Mr. Simpson, you seem to be a nice man. It's best if you don't know.

Back in the present, I grabbed the bar as an idea popped into my head. "Wait a minute. Bobby stole Desiree's car. Desiree reported him to the police. A few months down the line, Desiree turns up murdered at his aunts' nightclub."

Rambo scratched his bushy beard. "I see where you're going. You think maybe they bumped Desiree off."

"Yes, in revenge for what they saw as turning on their golden boy." Seven bumped my shoulder with her elbow. "They don't like to be crossed. You should see how fast they'll kick someone out of the Marlin for getting out of line. When are you going to talk to them?"

"I'd do it sooner rather than later, my friend," Wendell said. "We all know what happened with Desiree's car when she waited to report it stolen. You don't want to give them time to cook up a cover story."

"Maybe I'll swing by after work. See if I can have a chat with one of them before it gets too busy." I turned toward Seven. "And what exactly makes you think I've never seen someone thrown out of the Magnificent Marlin before? Are you insinuating that I'm old, like your dad?"

"Pssh. No. I'm saying it out loud. Everyone knows you're one of those early birds who likes to be in bed by, like, nine. Nothing interesting happens at the Marlin until later." She looked past me at Rambo. "And you can cut out the laughter, Rambo. I know you're no different than Early Bird Elmo."

"I'll have you know, young lady"—Rambo pointed a beefy finger at her—"I'm not old. I'm vintage. Besides, you try wrangling moody gators all day. You'd be in bed just as early."

The two of them started bickering about what was harder, dealing with drunk tourists or handling carnivorous reptiles. While they did that, I finished my lunch, saluted Wendell, and made my exit. If I was going to confront the mysterious and intimidating Farrell sisters, I wanted to do it without any bruises from officiating a spat between Rambo and Seven.

CHAPTER TEN

Aᴏᴏ FTER LUNCH AT the Riptide, it was tough to keep my head in the critter removal game. There were animals to be transferred from perilous situations and sales calls to make. In a perfect world, I'd do the inspections and service runs and leave the sales work to Jordan. He was a natural at connecting with people and I...wasn't.

It wasn't that I was an ogre, but people needed to peel through a few layers of the onion that was Elmo Simpson until I got comfortable with them. What can I say? I'm an introvert. It was little wonder that on our first Christmas together, Nic got me a Shrek plush doll.

I put him on my nightstand that evening. Other than to remove the dust from his outer *layer*, I hadn't moved him since.

My truck was our only mode of transportation big enough to hold all the equipment needed for removals. Because of that, Jordan and I developed a system for days, like today, when we had sales calls the same time as service calls.

He took the truck, and I rode an electric bicycle.

At first, I felt silly tooling around on a bike. The purchase had been made in a moment of desperation. Jordan was still learning, and I wasn't ready to drop thousands of dollars on a second vehicle I might not need if things didn't work out with him.

After a week or two, I began to notice a lot of tourists riding rental e-bikes around the area. All of a sudden, going to appointments in an eco-friendly way was cool. I knocked on the door of my first appointment using the bike a little sweaty but standing a little taller.

Fortunately, 90 percent of my sales calls were to businesses in the commercial district, which was sandwiched between the highway to the north and the Gulf, a couple of miles to the south. That meant short distances between stops. Which was a godsend because the temperature was hovering in the low nineties with the humidity to match.

At least the breeze created while I was in the saddle helped wick away the sweat. Thank the stars for small favors. And rechargeable batteries.

A few hours later, I was on my way home. The effort had been successful. Two of the three businesses I visited signed service agreements. We would be providing critter repellant along with strategically located traps, and would conduct weekly site inspections, both indoors and out, to look for evidence of any presence of small animals like mice snakes.

Jordan was getting better at the routine work every day, so it was work he'd be able to handle easy-peasy. That should leave me more time to respond to removal calls or kick back on the patio with a good book.

Life in Paradise Springs was far from perfect. Murders tended to support that statement. Which meant after a meeting with Jordan to recap the day and make a game plan for tomorrow, I was off to the showers.

To prepare for a date with the Farrell sisters.

I arrived at the Magnificent Marlin a little before seven. The early bird crowd had already enjoyed their senior citizen discount specials and moved on. The family crowd was just arriving, filling the parking lot with SUVs and minivans sporting license plates from as far away as Minnesota and New York. Vacation time in the Springs, indeed.

Before entering, I took a walk around the establishment. I wanted to get a sense of it before entering. A huge sign depicting a blue and gray marlin jumping through the outline of a yellow star was affixed to the top of the building. You could see it for miles. If nothing else, the garish sign was effective in warding off low-flying aircraft.

Near the restaurant, a flight of wooden stairs led from the parking lot down to the beach. Paradise Springs maintained a number of these amenities, which included a trash receptacle next to the bottom step. I tossed a granola bar wrapper in the barrel and made my way toward the ocean. The sound of the waves crashing against the beach never got old. Halfway to the water's edge, I turned around. The view from the beach revealed all three of the Marlin's floors.

In one corner of the beach bar, a musician was strumming an acoustic guitar and singing a tolerable version of "Brave" by Sara Bareilles. Customers hung out on the stairwell that went up to the main floor. A door that offered entry into the restaurant was open. I could catch a hint of beef sizzling on a grill. Windows on the main and upper floor that faced the ocean were open to take advantage of the pleasant breeze coming from the south.

I made a mental note to find out if the windows had been open the night of Desiree's murder. If so, maybe an employee or a customer heard something important. Even if they didn't know it.

I'd learned during my years maneuvering around cramped crawl spaces how important it was to practice active listening. It had helped me locate and remove countless critters.

And, I'd like to think, the skill would make my elementary school teachers proud.

The crime scene was easy enough to locate. A mound of flowers, teddy bears, and other mementos had accumulated in a stand of sea grass by the wall to my right. At first, I couldn't understand why nobody from the beach bar had noticed anything was amiss. As I got closer, the answer became clear. The murder had taken place a good twenty feet back from the side of the building open to the beach. It would have been dark. Any argument would have been drowned out by either the music from above or by the TVs in the beach bar that would have been broadcasting sports of some sort.

"Well, murderer, you picked a good spot. You're not going to get away with it, though." With that promise in mind, I scaled the stairs to the main floor. It was time for a sit-down with the owners of the Magnificent Marlin.

I found Cheryl near the host station. Her bright green hair made her impossible to miss. Dressed in a blue-and-yellow sundress with giant sunflowers on it, the woman radiated approachability. Her smile when I greeted her reinforced the reputation that she was a friend to one and all.

"It's good to see you again, Mr. Simpson. What can I do for you?"

A few feet from us, the host was busy with a family of five. Other than that, we were alone for the moment. Still, I didn't want to be overheard asking about a murder. Those questions could wait until we were someplace private.

"I was downstairs, paying a visit to Desiree's memorial."

"Awful news." She shook her head. "I still have trouble believing it. Do you know if they've made an arrest yet? I heard they were talking to Ms. Beecham the other day."

The casual way Nic was brought up put me on guard. Was I being overly sensitive or was it a move to direct attention from the woman's nephew?

"No arrests that I'm aware of. Chief Eikenberry wanted to talk to Nic since she and Desiree worked together and were seen together here the other night. I have it on good authority that she's been cleared of any wrongdoing."

Cheryl brought her hands together in a light clap. "I'm sure the two of you must be relieved."

"We are. That's why I'm here, actually. I was wondering if I could talk to you and your sisters about that night. You see, while I'm happy Nic's no longer under suspicion, I knew Desiree. I want to do my part to bring the murderer to justice."

"That's very noble of you. The police seem to have the case well in hand, though. They were here for quite a while.

84

They talked to everyone on staff, including my sisters and me."

I tugged at the collar of my polo shirt while I reminded myself to be patient. Just because it seemed like she was stonewalling me didn't mean she was. A horrific event had occurred at her business. It was natural for her to want to divert attention away from it.

"The chief and her team are great. I'm just concerned they're overwhelmed at the moment, between the recent vandalism and the tourist-related problems. I guess I'm hoping that I might find something that will help them. You know, like I did a few months ago."

"I see." She glanced over her shoulder, as if hoping someone was coming to rescue her. Nobody was. I'd boxed her in. She knew it, too. "Perhaps we can have a quick chat in my office."

"Excellent. I'd like to talk to Beryl and Meryl, too. If we could all sit down together, that would save everyone time, don't you think?"

"How can I say no?" She let out a shaky laugh, then stepped away to say a few words into a microphone attached to her dress. After a nod, then a few words, then a shake of her head, she returned to me. "Come with me, please."

Cheryl was a reliable source of positive energy. That was one reason she was the face of the Farrell sisters' empire. Instead of her usual smile, though, she was frowning. Something had her rattled. While it could be my insistence on chatting with her, it was more likely that her sisters weren't pleased with her.

Well, as my grandma used to tell me when I didn't want to do the dishes or take out the trash, *Tough toenails.* She was a stern one. That was for sure.

Meryl Farrell was sitting at a desk with a glass top and stainless steel frame, staring at a trio of computer monitors when Cheryl and I entered the office.

"Elmo Simpson, it's been a month of Sundays since you've graced us with your presence." She stood and offered to shake my hand. The royal blue of her nail polish matched the color of her business suit and her bob-style haircut. "Whatever can we do for you? Are you here to pitch your services again?"

"Not tonight." I eased into a leather chair Meryl gestured for me to take. Cheryl perched herself on a corner of the desk. "When someone tells me thanks, but no thanks, I leave it at that. If your situation changes, I figure you know how to find me."

"Why are you here, then?" Beryl, the third Farrell sister, asked. She shut the door behind her with a bang and leaned against it. She had long flame-red hair that was pulled into a side braid. Wearing a yellow tank club dress and hoop earrings large enough for me to put my hand through, she looked like she belonged in a fashion magazine. She was in charge of the night club. Apparently, she believed in dressing the part of someone keeping the party going until the wee hours of the morning.

"Now, B," Cheryl said. "Give the man a chance."

"Please excuse our sister." Meryl filled a tumbler with water from a carafe, then handed it to me. "We're all reeling from the events involving Ms. LaFontaine and are each dealing with it in our own way."

"I totally understand." I took a drink. The clear, cold beverage settled my nerves that had been upset by Beryl's fiery entrance. Until I began to wonder if it was poisoned. "I promise not to take up too much of your time."

"Save it. What do you want?" Beryl crossed her arms. Any information from her would come begrudgingly.

The other sisters seemed more open to my presence. It was two to one. I had numbers on my side. Hopefully.

"To make sure we're all on the same page, the police cleared Nic Beecham in Desiree's murder. With the killer still out there, I'm hoping you can tell me what you remember about that night." I stopped. If they were going to cooperate, they would. If not, I couldn't force them.

Though, any resistance would be odd. And if word about that got out? It would cast the sisters in a bad light. Hopefully, it wouldn't come to that. Getting on Beryl's bad side was something I'd probably regret for years to come.

Meryl spread her hands wide. "It was a typical Monday night. There was that buzz that comes with tourists who are new in town. Business was brisk. Not quite on par with the weekend, but close. I spent the evening in the office here. It's where one can usually find me."

The office had a single window that overlooked the parking lot. There was no way to see the crime scene from there.

"And how did you find out about Desiree?"

"Our head bartender was moving stock to the beach bar on Tuesday morning. She stepped outside for a moment and saw the body. She called 911, then called us."

"Who did she talk to first?"

"She sent a group text that she needed to talk to us all ASAP." Cheryl scrolled through her phone. "That was at around ten."

I asked Cheryl what she remembered.

"The restaurant slowed down around ten. I went downstairs to have a drink at the bar. I don't recall seeing or hearing anything out of the ordinary."

"You didn't notice the harpoon was missing?"

"I'm afraid not. It may have been there, for all I know."

"How about you, Beryl?" I locked gazes with the woman. One of her nostrils flared. I made a mental note of the tell.

"I spent most of the night behind or around the bar. I was the one who had to break up the quarrel between your girlfriend and Mr. Abbott. It was an ugly scene. Don't take my word for it. Talk to him. He was the one who got a drink in the face."

"I'll do that." I kept my tone friendly. The *drink in the face* part was new. I'd have to ask Nic about it. "Along that line, I was hoping to talk to your nephew. Do you how I can get in touch with him?"

"Why? He wasn't here that night." Beryl stared at her talon-like fingernails. They were painted an intimidating shade of crimson. It would take a while to recover from being clawed by them.

"I understand he and Desiree used to be together. That when they broke up, they didn't exactly part ways on good terms."

"That's true. On both counts," Meryl said with a sigh that carried the weight of the world on it. "It was really an unfortunate misunderstanding. I wish young people knew how to communicate better. Like my sister said, though, not only was Bobby not here that night, but he also wasn't even in town."

Cheryl nodded. "He's in New Orleans. Scouting out locations for a new Magnificent Marlin location. We've had so much success here, we're hoping to take that magic beyond Paradise Springs."

"Very cool. I hope he found a good site." Honestly, I didn't really care one way or another, but I figured it couldn't hurt to play nice. "Have you heard anything from him?"

"Why should we tell you if we have?" Beryl cracked a half smile, which was more of a sneer. The woman either hated me or was just plain mean.

It could have been both, I suppose. Negative energy emanated from her.

"I thought he might have any thoughts about who'd want to hurt Desiree."

"We'll save you the trouble," Meryl said. After a glance in Beryl's direction, she brushed a rogue strand of hair from her face. "You should take a hard look at Paul Rudd."

"The guy who's Ant Man? What's he—"

"No, you idiot." If looks could kill, the one Beryl was giving me would have me dead and buried where nobody would ever find my remains. "Not the actor. Paul Rudd, the handyman. I believe insensitive people refer to him as Drunk Paul."

Touché. Getting called out for being unkind by someone who could be on a poster for aggressive behavior hurt. I'd survive, though. There were bigger issues at hand than my feelings.

"What's the deal with Dr… I mean, Mr. Rudd?"

Meryl stepped forward. "Paul had a high school crush on Desiree. He made a big show of it when he asked her to their senior prom. If I remember correctly, it involved sparklers and smoke bombs and other fireworks. It was a disaster."

I saw where she was going. "Let me guess. She turned him down."

"Yes. In her defense, she'd already agreed to go with Bobby." Meryl held out her hands. "What was the girl going to do? Anyway, Paul never got over the humiliation from the regrettable episode. He's held a grudge ever since."

"Really? I didn't know." It was an intriguing story. Assuming it was true, of course. The sisters could have been simply working together to send me after someone other than their nephew.

"It's always our pleasure to help." Meryl handed me a business card as she got to her feet. "If you'll excuse us, we really need to get back to work. Give me a call tomorrow. It's been a while since you offered your critter removal services to us. We should revisit that."

Cheryl ushered me out of the office with some small talk. Even Beryl shook my hand and offered me a drink on the house. Since she struck me as a woman I shouldn't say no to, I took her up on the offer and made my way to the beach bar.

A few minutes later, I was seated at a corner table with a spiced rum on the rocks. There was an outline on the wall where the harpoon had been. How could it have gone missing without anyone noticing?

I nursed the drink as I revisited my conversation with the Farrell sisters. They were an odd trio. Which made them typical residents of Paradise Springs. Still, it was as if they were playing assigned roles. Cheryl was the friendly, helpful one. Meryl was the no-nonsense businessperson. And Beryl was the enforcer.

To be fair, they had their nephew's interests, and his freedom, perhaps, in mind. The revelation about Drunk Paul was news, too. I'd have to verify it, though. Just because they told me the story didn't make it true.

I turned to face the ocean. Parents with young children were frolicking in the shallows. Teenagers and couples had ventured out until the water came up to their necks. A few groups were lounging in folding chairs, intent on sticking around to soak in the last bit of sun. They didn't seem to have a care in the world. Good for them.

Their tasks were to enjoy the best Paradise Springs had to offer. I had another, less enjoyable one. Track down and talk to not one, but two murder suspects. Both of whom were good at being hard to find.

CHAPTER ELEVEN

"**A**RE YOU SURE you really want to do this?" My attorney, Georgia Phelps, raised a manicured eyebrow. "It's not too late to back out."

We were in her office on the top floor of a ten-story commercial building in the middle of Paradise Springs' business district. The workplace offered a gorgeous view of the Florida coastline. It was a reminder of how lovely the region was.

And a reminder of why her hourly fee was high enough to give me vertigo.

Georgia was worth every penny, though. Nic had referred me to her when I first floated the idea of starting Elmo's Critter Removal. Since then, she'd been an unerring source of excellent legal work.

When I told her I wanted to buy the Sea Breeze, her only response was to raise an eyebrow. It was her go-to response. Then, she asked me a single question.

Why?

Normally, I'm not one who goes for introspection. This potential deal had brought out the deep thinker in me, though. For a long time, I believed that if I worked hard and treated people the way I wanted to be treated, things would work out. I reached the top of the corporate ladder, running my own app development start-up and making more money than I could ever hope to spend. At first, life was great, and my philosophy was proving to be spot-on.

That changed when the pressures of the job, including the theft of some intellectual property, led to a breakdown and a week in a mental health facility. The series of unfortunate incidents revealed to me in crystal-clear terms how many true friends I had from my time in the tech world.

I had none.

The people I'd worked and hung out with were part of my life because of one thing. The job. It cut me to the bone to learn that my associates cared about my company's money, not me. So, I sold the company, put most of the proceeds in the bank, and set out to live a life where the complications were few and the gorgeous sunsets were numerous.

Sure, I'd been on the run from the past ever since. That included doing everything I could to avoid accessing the proceeds from the sale. It brought up too many bad memories. Instead, when I left Indiana, I made myself a promise.

I'd tap into the money when it could be used to make a difference. At the time, I didn't know what that was. The only thing I was certain about was that I wanted to do more than write a check to a good cause. I hoped the answer would come in good time.

Buying the Sea Breeze was the answer.

The resort was the largest employer in the area. The previous owner may have been a criminal, but he paid his employees competitive wages and offered them decent, if not overly generous benefits. Sure, it may have been nothing more than a ploy to keep his staff happy, so they didn't stir up trouble. The fact remained that the resort's personnel needed their jobs. On top of that, over two hundred folks lived at the resort year-round. It was their home. They needed someone to look out for them, too.

I couldn't stand by and let the place shut down or be bought by a firm that would slash pay and services to save a buck. Too many lives were at stake for me to stay on the sideline.

My money was finally going to make the difference I'd been looking for. I gave Georgia a smile.

"I'm sure. Like 150 percent sure."

She stood and straightened her navy-blue suit jacket. "Then let's go sign some papers and make you a real estate magnate."

A little while later, after electronically signing too many documents to count, I shook hands with the resort's representative. The deal was done. Georgia's assistant escorted the former owner's representatives from the room. When we were alone, I raised my hand.

"I'm the owner of the Sea Breeze Resort and Condominiums. How about that?"

We exchanged a fist bump. "Well, technically, the LLC we created is the owner, but why split hairs. I'm proud of you, Elmo. Are you sure you want to keep your ownership anonymous? I'm sure there are a lot of people who'd like to say thank you."

"People are going to find out eventually." I told her about my conversations with Goob and Gretchen. "I didn't do it for any pats on the back, though."

"I know." She gestured to follow her. "You did a good thing. I've got a present for you in my office to mark the occasion."

The present was a bottle of champagne that I assumed was expensive because I couldn't pronounce the name on the label. Georgia joked that it was the least she could do given the bill she'd be sending me at the end of the month.

At least, I thought she was joking.

We clinked glasses and took a small drink, then she asked me how my investigation was going. After assuring me she wasn't going to bill me for the time spent discussing the matter, I told her about my initial group of suspects.

"You grew up around here, right? Did you know Paul had a crush on Desiree back in the day?"

"Not until the whole *promposal* disaster. I was in town, interviewing for clerk positions between my second and third years of law school, when it went down." She shook her head. "Somebody posted the whole thing on social media, which just added to Paul's humiliation. I feel bad for the guy just thinking about it."

"I totally get that things must have been embarrassing. But for him to carry a grudge all this time? That seems extreme."

"Let me tell you a little something about Paul. I don't think he's ever fully recovered from when he got hurt. Whether his existing injuries are physical or psychological, I don't know. If I were you, though, I'd be more worried about the Farrell sisters."

"An interesting group, that's for sure. I didn't buy for a second that they can't get ahold of Bobby. I'll give them points for looking out for a relative, though."

"Don't be so sure. Those women are as ruthless as they come. At least Beryl has the decency to be herself. The other two? Not what they seem. They didn't develop the Marlin out of the goodness of their hearts, despite what they say. They knew a goldmine when they saw it."

I processed Georgia's words as I took another drink of the champagne. I trusted her almost as much as I trusted Nic. She was holding something back, though. Something she wanted me to figure out on my own. No doubt to prevent anyone from claiming she was engaging in behavior unbecoming of a member of the bar.

"You think they might have had something to do with Desiree's murder." I began pacing back and forth in the office. "It makes sense. Desiree died on the property. They were mad at her for reporting Bobby to the police. The stab wound might be a cover. It would have been easy enough to slip poison into one of her drinks. I don't believe their story that they didn't notice the harpoon was missing."

She put up her hands. "I didn't say anything of the sort. It's something worth looking into, though, don't you think?" She gave me a pronounced nod.

I laughed. It was either that or run home and curl up under the covers with Oscar until the murderer was behind bars.

The former was always better than the latter. Especially since I'd promised to get justice for Desiree.

"It looks like my suspect list just got a lot longer." I drained the rest of my drink and placed the champagne flute on Georgia's desk. "But first, I'm going to take a look at the new addition to the Elmo Simpson empire. Who knows? Maybe I'll catch the murderer on the way."

CHAPTER TWELVE

WHILE I FAILED to apprehend any murderers after my departure from Georgia's office, I did manage to visit the Sea Breeze. My Sea Breeze. My ten-million-dollar Sea Breeze. I forced a surge of panic back into its shell by snapping a few photos and sending them to Nic.

That was a lot of cash, after all. When I told her I wanted to buy the property, she questioned my sanity. To be fair, that was something she did on a regular basis. She warmed to the idea when I explained why I wanted to do it. She came fully on board when I showed her the numbers I'd run.

"I still think you're crazy, but I can't argue with the math," she said at the time. "Not going to lie. I wish I had ten mil to drop on a whim."

I debated telling her that if she married me, she'd have access to about fifty mil. I held that one back when I ran it through my head. Me marrying Nicola Beecham? I'd do it in a snap. The real question was whether she'd marry me. Instead, I told her something much more practical.

"I'd be happy to finance the purchase of a new boat to add to your fleet."

After a moment's hesitation, she told me she'd think about it. Then, Desiree quit and any plans for the expansion of Nic's operation sunk like a stone tossed into the Gulf waters.

My thoughts returned to the present. After sending the pictures to my mom, I sauntered into the resort's welcome area. It wasn't three o'clock yet, so the check-in line was empty. A young man wearing a light blue polo was standing at the registration counter. He was staring at a computer monitor as he ticked away at a keyboard. I resisted the temptation to say *hi*, and instead wandered over to the concierge desk.

"Tickle Me Elmo, what's shaking?" Gretchen extended her fist for a knuckle bump.

"You know, just signed off on a little purchase. Still getting my head around it."

She jumped to her feet and placed her hands over her heart. "Yes! You have no idea how much of a relief it is to hear you say that. Can I start spreading the word?"

"Not just yet. The previous owner will be sending a company-wide email before the end of the day. All it'll say is that the new owner's a local group that's looking forward to naming a new resort manager soon."

Gretchen practically swooned. My friend might be a little heavy with the drama, but her excitement was genuine. As was her desire to maintain the Sea Breeze's reputation as the best-kept secret on Florida's Emerald Coast.

After settling back into her seat, she asked me how long *soon* meant.

"Give me a week. I want to make sure nothing pops up that will torpedo the deal. I'd like to get Desiree's murder solved before making any announcement, too."

"I guess I can live with that." She winked. "Have you talked to Bobby yet?"

"Afraid not. I talked to his aunts last night, though. They claim he was out of town the night in question. It's been suggested that one, or all three, of them might be the murderer. A revenge killing."

"I'd totally believe Madame Fire or Madame Water doing it. Not Madame Earth, though. She's too nice. The only good person of the three, if you ask me."

"You lost me. Who are Madame Fire and the other two?"

"Sometimes, I forget you're not a Springs native." She gave me a friendly slap on the hand. "The Farrell sisters' parents were magicians. They traveled all over the world. When the girls got old enough, they became part of the act and were introduced as the Four Elements—Earth, Air, Fire, and Water. Cheryl was Earth and always dressed in green. Beryl was Fire and dressed in red. Meryl was Water and had a blue costume. Carol, Bobby's mom, was Air. Yellow was her color."

All of a sudden, the sisters' appearance, from the shades of their hair to the palettes of their outfits, made sense. Well, it added up. I wasn't sure if it made actual sense from a real-world perspective.

Once again, that was Paradise Springs for you.

"Now I get it. Fire sure fits Beryl." I shivered. "Wouldn't want to cross paths with her in a dark alley."

"Or in a shadowy patch of seagrass?" She adjusted her name tag. "Just saying. Anyway, I've got some things I need to get done before my shift is over. Don't want the new boss to think I'm a slacker, whoever they may be."

I laughed. That was one thing I always liked about Gretchen. She made me laugh. Inevitably, I felt better after seeing her. She was that way with everyone. Paradise Springs was a better place, a kinder place, with her around.

The world needed more people like Gretchen.

"I have a feeling the new boss has an inkling of how much you do for this place. See you around."

The next few hours were spent doing critter removals. It felt good to do something I was familiar with. It was reassuring to have work that paid the bills, too. I didn't want to live off my nest egg, after all. That money wasn't for day-to-day expenses. While an accountant I hired to study the resort's books couldn't find evidence that the previous owner cooked the books to make sure the resort stayed afloat, I had my doubts.

Sometimes, paranoia was a good thing.

I could subsidize the Sea Breeze to keep it in the black, if needed. I didn't want to do that indefinitely, though. It was nice to have a nest egg for other things, after all.

At seven o'clock that evening, I logged onto my laptop. It was time for my weekly video chat with my mom.

"Elmo, dear, you look tired. Are you getting enough sleep?"

So much for exchanging pleasantries. Then again, Mom had a full social calendar on top of her job as a nurse. Sometimes, she got to the point on these visits so she could wrap them up and then go have fun with friends.

At least I knew my place in the pecking order.

"I'm good. Been a busy few days. Messing around in crawl spaces and attics in ninety-degree heat can take it out of you."

"Make sure you're staying hydrated. With healthy things like water and green tea. Not those sugary concoctions they sell at all the bars down there."

Sometimes, my dear mother said things that made me laugh. This was one of them. I choked it off as quickly as I could. She meant well, after all. I needed to remind myself that despite what she seemed to think, I wasn't living a life straight out of a Carl Hiaasen novel.

"You have nothing to worry about. I haven't drunk on the job since before my breakdown. I did have some champagne at lunch, though."

She sat up straighter in her chair. "The deal went through? That's excellent news. I'm so proud of you. Sometimes, I think you're too good for that town."

Alana Simpson loved to remind her son that he was too good for his adopted hometown. I appreciated that she didn't have a problem telling me how much she loved me. From time to time, though, I wondered if she would be happier if I had settled in a place more cosmopolitan, like Miami or the French Riviera.

Now, I had a surefire way to have her visit without complaining about the accommodations. Her kindest term for my trailer had been *efficient*.

"Yeah, well, the Springs has been good to me. Anyway, one of the perks of owning the Sea Breeze is that I have a personal condo there. I can put you up in the lap of luxury anytime. Can you get away for the Fourth of July?"

"Absolutely." She licked her lips. "I'll make flight arrangements tonight. Is it okay if Brian comes? There's something the two of us would like to talk to you about."

Brian was Mom's boyfriend. They'd been seeing each other a few months, so I'd only met him via video chat. He seemed nice enough, if a bit nerdy. That was saying a lot, coming from a tech nerd like me.

"Um, yeah. He can totally come." I swallowed. A bead of sweat broke out on my forehead as a question formed in my mind. "You want me to get him his own unit, right?"

It was her turn to laugh. "I think one unit will be enough. Though, I do appreciate your concern for my virtue."

My cheeks started burning. "Oh, come on, Mom. Don't talk like that around me, please."

"You're the one who brought it up."

She winked. My mother actually winked at me. What was with all the winking recently? I covered my ears. "La la la. I'm not listening. I don't want to hear any more."

We both broke down in fits of laughter. For years, I'd encouraged her to find a special someone. Now that she had, I was suddenly acting like a moody high schooler. Still, the thought of my mom getting busy with someone made me want to make an all-out run for one of those alcohol-filled sugary drinks she'd been complaining about.

We chatted for a bit about safer topics. After asking how Nic was, Mom turned the conversation toward heavier matters.

"I heard about that poor woman's murder. Did you know her?"

"Yeah. It's really sad." I told her about Desiree's split with Nic. "There were some hard feelings when she left that they never seemed to get over. They got into an argument the night Desiree died. I didn't ask her what it was about. Figured she'll talk about it when she's ready. It was tough enough for her to deal with Desiree's murder and then having to talk to the police about it."

"Have they made an arrest yet?"

"No. Nic's got an alibi, but a multitool that belongs to her was found in the victim's hand. I told her I'd try to find out how it ended up there. And, in the process..." I shrugged.

Mom shook her head. "You're crazy for sticking your nose into a police matter. One time should have been enough for you, for anyone, really. Promise me you'll be careful and watch your back."

"Will do."

"Good, because if I'm going to book a flight down there, I don't want you going and getting yourself killed before I can enjoy this condo."

"You're all heart, Mom."

"Yes, I am. Hey, I just had a thought. It's from one of my true crime podcasts. Remember, unless you get lucky enough to catch the murderer actually holding the murder weapon in their hand, the murderer is never who you first think it is."

After the video chat, I sat at my desk scratching Oscar. He'd climbed onto my lap. Mom's parting words resonated in my mind. She was right, of course. The initial consensus had been, by virtue of her multitool's presence, Nic committed the murder. That thought was obviously proven incorrect. While that was great, it still didn't answer the fundamental question. Who murdered Desiree LaFontaine?

"Time for some detective work, buddy." I opened my laptop. I'd asked enough questions. It was time to put my tech skills to use.

CHAPTER THIRTEEN

THE WEEKEND BEGINS on Friday in Paradise Springs, Florida. A lot of us still had to work the first day of the weekend. For me, that meant spending the morning doing the bookkeeping for Elmo's Critter Removal. With Jordan on our massive team of two, I'd turned payroll and benefits over to a third party. I still handled the income and expenses, though.

What can I say, I'd been a numbers person all my life. Math came naturally to me. That's one of the reasons I studied computer science in school. With enough patience and attention to detail, any problem could be solved through the application of mathematics. Shoot, to this day, I often relied on principles learned in Geometry class to help me narrow the search for a critter hiding in the dark somewhere.

So, while paying bills and depositing payments wasn't exactly fun, it was a great way for me to forget about the rest of the world. I also got to use a part of my brain that didn't get as much exercise as it used to. An added bonus was the fact that it was a way for me to stay on top of how the business was doing. While Jordan and I were busy, paying a new employee a decent wage wasn't cheap. When you added benefits like a 401K and health insurance, keeping an eye on the bottom line was critical.

"Good news, buddy." Oscar was sitting on the corner of my desk. It was his usual spot during bill-paying time. He'd learned over the years that when things were going well, he got lots of kitty treats in celebration. When things were not going so well, he got kitty treats as a reward for putting up with my grumbling.

He was no dummy.

I dropped a few beef-flavored treats in front of him. "Still in the black. In fact, we're a little better than last month. Jordan's definitely earning his pay."

The cat didn't even look at me. Instead, he gobbled up his reward like he hadn't seen food in weeks, if not months. I glanced at the clock. He'd eaten his breakfast all of two hours ago. Oh, the life of a spoiled house cat.

Spoiled house cat. That's redundant, isn't it?

With the financial work complete, I checked my calendar. Jordan and I were conducting the weekly inspection at the Bayside Inn, the most exclusive restaurant within three hundred miles. The owner was Chef Claudine, a world-famous chef who had the sharpest knives in the business. And an even sharper tongue. When someone displeased her, she didn't hesitate to wound them with a few words.

And those wounds cut deep.

I knew that firsthand. Which was why I insisted on accompanying Jordan on the Bayside inspections. My protege was smart, thorough, and a fast learner. Claudine didn't care about those things. Until I was certain beyond the shadow of a doubt that he knew the job as well as me, I was going to stick right by his side.

The appointment wasn't for another hour, though. That meant I had time for some snooping. With a serving of amateur psychologist on the side.

Initially, my plan had been to talk to Susan about the case. After a good night's sleep, I figured she wouldn't want to see me unless I had solid information for her. Which I didn't have.

Yet.

She'd be following police procedure, which was as it should be. That's why I'd come up with a different plan. Who wanted to be a detective? Who really, really tried, but often failed, to impress his boss? Therefore, who would love to take a potentially key lead to her?

Officer Thomas Nimoy. That was who.

Good old Spock would eat the information I had up. In turn, hopefully I'd be able to coax the true cause of death from him. It'd be a win-win situation.

Now, all I had to do was find the guy.

Lucky for me, Spock wasn't the most imaginative fellow. A couple of years ago, the Riptide had hosted a costume contest for Halloween. Spock had entered. As a cop from Miami.

He had a friend down there who let him borrow an MPD baseball cap and polo shirt. He'd been so disappointed those in attendance didn't share his enthusiasm for the choice of costume that Wendell made up a new category just for him—Best Reality-Based Costume. Goob threw in a ten-dollar gift card as a prize.

Spock's reaction when Wendell announced him as a winner was worth all the sunken treasure in the Gulf. The guy practically floated through the crowd to receive his winnings. He stood as tall as I'd ever seen him when Seven gave him a peck on the cheek while his picture was being taken.

People in the Springs took care of their own. That included Spock. He might be a predictable doofus, but he was our predictable doofus.

Which made it easy to find him. He spent every Friday morning monitoring traffic in the entertainment district with his trusty radar gun. The practice annoyed some of the tourists, but he had the full support of the powers that be. It slowed traffic, which made it safer for pedestrians. It also reduced the number of folks who drove impaired.

Paradise Springs was all about letting your freak flag fly. Not if you were going to put others in danger, though. Which was why, thanks in part to Thomas Nimoy, folks used nonautomotive options to get around our fair town.

The income generated from speeding tickets helped pay for the walking and bike paths in the area. Which were plentiful because Spock was unforgiving to motorists who exceeded the speed limit. He wasn't a barbarian, though. The only people who got pulled over were those who were going more than ten miles per hour too fast.

Over the years, I may have received a ticket or two from Spock. There were no plans to broach that subject, though. I was still too annoyed from the last time he got me. I claimed that the speedometer indicated I was only eight miles per hour over the limit. Spock told me I should know better.

The worst part of the episode was that he'd been right. Nic said it served me right by lying to him. She'd been right, too. Oh, well. Lesson learned.

"Officer Nimoy, how are you this fine morning?" I slipped into the passenger seat of his cruiser and placed a cup of iced coffee in a holder.

"Keeping the town safe, Elmo. You know I can't accept that drink. Don't want people thinking I'm open to bribes."

I counted to ten. If the coffee had come in a twenty-four-carat mug, I could have seen his point. That wasn't the case here. Yes, I had money. If I was going to bribe the Paradise Springs PD, I wasn't going to do it with a single cup of coffee, though. And Spock wasn't the person I'd try to bribe, either.

"It's a cup of coffee, man. I have it on good authority that Chief Eikenberry won't fire you for accepting it."

He gave the cup a sniff. "Nonfat milk?"

"Yep."

He took a tiny sip. "Three packs of sugar? Natural, not any of that artificial stuff?"

"Just the way you like it. Comes with the territory to know what customers and friends like." That was mostly true. As a small business owner, it definitely helped my relationships with customers when I remembered their preferences.

In Spock's case, I knew his coffee order because it was so ghastly. I mean, how could he taste any actual coffee after all the milk and sugar had been added? It didn't even look like coffee, either. More like weak chocolate milk.

Whatever floated his boat, though. After all, as a tea drinker, I was in no position to judge. If the man took his tea like he took his java, then we'd have words, though.

After a few moments, he took a drink. "Thanks. You're not here to just pay me a friendly visit, are you?"

I laughed. Despite his shortcomings as a police officer, the man could be decently perceptive at times.

"Guilty as charged. I wanted to talk to you about the LaFontaine case." I waited while he checked the speed of a black SUV that motored by. "I have information that may be relevant."

Just like the character from *Star Trek*, he raised one eyebrow. Well, mostly raised. He had to squeeze his right eye closed in order to get the left brow to go up high enough to be noticeable.

"I'm listening."

"First, let me ask you a question. Have you gotten the coroner report yet?"

"Please." He let out a little chuckle. "You've been watching too much TV. It's only been three days. We'll be lucky to get a final report in three weeks. That's how it works in the real world. And it's *medical examiner*, by the way."

"Okay, but what about a preliminary report?" I knew the proper term for the person performing Desiree's autopsy, but sometimes my Hoosier roots came back to haunt me. *Coroner in Indiana. Medical examiner in Florida.*

"You said you had information for me."

From Spock's tone, it was time for cards on the table.

"What if the stab wounds weren't fatal? What if they were a cover for something else?"

"What? Like another knife?"

I opened my mouth, then shut it again. His response was weird. Cops were good at being vague. Somehow, the practice helped them get confessions out of suspects.

At least that's what I'd heard. Secondhand, of course.

"What do you mean?" If it was a slip of the tongue, I wasn't going to let him off the hook. "About another knife, I mean."

"Darn it." Spock smacked his forehead with the heel of his palm. "Me and my big mouth. I'll never make detective."

"One step at a time, buddy." I gave his shoulder a friendly squeeze. "You help me, and I can help you. All that matters is finding Desiree's murderer."

He took another drink of his coffee. "I guess that's true. According to the medical examiner's preliminary report the wounds to the chest and armpit were too deep to be caused by Miss Nicola's multitool. They didn't align with the harpoon, either."

"Does Nic know?" A massive wave of relief washed over me. Spock's information put to bed any worries about her involvement in the case. It raised other questions, but those could remain unanswered for the moment.

"The chief said she was going to talk to her today. With the depth of the wound, we don't need to know how the multitool ended up at the scene to clear her."

"That's huge news. Thanks, man. My turn. I was talking to the Farrell sisters the other night."

"And you lived to tell the tale?" Spock shuddered. "Those ladies creep me out."

"Same here." I told him about my conversation with them. "What if they slipped something in one of Desiree's drinks that night and then used a knife to cover their tracks?"

"Huh." He nodded. "That's an interesting theory. The sisters had motive, means, and opportunity. I wouldn't put it past Beryl to do it. I pulled her over one time, and she let me have it for a good twenty minutes. When I wouldn't let her off with a warning, she put a curse on me."

The fiery Farrell sister did not like to be crossed. There was no doubt about that. All three of them seemed to be protective of their nephew. So, maybe Beryl administered the poison and the other two helped cover up the crime. It seemed farfetched, but there was enough plausibility that I couldn't discount it.

"Thanks for the intel. Let me know what you find out from the tox screen. Live long and prosper." I exited the cruiser before he could respond to my little joke. Sometimes, I couldn't help myself.

One thing was for certain. I needed to nail down Desiree's movements the night she died. Maybe even down to the second.

It wasn't going to be easy. It'd be time well spent, though.

CHAPTER FOURTEEN

WITH MY VISIT with Spock complete, I headed to the Bayside in a state of relative tranquility. Which was a welcome change.

Normally I approached appointments with my most demanding client certain that Claudine would find a mouse dropping or a snakeskin fragment and fire me. In front of her entire staff. In a loud voice that left no doubt I was never welcome to come within a hundred meters of her establishment again. Probably on video, too, so she could use it as part of a reality TV pitch.

At the moment, I had bigger things on my mind. Like the police confirming Nic's innocence. I debated calling her but thought that would be jumping the gun. That was news Susan should deliver.

Instead, tonight I'd bring her a bottle of the finest rum in Paradise Springs. As shorthanded as she was, I'd volunteered to crew for her whenever she needed me. That usually meant Friday and Saturday evenings. Those were the times her crew of folks in their late teens and twenties wanted off to have fun. The arrangement helped keep Nic and her employees happy.

Showing up with her favorite grown-up beverage in hand

would be a bonus. My girlfriend made me a happy guy. I was always on the lookout to do things to return the feeling. Cheap labor and good rum. Yeah, those were two things I could provide.

When Jimmy Buffett's "The Wino and I Know" came through the truck's speakers, I started singing along at the top of my voice. The Springs had never been the same since the legendary storyteller made his way to the Great Margaritaville in the Sky. Yes, his tunes were played every bit as often in the bars and restaurants as before his passing, but since then, the locals took a moment to bow their heads in his memory.

I chose a different tack. I played his music even more often than I had in the past and sang along to every single one of them. And I played it a lot. I was also rereading his books and had joined an effort pushing the local community theater group to perform his musical *Don't Stop the Carnival.*

Jimmy made the world a better, kinder, and more fun place. The least I could do to repay him was keep his music alive in my little corner of paradise and, like the Wino, keep living my life like a song.

Before I knew it, Jordan's house came into view. It was a single-story bungalow painted the pale pink shade of the inside of a conch shell. A wooden porch ran along the front, where three rocking chairs sat empty. Later in the day, Jordan's parents would be occupying two of them. Porch sitting was one of their favorite pastimes. It was something my employee shared with them. It made me happy that he valued time with the people who raised him.

As I pulled into the driveway, I wiped a tear from the corner of my eye. What I would do to be able to spend an evening sitting in a rocking chair hanging out with my dad. I shook the thought away as I turned off the engine. Someday, maybe, on another plane of existence, I'd get that chance. For now, I had things to do right here.

On either side of the house, palm trees rose twenty feet into the air, giving the home a quintessential tropical vibe. Jordan was seated at the foot of the palm tree to my right. His legs were crossed in a classic meditative position with his wrists resting on his knees and thumbs and second fingers touching.

"What is up, boss?" He opened one eye. "Ready to go slay the dragon?"

Despite myself, I laughed. "You shouldn't talk about a client that way, man." I extended my hand to help him up. He waved me off and popped to his feet like a human pogo stick.

"True. You shouldn't, either." He wagged his finger at me. "You'd be surprised what these ears pick up."

"Guilty as charged. How about we keep this between the two of us and go see our valuable client Chef Claudine?"

The restaurant's kitchen area was bustling with activity when we arrived. The dining area was quiet. Such was the life of a restaurant thirty minutes before opening. The head chef informed me that Claudine was in her upstairs office and wanted a word with us before we left. When I asked her what it was about, she shrugged and went back to supervising the preparation of the day's special, grilled sea bass with seasonal vegetables served on a bed of rice pilaf.

I had to practically drag Jordan out of the kitchen. The man loved his seafood.

With me by his side, he checked the front of the house first. I smiled when he stopped to check two questionable spots where the baseboards met the floorboards. While there was no evidence of any presence of critters, his attention to detail was impressive.

The situation was the same in the back of the house. All good news. Since we were nearing hurricane season and the monsoons that came with them, Jordan asked if we should put out any traps in anticipation of unwelcome visitors seeking shelter.

"Let's discuss it with Claudine." I didn't think it was necessary, but the fact that he was thinking ahead impressed me. It would be a chance to show our client he had a good head on his shoulders, too.

Even if sometimes he could make it look like he didn't have any shoulders.

I let him do the outdoor inspection solo. On his return, he reported there were no problems.

"Excellent. Let's go see Chef."

The woman was seated at her desk. She was writing in a notebook when we knocked on the door frame.

"Come in, gentlemen. I've been working on a new menu item for the Independence Day holiday. I wanted Mr. Selassie's thoughts."

"How may I be of service?" With a wide smile, Jordan took a seat. He was a born salesperson.

And a bold one, too. I'd never had the guts to sit down in Claudine's office without a specific invitation to sit. Then again, she'd never asked me for input on one of her recipes, either. Double points for him.

She opened her mouth, then closed it and turned her attention to me. "As this is a matter regarding proprietary recipe information, you may be excused, Mr. Simpson. Good luck on your investigation. Unsolved murders are bad for business. Even mine."

I bit back a snarky response and instead shook her hand and left. It wasn't a good idea to tangle with Claudine. Thanks to my previous investigation, I had information about Paradise Springs' preeminent culinary expert. She knew that I had it. Even with that ace up my sleeve, the wrong word could get me fired.

If it was still only me involved with Elmo's Critter Removal, losing her business, and the headaches that came with it, wouldn't be much of a loss. With Jordan on board, I didn't want that to happen. I had no idea if owning the Sea Breeze would monopolize my time so much that I'd have to let go of my current day job. If that happened, I wanted to be able to turn it over to Jordan in the best financial condition possible. Maintaining Claudine as a client would help accomplish that goal.

Jordan found me in the bar, sipping an iced tea and pondering the case. I got up, but he waved me back into my seat.

"Chef said for us to enjoy lunch on her today." With the grace of a ballet dancer, he slid onto the chair across from me and gestured to the bartender.

"What did you do?" In all the years I'd provided the restaurant my services, I'd never received so much as a Christmas card from the woman. She was as notoriously tight-fisted with her suppliers as she was as volatile with people who got under her skin.

He ran his long fingers along the collar of his shirt. "My mom wanted to have her own restaurant when she was young. She's amazing in the kitchen. Chef's had her food and wanted to know what my mom would think of a new seasoning mixture she's working on."

"Why doesn't she ask your mom?"

"Mom won't share her secrets to anyone outside the family, so people come to me instead." He tapped the side of his head. "That information's good for two or three free meals a year. And I never have to give any of her secrets away."

I shook my head. I had no idea the guy was so talented. I also wasn't going to let an opportunity like this pass me by.

"What do I have to do to get you to make some gourmet burgers on my grill at the trailer?"

He laughed, then grew serious. "Tell you what. You figure out who killed Desiree, I'll make a meal for you and Miss Nicola that you'll never forget."

I couldn't agree to that offer fast enough.

I had an amazing feast of spicy gumbo with andouille sausage and melt-in-your-mouth garlic bread for lunch. Jordan went through a double order of blackened fish tacos that had him uttering phrases like *over the moon*, and *best lunch ever*. To be fair, providing a service to Claudine did have its perks.

We'd barely left the parking lot after our meal when he asked me how the investigation was going.

"Making progress." I recounted the relevant conversations I'd had over the past few days. "Know anything about the elusive Bobby Darrin?"

"That dude is bad news. He's a con artist who's convinced his next score will set him up for life. Except he doesn't have the charisma to pull any of his schemes off."

I raised my eyebrows. Jordan was one of the nicest folks I knew. The worst thing I'd ever heard him say about someone was that maybe they were having a bad day.

"Why don't you tell me how you really feel about him?"

"If it wasn't for his aunties, he'd be in jail. How's that?" Jordan wrapped his arms around himself. A feat he could literally do thanks to his slim frame and contortionist skills. "He ripped me off one Saturday night. Had someone distract me, then grabbed my tip hat and took off. I was having a great night. There was at least a hundred bucks in there."

"Yowza, not cool." I felt for Jordan. The Paradise Springs street performers were hardworking souls who played a big part in the town's funky vibe. Like the classic film character Blanche DuBois, they depended on the kindness of strangers to help them get by. I'd be angry with Bobby if he'd done the same lowdown, dirty, rotten thing to me, too.

"I had eyewitnesses and everything, but by the time the cops tracked him down, the money was gone. He said he swiped the hat as a prank and that it was empty when he took it. He gave me that hat back and was acting all, *Sorry for the misunderstanding, buddy.* He's the worst."

"Do you think he's a killer?"

"If there was enough money in it for him, yeah. Him and Desiree weren't married, though, so it's not like he's in line to cash in on a life insurance policy."

I nodded as we came to a stop at a red light. Traffic on a Friday afternoon in June was heavy. It was one of the things that helped teach the locals the value of patience. Traffic meant tourists, which meant money. We were all willing to put up with the congestion since it meant dollars were going into local coffers.

Jordan interrupted my musings about the local economy when he let out a low whistle. A spotless gold Range Rover, complete with spinning rims that matched the paint job, crossed through the intersection.

"Man, that is one sweet ride."

It was way too gaudy for my tastes, but I didn't want to rain on his parade. "Where do you think they're from?"

"That's not a tourist. That's Craig Abbott. You know—"

"I know exactly who that is. If he hadn't have come to town, Desiree would have never left working with Nic."

He nodded. "Sorry I brought it up, man."

"Don't be." I turned left to follow the vehicle. "I'd like to have a word with him."

CHAPTER FIFTEEN

A S WE FOLLOWED the garish SUV, I had flashbacks to another time I'd chased a vehicle while investigating a murder. I loosened my grip on the steering wheel. This time, I was going along at a few miles per hour below the speed limit.

Nothing like the previous race through town at twice the speed limit.

Eventually, Craig came to a stop at his company's ticket booth near the marina. The canary-yellow fiberglass structure was an old travel trailer that had been converted to serve as the base of operations for Craig's Cruises. In the middle of the structure, a small flight of stairs led to a door. To the right of the door, a canopy provided customers relief from the sun while they conducted business at the ticket window.

"What are you going to say to him?" Jordan opened the passenger-side door.

"Not sure. But he was at the Magnificent Marlin the night Desiree died. Maybe he can help establish where she was and when."

"Do you think she really was poisoned?"

"Don't know. Only way to find out is to keep poking." I opened my door. "And hope we don't find ourselves face-to-face with a hornet's nest."

Craig was lugging a cardboard box from his car when I came up alongside him. He was dressed in a light blue long-sleeved dress shirt, tan pants, and loafers. Not exactly the attire for carrying around heavy work materials. I couldn't help wondering if he was doing chores that had been Desiree's responsibility.

"Gentlemen, care to book a cruise? I'd be happy to answer any questions you may have. We have sunrise cruises, sunset cruises, dolphin cruises, fishing expeditions, Jet Ski excursions, and party boat rentals." He gave my hand a vigorous shake. "Mr. Simpson, since you're a fan of the competition, you and your associate can take your pick of two tickets to any cruise, free of charge if you book right here, right now."

Jordan's eyes went wide at the offer. I could practically see the wheels in his brain turning. He fancied himself a flirt and was probably figuring out how to parlay the offer into an opportunity to ask someone out on a date.

I wasn't so easily swayed. Though it was a decent sales pitch.

"I believe my friend Jordan would like to take you up on your offer. I was hoping you could help me out with something different."

Craig hesitated a moment, then his wide grin returned. With a nod, he took Jordan by the shoulder and guided him to the ticket counter line. After conferring with an employee, he returned to me.

"How may I be of service?" He put on a pair of dark

sunglasses. Slick move. It made it more difficult to get a read on him.

"I wanted to ask you about the night Desiree LaFontaine was murdered. I understand you were there." A better man might have offered him condolences on the loss of his operations manager. Given what Craig did to Nic, I'd be the better man some other time.

"I was. I talked to Chief Eikenberry about it the other day. Told her everything I could remember from that awful night. Are you working with the police?"

"Alongside them. I was asked to look into some things related to that night."

He raised his eyebrows. "Like a private investigator? I thought you were the local exterminator."

"Animal removal specialist, yes. I'm conducting an investigation at a client's request. I have experience with this sort of thing." It wasn't a lie, even if it was a serious case of me splitting hairs. "How was Desiree feeling that night?"

"Well." He rubbed his chin in apparent thought. "It's not like we were joined at the hip, but as the night went on, she did get a little tipsy. She'd been working hard, though. I didn't see anything wrong with her cutting loose a little. Man, I'm going to miss her."

"Do you remember where she was getting her drinks? Was a server bringing them to her or was she going to the bar?"

"Beats me. She talked to a lot of people throughout the night. The only time we sat down together was when we chatted with Ms. Beecham."

I'd been hoping to ask Nic about that very conversation when the evening's cruise was over. Our jobs kept us super busy this time of the year. In the past, days might go by with the only communication between us conducted via text message. That arrangement was easy. If I wanted more out of the relationship, though, I needed to up my game. She deserved more than what I'd given her in the past and more was what I was going to do.

"Yeah, I heard about that." I wasn't going to waste my time asking this guy about the argument. Nic's version would suffice. "What time did you leave?"

"I'm not sure exactly, thought it was about eleven when I got home. I remember checking the time on my phone. I had a business meeting in Houston at nine the next morning. I was on my way back here when I got word about Desiree. It's a huge loss."

"I'm sure. How did she seem when you last saw her? You said she was tipsy. Was she in a good mood or a bad one?"

"She was upset with the result of our meeting with Ms. Beecham. Is there a point to all of this? I thought she was the police's main suspect."

I shrugged. He'd find out about Nic's innocence soon enough.

"The multitool that was found at the scene didn't match the stab wounds. Desiree was murdered by something else. I'm trying to figure out what, exactly, that was."

Craig's jaw dropped. It was too bad he was wearing shades. The look of utter astonishment on his face would have been priceless to see.

After a few seconds, he pointed at me. "Now I get it. With all the question about where she was getting her drinks and how she was feeling, you think she was poisoned, don't you?"

"I'm not ruling anything out."

The door behind Craig opened. A short fellow with thinning hair on top stepped outside. "Hey, Mr. Abbott. Sorry to bother you. We're having some trouble with the credit card machine. Can you take a look at it?"

Craig balled his hands into fists. He relaxed them, then looked at the man. "Isn't that something that falls under your job description, Oliver?"

"Well, yeah. I'm still learning the system, though. Desiree always—"

"Yes, I know. Desiree always took care of things like this. If you're going to be my new Number One, you need to learn to handle these things yourself." He let out a dramatic sigh as he turned back to me. "If you'll excuse me, Mr. Simpson, duty calls. If there's anything I can do to help with your investigation, let me know."

As we shook hands, I told him I'd do just that. Jordan came up alongside me as Craig closed the door behind him.

"How'd it go, boss? Get anything good?"

"Maybe. Apparently, he's got a replacement for Desiree already in place. Know anything about this Oliver guy?"

"I know he used to live here. Came back to town with Craig and helped him get things set up, but that's it. Why?"

"Because now that Desiree's gone, he just got a promotion. Did he kill her to get the job? I don't know. It's worth looking into, don't you think? I know I do."

CHAPTER SIXTEEN

"*SALUD.*" NIC CLINKED her plastic cup against mine. We were sitting on the deck of her tour boat, taking a well-earned breather. The sunset cruise had been a sellout, which was great news. Even better news was that the crowd had been mostly families with young kids. That meant they were well-behaved.

And were good tippers, too. Even if one little boy did get seasick.

I took a drink of my rum. The spicy liquor danced on my taste buds until I swallowed. The rums available in Indiana when I was younger couldn't hold a candle to the ones available here on the Gulf Coast. While I would deny the claim that I only started drinking rum because that's what Nic liked, it was probably true.

The woman had good taste in just about everything. I liked to think in men, too.

"It was a good crowd tonight. I would swear that one pod of dolphins knew we were carrying a bunch of tourists. I don't know how many people showed me pictures on their phones."

She chuckled. "The sci-fi author Douglas Adams claimed dolphins are smarter than humans. He might have been joking. He might have been onto something, though."

"Speaking of being onto something, or moving on, I guess, it must be a big relief that the cops are moving on from you."

"That it is. Susan's visit was the best thing to happen to me in a long time." She downed the contents of her cup. "With that in mind, I'm in the mood to celebrate. Hit me."

I poured a shot into her cup. She slammed it down like it was water, then asked for yet another one.

"How about I make dinner? I've got some kebabs marinating in the fridge at the trailer. And some sliced peppers and onions to go with them. Besides, Oscar misses you."

"Ha." Nic tossed her cup into the trash bag we'd taken with us when we disembarked. "The only thing that mangy cat misses is seeing more food poured into his bowl. You spoil him. You know that, right?"

"I do. He's put up with me all these years, it's the least I can do." I wanted to throw in a line about how I liked spoiling her, but she'd respond by rolling her eyes or shaking her head and calling me a blockhead or something like that.

She smiled when I offered her my hand as she stepped off the boat. Didn't object when I opened the truck's passenger door for her, either.

The little things were her love language. Even if she didn't want to admit it, I knew.

A bit later, the kebabs and peppers were sizzling on the grill. Nic had her feet up on a spare patio chair. She was munching on pita chips and hummus. Oscar was on her lap, purring away as she scratched him between bites of the appetizer.

"Did Susan give you hints about suspects?" I kept my thoughts about the poisoning to myself. I didn't want to ruin Nic's mood by delving too far into the case. I'd take it one question at a time and let her responses guide me.

"No. To be honest, I was too relieved to ask any questions. I mean, I know I was out on the boat when Desiree died, and Susan told me she never really suspected me. I'd still like to know who stole my multitool, though."

I turned the kebabs. Since she seemed willing to discuss the case, another question couldn't hurt.

"I ran into Abbott today." Yes, I'd done more than that, but discretion was the better part of valor. Especially when mentioning the man to Nic. With kebab skewers within her reach.

"What did that jerk have to say?"

"Not a lot. I asked him about Desiree's actions that night. Trying to get an idea if she was poisoned by the Farrell sisters as revenge for her breaking up with Bobby."

"Huh. I thought you promised me you were going to stay out of it and keep any sleuthing to finding out who stole from me."

"I did. I think the two are related, so I decided to do some poking around. I mean, regardless of how low it was for her to jump ship, she didn't deserve to have her life taken."

"That's true. It still hurts, you know? I thought we had something good together. Something more important than money. I had plans." She wiped her cheek with the heel of her hand. "And now I'll never get to tell her how sorry I am for getting mad at her for leaving."

Nic wasn't one to wear her emotions on her sleeve. She confided in me years ago that she worked hard at keeping an even keel in public. The sexist old-timers at the marina jumped at the chance to dismiss her as a *hysterical woman* the one time she got emotional while on the job.

Even in private moments, she was the stoic one. When we watched a romantic or heartfelt movie, I was the one with a pile of used tissues, red eyes, and stuffy nose at the end. The only time I'd seen her full-on weep was when her grandfather, the man who taught her how to navigate by the stars as a child, passed away.

For her to shed a tear, even after a few drinks, showed how tough it was for Nic to lose Desiree, first as a coworker and friend, and then for good.

At times like this, I liked to use the approach my mom used when I was feeling blue.

"Do you want to talk about it?" *It* was Desiree's unpleasant departure from Paradise Springs Charters. *Unpleasant* was being kind. *Acrimonious* was more accurate. Nic had refused to discuss what had happened every time I brought it up.

Now seemed like a good time for her to get some things off her chest.

"No."

"It'll make you feel better." I emulated my mom's sing-song tone while I plated the kebabs and grilled veggies. I dropped a few morsels of the grilled chicken in a small bowl for Oscar. If he was going to hang out with us, he was going to expect dinner, too.

"Food that I don't have to make is what'll make me feel better." She cut her chicken with the ferocity of a lioness who hadn't eaten in days. In midcut, she lost her grip on the utensils. They fell to the ground with a clatter that sent Oscar scrambling under the table for shelter. After dropping a string of curse words, she put her head in her hands.

"All right, you win."

I fetched a replacement set of utensils, then took my seat in silence while I placed Oscar's bowl on the floor.

"I was caught totally off guard when Desiree told me she was quitting. Shoot, when she showed up at my place that night, I was working on a business plan to buy another tour boat. She was going to captain it. Instead, before I could even say anything, she handed me her keys and told me she was quitting. That Abbott had given her an offer she couldn't refuse." She shook her head. "Can you believe that?"

"This offer she couldn't refuse didn't involve a horse's head wrapped up in her bedsheets, did it?"

"What?" Nic furrowed her eyebrows. "Oh, wait. Now I get it." She chuckled. "No, nothing like that. Two stars out of five for the joke. And that's for trying to lighten the mood."

"Sorry." My sense of humor wasn't for everyone. Lucky for me, Nic got it. Most of the time.

"Yeah, well." She chewed on a forkful of grilled peppers. "I'll admit, I didn't respond well. Said some things I shouldn't have."

"Who can blame you? She didn't give you any notice and didn't even give you the courtesy of letting you make a counteroffer." Sure, I cared more for Nic than anyone else on the planet, so my perspective might have been a little skewed. It didn't change the fact that dropping a bomb on her like Desiree did was unprofessional at best, and a stab in the back at worst.

"I tried. I showed her the plan I was working on. She said she needed the security Abbott offered her. And, get this, she was tired of me taking advantage of her."

The accusation made my blood boil. I'd seen Nic's financials. She wasn't getting rich by any means. And, as sure as the sun was going to come up tomorrow, she wasn't taking advantage of Desiree, or anyone else. That was part of the reason she lived on her boat. The slip rental was way less expensive than anywhere she'd want to live on land. The work, and money, simply hadn't been there to keep Desiree on the payroll full-time all year-round. The woman had known that for years.

"That doesn't sound like Desiree. That sounds like something Abbott told her to say to make her feel better about leaving you in the lurch."

"Doesn't matter much now. Does it?"

It did to me, but I wasn't going to argue the point. Instead, we ate in relative silence, only speaking about the weather and marveling at how fast Oscar had gobbled up his chicken. When we were finished, I took the dinnerware inside and returned with another question.

"What did Abbott say that made you so mad the other night?"

"So, it's turning into Nic's night of confession, I see." She drained her glass of rum. "May as well get it out all at once. Pour me another drink, and I'll tell you."

I did as requested, making a point to add extra ice and less rum this time. Nic had a long day tomorrow with three cruises scheduled. I wouldn't be much of a boyfriend if she ended up working with a hangover.

To be fair, not once in the ten years or so that I'd known her had I ever seen Nicola Beecham hungover. Whether it was due to an admirable level of discipline she maintained when she imbibed or some gift of genetics, I didn't know. All I knew was I was jealous of her unique power.

Especially on those mornings when I'd shown a lack of Nic's discipline the previous evening.

She raised an eyebrow when I handed her the cup but chose not to comment on the ratio of ice to rum.

"Desiree texted me Monday night. She said Abbott wanted to run a proposition by me."

I took a drink of my ice water, then wiped my brow as Oscar jumped back onto Nic's lap. The sun was setting, but it was still hot enough to melt the ice in my cup in no time.

"I didn't want to go, but Abbott's operation is killing me. He can afford to pay the seasonal workers more than I can, so it's been tough to hire and keep people, even though I raised my pay scale. Income is flat while expenses are up. I figured it wouldn't hurt to hear what they had to say."

"You're a better person than me. I would have told him

to take a long walk off a short pier."

She winced. "I wish I would have told him that. Instead, I went. We did the typical small talk thing, had a drink. On his tab. Then we got down to business. Abbott said he knew how much I was struggling and thought he could help by us working together."

"Working together? Color me suspicious."

"Same thought that I had, so I asked him to elaborate. That's when Desiree started tapping her thumbs and index fingers together. That's her tell that she was nervous."

"Any idea what about?"

"Yeah. He told me he wanted to buy me out and roll my operation into his. He'd be in charge of the company. Desiree would run the operation here. I could still be captain of my boat."

I almost choked on the piece of ice I was chewing. The nerve of the man.

"That's not like any definition of *working together* that I've ever heard of."

"Same here." Nic cracked a half smile. "That's when I threw my drink in his face and told him to get lost. In so many words."

"Get lost? I heard you told him to commit a sexual act with himself."

"Like I said. In so many words." She rubbed the back of her neck. "Anyway, some less-than-pleasant words were exchanged. Desiree got between us before things got out of control. A good thing, too. I was about ready to slug the guy."

Nic wasn't much for exercise. As hard as she worked, she didn't need to. The physical exertion she put into maintaining her watercraft left her with a physique as solid as any fitness guru.

She was strong, too. I knew that from all of the arm-wrestling contests I'd lost to her. There was no doubt in my mind a single punch from Nic would have laid Abbott out cold on the floor.

"I guess it was good that Desiree was there."

"Yeah. At least I got to thank her for preventing a fight." Nic tapped her finger against her cup. "Now that I think about it, she seemed pretty miserable during the whole conversation."

I considered the observation for a moment. Craig had mentioned Desiree getting a little drunk but not anything about her being down. The guy was hardly trustworthy, though.

"She was probably dreading the idea of the two of you working together again. That would have been awkward with a capital *A*."

"True." She gave Oscar a scratch under his chin. "If that was it, she got herself worked up over nothing."

"Why do you say that?"

"Because I'd never sell my business. Not to him or anybody else."

"Did Desiree know that?"

"Of course she did. The stars above know we talked about our plans for running the operation until we were too old to do it. Then, we'd sail off into the Gulf and let the sea guide us to our next adventure."

"That's a nice thought." Cruising into the sunset with nowhere to be sounded like a fun retirement plan.

It made me wonder, though. If Desiree knew there was no way Nic would sell, why did she go along with her boss while he made the offer? Maybe she didn't want to. That would explain her sour mood. And would also explain why Craig failed to mention it during our conversation.

It also left me with another question. Was Desiree murdered because she knew something? Had she stumbled upon a secret? Perhaps a secret so loathsome that someone was willing to kill to keep it under wraps?

I could think of at least one person who'd fit into that category. Now, if only I could find him.

CHAPTER SEVENTEEN

I TOOK NIC home before it got too late. With the weekend in full swing, she was going to be working nonstop for the next two days. After she gave me a good night kiss, I asked her to text me if any of her employees called off. With her now out from under the cloud of suspicion, the last thing she needed was to take a hit on one of the busiest weekends of the year because of staffing shortages.

The stars shone like tiny little beacons as I meandered back my truck. I tried to count them but gave up after getting to one hundred. There were simply too many.

Just like the questions I had about Desiree's murder.

Not far away, the neon lights of the Magnificent Marlin beckoned. It was only ten o'clock. The real party hadn't even begun. Maybe I could pay the Farrell sisters another visit to see if Bobby had been in contact.

There was a line out the door of the nightclub, so I turned to head back to the truck. My questions could wait another day.

As I turned, Drunk Paul came into view, cruising along on his two-wheeler. I made a move in his direction. Apparently, I surprised him, because he stopped short, almost dumping his bike on its side.

"Hey, dude. Got a minute?"

He gave me a long, unblinking look. His eyes were more glazed over than usual. He smelled like someone had poured a pitcher of cheap beer on him. Sure, it was Friday night, but I'd never seen the man this intoxicated.

"I'm busy, Elmo." He waved a hand in the air. He was either trying to use the mystical signal Obi Wan Kenobi made in the first *Star Wars* movie to convince me those weren't the droids I was looking for or he wanted me to move out of his way.

"I know you are. I wanted to apologize for the other day. I didn't know about your connection to Desiree. I'm sorry."

He looked away and shook his head, pounding one fist on his handlebar. Eventually, he returned his gaze to me. His cheeks looked damp.

"Desiree did me wrong. Made me look stupid. That was a long time ago, but it still hurts."

I had him talking. Despite his appearance, he seemed lucid. Maybe I could get him to open up this time.

"Whoever said time heals all wounds never got hurt." I forced a laugh.

"Got that right." He extended his fist but leaned too far and lost his balance. I had to grab him by the shoulders to stop him from tumbling to the ground. "Thanks. You're not all that bad, Elmo. You know that?"

"I try. And I'm sorry for what she did to you. I remember my high school years. It was tough enough surviving without someone screwing you over like she did."

"Yeah." He picked at a scab on his arm. "Made my last

month of school a nightmare. Some people still bring it up. Like to laugh at me about it. The jerks."

"That's tough." I put my hand on his shoulder. Partly as a gesture of moral support and partly to make sure he remained on his feet. Regardless, his pain was real.

Every now and then, something would trigger memories of being bullied in high school. A group of meatheads had themselves a lot of fun by calling me Tickle Me Elmo the year that toy came out. I was fifteen at the time and kind of nerdy, a prime target for idiots who needed to make someone else feel small.

Almost thirty years later, I could laugh about it. Of course, having fifty million dollars in the bank made it a lot easier to brush off injustices from my childhood. Paul didn't have the resources I did.

He shrugged my hand off his shoulder. "Doesn't make a difference now. It's not like she can apologize from beyond the grave."

My sleuthing radar started pinging in my head. Paul's comment seemed to indicate a certain lack of remorse at Desiree's untimely death. What if he still harbored ill feelings toward the victim?

And what if something triggered him to act on those ill feelings?

"The other day, we never finished our conversation. Did you happen to be in the area the night Desiree was murdered?"

He stiffened and placed one foot on a pedal. "I don't know anything about it."

"You sure? Did you come this way on your way home? Maybe you saw something that didn't seem important at the time. It might be."

"I told you I don't know anything." He pushed me aside and pedaled away. Before I could regain my balance, he was out of sight.

There was no doubt that Drunk Paul had problems that only a professional could help. Chronic medical issues, either physical or mental, were tough to live with. I could empathize with his plight.

There was also no doubt that he was hiding something. And that something was connected to Desiree. Could he have harbored a grudge that festered untreated over the years until, like a metastatic cancer, it overwhelmed him and compelled him to do something horrible? If so, what triggered the act? I made a note to ask more questions about Paul and his star-crossed past with Desiree. Rambo would know. That guy knew everyone.

Sybil might know something, too. Though, with her, I never knew if she really could make contact with the other side or if she was just making stuff up.

With a sigh, I peered at the Gulf. A few lights were low on the horizon. A cargo vessel was on the move. That was one of the things about the ocean. It was alive and active, twenty-four hours a day.

Out of the corner of my eye, something down in the seagrass caught my attention. There was a difference in color of the shadows near the nightclub. It was like a spot of the deepest shade of obsidian was hovering around the area where Desiree was found.

I blinked to clear my vision. The shadow was gone.

"What the heck?" I walked to the edge of the parking lot. A concrete curb and rope fencing separated the asphalt tarmac from the sandy incline that led to the beach. I eased myself over the three-foot-high rope and made my way toward the spot in question, my sandals kicking up puffy clouds of white sand with each step.

When I reached the area in question, nothing seemed amiss. I bent over and tiptoed through the seagrass. My right hand brushed aside the blades while I used my left hand to pan back and forth with the flashlight on my phone. Twenty minutes of diligent looking failed to turn up anything other than a few plastic water bottles and a condom wrapper.

I was relieved that I failed to come across the contents of the wrapper. *Good golly, I'm getting old.*

With a sinking spirit, I went back to the place where Desiree had been found. Maybe I'd imagined the whole thing. It wouldn't be the first time. Weirdness abounded in the Springs.

One time, I thought I'd seen an alligator walking upright out of Goob's store. It turned out to be a high school kid filming a horror flick with his buddies. But that was the thing. I'd lived here long enough that I believed, until proven otherwise, that there might be a carnivorous reptile strolling around the marina area like there was nothing to it.

"Good evening, Elmo."

I let out a yelp, crouched down, and covered my face with my arms. My standard defensive move since high school. When I realized I wasn't going to be shoved inside a utility closet or pushed outside during a snowstorm, I lowered my arms.

"My apologies. It wasn't my intent to frighten you." A tall, thin man dressed head to toe in black emerged from the darkness. He offered to help me up.

"Thanks, Mr. Longfellow." I took his hand. It was as ice cold as it was snow white. Normally, he wore gloves. I guess since it was the middle of the night, he didn't need them. After all, Abraham Longfellow was the Vampire.

Well, it was rumored he was a vampire. Science and logic said he was simply a man who lived with the disease porphyria. It was a rare medical condition that caused an intense sensitivity to sunlight, among other symptoms. The thing was, nobody knew the man's age. His salt-and-pepper hair indicated he could be anywhere between thirty and seventy. The car he drove was built in the 1960s. He lived in a secluded mansion on the outskirts of town with a butler for company, but his only known source of income came from the aluminum and steel he collected and then sold for recycling.

"Please, call me Abraham. All my friends do." He smiled, revealing teeth as white as fine porcelain. And canines that were abnormally prominent. "We're friends, are we not?"

"Yeah, of course." I brushed sand off my legs to give me a moment to gather my wits. And to avoid looking at his fangs. They could puncture a young maiden's neck with ease. "It's been a while. How've you been?"

He waved his hand. The enormous ruby on his ring finger glowed in the dim light cast from the marquee above. "Oh, you know. Like everybody else, this is a busy time for me. More tourists means more recyclables which means more work for your friendly neighborhood recycling agent."

"Yeah, I imagine so." I pointed toward the top floor, where the thumping bass grooves the deejay was producing spilled out the open windows. "What brings you by? A little early to be picking up here, isn't it?"

"Indeed." He reached into a pocket of his trench coat. "I have something I'd like to give you."

I tensed, my fight-or-flight instinct in full-on *ready to scamper* mode. Yes, the Vampire freaked me out.

He withdrew a brown paper lunch bag just like the kind my mom used when I was in elementary school.

"Go ahead. It shan't bite." He chuckled. "I won't, either. Unless you want me to."

It took all my willpower to refrain from snatching the bag from him and dashing away. Distance equated to safety, after all. Instead, I reminded myself that Nic was friends with him. If she trusted the guy, I should be able to do the same.

After giving it a little shake, I moved to an area with more light, then opened the bag. There was a multitool in it. *What is it with these things?* This contraption was larger than the one found with Desiree.

"Okay. Um, thank you?"

He handed me a surgical-type glove that he used when he was picking up his recyclables. "If you take a closer look, you will find something intriguing."

Once my hand safe inside the glove, I removed the tool

and stared at it. Even in the meager light, the dull discoloration all over the steel blade was impossible to miss. I turned my phone's flashlight on. With better illumination, the discoloration took on a familiar dull brownish color. I slipped the tool back into the bag.

"Zoinks, that's blood."

"My assessment, as well." He grinned, which sent a shudder through me.

"Do you think this is connected to Desiree LaFontaine's murder?" There was little other reason for the Vampire to give it to me. I didn't want to assume, though. Not with a killer still on the loose.

"That is my assumption, yes. With news of dear Nicola and her device being cleared of wrongdoing, it's logical to deduce this gadget is the murder weapon. I thought the authorities should be made aware of it."

It was tough to be certain, but the blade seemed to be longer and wider than Nic's. Which would fit with the information in the medical examiner's report.

The Vampire distrusted the police due to problems he'd experienced with them in the past. He didn't specify which authorities or whether pitchforks and torches had been involved. I was too afraid to ask.

"This could be huge, Abraham. I'll take it to the police station right away. If you don't mind me asking, where did you find it?"

He clapped. "I knew giving it to you was the right decision. Big Baby assured me that if you're good enough for dear Nicola, you're trustworthy enough to ensure this is presented to Chief Eikenberry in the appropriate manner. I'm afraid I don't know, precisely, other than it was during my rounds. I'll leave that to you to investigate further. And now, I must be off. Farewell, Simpson. Good luck in your pursuit."

He bowed, then ascended the incline without disturbing so much as a grain of sand. Almost as if he was floating. I tucked the bag into a pocket and headed for the beach bar. As was usually the case after I had an encounter with Abraham Longfellow, I needed a drink.

CHAPTER EIGHTEEN

"**Y**OU LOOK ALMOST as bad as the two morons I've got locked up in the drunk tank." Susan Eikenberry shook her head but still gestured for me to take a seat across from her. "At least you don't smell as bad."

Looking down, I realized that my shirt, while clean, was inside out. A glance in the mirror while brushing my teeth earlier had revealed dark circles under my eyes. Yeah, I did resemble someone who'd been out too late carousing and hadn't gotten enough sleep. Without bothering to ask permission, I whipped my shirt off and put it back on, right-side out.

"Better? Didn't sleep well last night. This is the reason." I pushed the paper bag containing the murder weapon across her desk.

The chief looked at it like I'd offered her a cup of week-old coffee. "It's too flat to be dog doo. I assume there's something inside you want me to take a look at."

"Yeah. I think it's the weapon used to stab Desiree."

She raised an eyebrow. The real way. Not the pained attempt Officer Nimoy made. After donning a pair of latex gloves taken from a desk drawer, she removed the piece of evidence.

"What is it with multitools in this case?" Even though she'd asked the question under her breath, it was loud enough to make me laugh.

"I had the same question last night." Using a pencil from a pineapple-shaped jar on her desk, I pointed out the brownish smears. "That looks like dried blood to me. I didn't open the blade, but I'm betting it's longer than the one in Nic's multitool."

She opened the blade. It was covered from point to heel in blood. We looked at each other. There was no doubt that it was both larger and longer than Nic's blade. The million-dollar question hung in the air, like the Sword of Damocles.

"It's the murder weapon, isn't it?" I couldn't help myself. I should have kept my mouth shut. The chief didn't like jumping to conclusions.

"Possibly." She pressed a button on her desk phone and asked Spock to join us.

Mere seconds later, he entered. "Officer Nimoy, reporting as requested, Chief."

"At ease, Officer. This isn't the military." She smirked as she shot me a quick glance. "Please enter the contents of this bag into evidence in the LaFontaine case and send it to the lab for testing. I want fingerprints, DNA, blood type, anything else they can get."

"Yes, sir, I mean, ma'am." The poor guy's cheeks turned bright red as he took hold of the bag. "I mean, yes, Chief."

Once the door shut with a click, she let out a sigh. "He wants to be promoted so much."

"Is that a bad thing?"

"No. I love his drive and his desire to please. He's like a puppy. He's got a long way to go before he's detective material, though."

I considered Susan's words. Apparently, she wasn't ruling a promotion out. The thought made me smile. Spock was a dork, but he was our dork. The man only wanted one thing. To make Paradise Springs a safe place for everyone.

"Well." I got to my feet. "With my work here done, I'll be going. Those critters won't remove themselves."

She put her hand up like a STOP sign. "You're not going anywhere, Simpson. How did that multitool come to be in your possession?"

"A concerned citizen gave it to me." I'd been ready for the question. A sleepless night mulling over the find's implications wasn't without benefits. I told her about my meeting with the Vampire. Without mentioning his name.

She tapped the desktop with her index finger, her blue eyes boring into me. "How do you know this *concerned citizen* isn't the murderer?"

Any number of images came to my mind when the name Abraham Longfellow was mentioned—mystery man, lothario, recycling maven, classic car owner, vampire. Murderer was not among them.

"I don't. But I don't see this person as the murderer. Not in a million years."

He might have murdered other people. If those fangs were used for sucking blood and not just abnormally long. The jury was still out on that in my mind. No way he murdered Desiree, though. Otherwise, why would give me the potential murder weapon? For payback? For misdirection? To simply play games with me?

Nope. Things like that were beneath him. Someone else was the murderer.

"I hope you'll forgive me for not taking you at your word. I have to go with things like evidence instead of my gut."

"Which is what that multitool is." I took a step toward the door, but she stopped me by clearing her voice.

"Yesterday, you were convinced Ms. LaFontaine's cause of death was poisoning. Now, you're saying stabbing did her in. What changed?"

"Nothing's changed. I'm sure the autopsy found alcohol in her system, but it will be a while to get toxicology results."

Other than a slight hand gesture for me to continue, the chief's expression gave nothing away. She was known around town as a lethal card sharp, so the poker face wasn't a surprise. The stars above knew I'd lost a fair amount of cash to her over the years. That was why my wagers with her no longer involved money.

"Okay, cards on the table." I grimaced at the poker analogy. "Desiree had that big blowup with Bobby Darrin last December. His aunts are protective of him. What if one of the Farrell sisters slipped something lethal into Desiree's drink, then stabbed her in a misdirection ploy? You and your team spend your time looking for a stabber like Drunk Paul or Nic. In the time it takes to get a complete toxicology report back, Bobby and/or the sisters leave town, never to be seen or heard from again."

"What's their motive?"

"Revenge. They never forgave Desiree for getting you involved in the car fiasco and then dumping him. Or, Bobby poisoned her and they're protecting him. They said he was out of town the night of the murder but claim they don't know where he is."

"Interesting theory, Simpson. I'll give you that." She ticked away at her keyboard. "There's nothing in the ME's initial report about poisoning. If the full tox report comes back with something positive, I'll look into it. Until then, I have to follow the evidence. Sorry."

"Don't be. I get it. Appreciate your time."

"That's what I'm here for. I hope you realize I can't reveal the test results from that blade to you."

"I do. And no need. The blood will match Desiree's type and there won't be any fingerprints on it. I'd bet an order of the Riptide's screamin' hot wings on it."

"Deal." She gave me her famous sharklike smile that was universally known as the *I've got you now* look. There was no way I could back out.

Which, in this instance, was fine. I'd keep my investigation going. Identifying Desiree's murderer would be way more satisfying than suffering through a plate of hot wings. Maybe I could even get Wendell to slip me a few mild ones. I mean, catching a murderer ought to be good for a favor now and then, right?

On my way out of the police station, I stopped by Spock's desk. He was working on logging the multitool into evidence. I gave him a quick pat on the shoulder.

He kept his gaze on his computer screen. "Can't talk now, Elmo. Need to get this to the crime lab ASAP."

I leaned in close. "You didn't hear this from me, but the Vampire found it while making his rounds. He asked me to turn it in. You know how it is."

Spock turned to me, his mouth open in a large O. Then he nodded and returned to his task. "Message received."

Leaving the station, I tried to figure out what spurred me to share the tidbit of information with Officer Nimoy. It wasn't gratitude. The guy was annoying as much as anything else. He was trying the best he could, though.

His situation reminded me of when I was struggling to find my place in the world. A few kind words from a few Paradise Springs natives changed my life's entire trajectory all those years ago. Maybe I could do something similar by helping Spock on his quest to become a detective. If nothing else, it would be some good karma.

With the current state of my investigation—a lot of theories but not a lot of facts—I would take all the good karma I could get.

CHAPTER NINETEEN

I SPENT THE rest of the morning on service calls, then stopped at Goob's to grab some lunch. I was seated under an umbrella at one of the wrought-iron tables right outside the store, munching on a beef po boy, when Gretchen slid into the chair across from me.

"What's shaking, Tickle Me Elmo?" She laughed. "Or am I not allowed to call you that anymore, since, you know, you're my boss?"

"I have no idea what you're talking about. Though I did happen to see a blurb in the *Palladium* about some outfit called Lone Palm, LLC buying the resort. How was your workout?"

She wiped her forehead with a towel, then took a drink from a massive water bottle as big as Oscar. Sporting a neon yellow tank top and burgundy leggings, Gretchen must have recently finished a yoga session. The rolled-up mat sticking out of her gym bag was a bit of a giveaway. Shawn Spencer from *Psych* would have been proud of me.

"It was good. Got rid of a lot of stress that built up over the week. I'm thrilled with the promotion, but it's a big step. And not everybody is happy about it."

I'd become so focused on the day job and the investigation that I hadn't given any thought about the announcement of her move to chief of operations. I was getting dangerously close to juggling too many flaming torches. If I wasn't careful, one of them was going to burn me. I'd worry about that later, though.

"I know this is going to sound like a cliché, but the only person you really have to keep happy is your boss. I offered you the position because I think you'll be great at it. I have your back 100 percent. Hopefully, that relieves some stress yoga didn't take care of."

Gretchen laughed. "You're the best, Elmo. Nicola's lucky to have you." Her smile drooped. "I'm worried about Craig, though. I haven't seen him at yoga all week and he never misses a session. He's one of my best students."

"I ran into him the other day. Don't worry, only metaphorically." Gretchen, like pretty much everyone who knew me, was well aware that the guy wouldn't be getting a Christmas card from me anytime soon. "Seemed fine to me."

Gretchen sat back in her chair and took another slurp from her bottle. "Oh, good. I was afraid after losing Desiree, he might have done something rash or, I don't know, hurt himself."

Gretchen, bless her soul, chose to look at the world through rose-colored glasses. If it was raining, she'd remark about how the plants needed the water. Shoot, one time a kid tried to snatch her purse while she was hanging out at the Paradise Springs Pier. Due to the crowds, the thief didn't get far before Seven Banderas laid him out with a flying tackle that would have made the legendary football coach Don

Shula proud.

What did Gretchen do when Seven hauled the kid back to her? She took all the cash from her wallet and gave it to the scruffy boy. Sixty-seven dollars. Then she told Seven to let him go. Later, when someone asked her why, she said he had frayed clothes and sad eyes and clearly needed the money a lot more than she did.

I didn't have to like Craig, but I could choose to be like Gretchen and take the high road.

"I'm sure he's really busy right now. With Desiree gone, he's got to be scrambling. The guy he's got covering for her didn't seem to be cutting it."

"Is that Oliver King? He came back here with Craig. He's staying at the resort. I see him in the lobby from time to time."

When I nodded, Gretchen leaned forward. "I don't think he's very happy here. He's always in a rush, like he's perpetually behind on his to-do list. I don't think I've seen him smile since their first week in town."

Gretchen was a legend at reading people. It was one of the reasons she was an excellent concierge and would be an even better general manager. Her assessments of people were on the mark. This one gave me an idea.

"Does he ever stop to talk? Maybe to vent about his job?"

"Not to me. Whenever I asked him about his day, he'd give me a smile that made him look like he was constipated and say he was fine. Everything was always fine with him. He gets a lot of carryout from the Riptide. Maybe you could talk to Seven. If anyone could get the guy to spill his guts, it's her."

We both laughed. Seven could make a man weak in the knees with a glance. On more than one occasion, a smile had sent a man down on one knee to propose marriage to her. I'll never forget the time I admitted to Nic that I had a bit of a crush on Seven, even though I was way too old for her. My girlfriend told me she felt the exact same way.

Seven had that effect on people.

"I'll talk to her. Thanks for the tip."

Gretchen raised her eyebrows. "You think Oliver had something to do with Desiree's murder?"

"I don't know. He was happy when he got here. Then Craig stole Desiree from Nic."

"And all of a sudden, Oliver turned into a sourpuss. Co-incidence?"

"I don't know." A charge of electricity coursed through me. My next move became clear. "But I know who will. Thanks, Gretchen. You're a rock star."

Between work appointments and covering for one of Nic's crew mates who called off, the rest of my Saturday flew by faster than Oscar could inhale a handful of kitty treats.

That meant I wasn't able to track down Craig until Sunday. It also meant I had plenty of time to formulate a list of questions for the guy.

I didn't bother knocking on the office door. The element of surprise was part of the plan.

"Mr. Simpson, this an employee-only area." He grasped his phone as he started to get up.

"No need to get all formal on my account." I dropped

into the chair across from him. "I talked to Nic. Not much of a buyout offer. No wonder she threw her drink in your face."

He stiffened, then smiled. It was a gesture that matched the myriad framed photographs of him hanging on the wall. The guy must have been quite the sports fan. There were shots of him at high-profile sporting events like the Masters golf tournament, the Tour de France, and a Formula 1 auto race. He wasn't just a spectator, though. One photo caught him on a fishing boat, standing next to a marlin as long as he was tall. Another showed him in camo gear with a rifle slung over his shoulder. A multi-antlered deer lay at his feet. He was dressed in skydiving gear, giving the photographer a thumbs-up, in an additional photo.

All with the same smile. It said Craig Abbott was living the high life and loving every minute of it.

"I was doing her a favor by offering to buy her out. She shot herself in the foot by turning me down. One boat can't compete with my fleet."

"We'll see. What was the real reason you hired Desiree? Was it to get intel on Nic's operation?"

"Now you're sounding paranoid. Desiree knows, I mean, knew the area. She brought a lot to the operation."

"And by a lot, you mean a lot of inside knowledge that Oliver didn't have? Knowledge you needed to make sure your operation didn't founder the second it hit the water?"

"Mr. Simpson, I told you already, I don't know who murdered Desiree. My staff is having a hard enough time coping with her loss. You're not helping anyone by barging

156

in here and pestering me."

"Oliver wasn't happy with your decision to hire Desiree." I made sure my accusation sounded like a statement. If he thought I knew something, he might dish on his employee.

Craig scratched the sleeve of his suit jacket. "I've had enough of your little games. If you don't leave, I'm calling the police."

I stood. He could think he'd won this round. Which couldn't be further from the truth.

"No need for that. I want to find Desiree's murderer. Since she worked for you, I thought you might have some insight into what was going on in her life. My apologies."

"I want her murderer caught, too, Mr. Simpson. I prayed for it at church this morning."

Church. That explained him being all dressed up. The last time I wore a tie was when I went to a Halloween party at the Riptide. I donned my gray suit, parted my hair on the side, walked around with a pipe in my hand, and told everybody I was Cary Grant. The younger crowd didn't get it, but Nic said she loved it. I considered that evening a smashing success.

And way more successful than my meeting with Craig.

After exiting the trailer, I took a peek into the ticket booth. There was no sign of Oliver. That didn't mean much, though. Craig's new second-in-command might have been working on one of their boats. I headed for the water, pondering why Craig didn't answer my question about his new second-in-command.

I laid eyes on my quarry. He was at the helm of a pontoon boat that was backing away from the dock. We locked gazes for the briefest of moments. Maybe I was making a mountain out of a molehill, but it sure seemed like Oliver narrowed his eyes and curled his lip before he looked away.

I'd have to arrange a chat with the man.

While I hadn't cracked the case, my trip to the marina had given me some promising items to think about. Since I needed to talk to Seven about Oliver, I didn't need Sybil to divine that lunch at the Riptide was in my immediate future.

I was about to pull out of my parking spot when a surprising sight caught my attention. Chef Claudine and the Reverend Andrew Jackson were walking toward her luxury vehicle. Holding hands. I didn't like passing judgment on people. The stars above knew how many poor decisions I'd made in my lifetime. It was undisputed, though, that the reverend was married, while the chef was single. The fact that they were engaged in a public display of affection struck a sour note.

What two consenting adults did in private was their own business. Infidelity was uncool, though. Especially if one of the people being unfaithful was an alleged source of moral guidance. As they got in the car, I wanted to dismiss the image as nothing more than friends showing affection toward each other.

I knew better, though.

It bummed me out to find out the two of them were still carrying on. As the car left the parking lot, it occurred to me that they'd parked in a relatively secluded spot. Maybe they were still trying to keep the relationship on the down-low, and I'd caught them in a momentary slipup.

Regardless, it gave me another idea. What if Desiree's murder was the result of a secret relationship gone bad? Or what if it was a secret relationship that Bobby uncovered? What if he then took matters into his own hands?

While I needed answers about Mr. King, once again, Mr. Darrin was still looking like a prime candidate for murder. If only I could find the guy. He'd stopped posting anything online the night of Desiree's murder. His aunts claimed they didn't know where he was. A phone number Nic gave me had gone to a voicemail box that was full. It was as if the guy had fallen off the face of the Earth.

Who disappeared like that? Someone who was either dead or was hiding. If he was hiding, a question was why? Another question was whether his decision to go underground had anything to do with Desiree's murder. Both were questions only he could answer.

CHAPTER TWENTY

S EVEN WAS RUNNING the Riptide's open-air bar when I arrived. And I mean running, back and forth behind the bar to keep up. All eight barstools were occupied by patrons. Customers were lined up at the server station to place orders. The seats around the six tables in front of the bar were fully taken, too. I sent a prayer to the stars above that the ice machine didn't blow a gasket.

At least she had some help. A tiny Kansas transplant who went by the name of Skye and used they/them pronouns was sprinting from table to table. They were taking orders, clearing away dinnerware, and refilling drinks. All without slowing down. And sporting a big smile the whole time.

"Hey, Mr. Elmo, got crawfish *étouffée* on special today. It would go perfect with a Riptide Red." They waved me toward the bar. "Come on. We've always got room for one more."

With a laugh, I followed Skye. Between their short stature and slim figure, they looked like they'd get eaten alive by a crowd of partying, summer vacationers. They had the sharpest elbows I'd ever encountered, though. And a whistle that could get the attention of a dog five miles away.

That's not an exaggeration. I'd seen the act performed in

person. And went home twenty dollars lighter after witnessing it.

A few well-timed moves with their elbows, a sharp word or two, and a threat to use Krav Maga created a space at one end of the bar. They gestured me toward it.

"That was more impressive than Noah parting the Red Sea." I gave them a fist bump.

"No big. I laid a guy out the other night after he made one too many crude comments about Seven." They gave me a wink and urged me forward. "Word gets around fast."

It took a minute once I was in position, but I managed to make eye contact with Seven. She lifted her chin and without speaking a word, served me a double Irish whiskey on the rocks. It was good to have friends; it was even better to have friends who knew what your favorite adult beverage was.

Intent on enjoying the sharp taste of the drink, I took small sips and let the liquor dance around on my tongue before swallowing. In no time, the cacophony surrounding me faded away and it was just me, my drink, and my thoughts.

Which went straight to the investigation.

My drink disappeared down my throat at a tortoise's pace compared to the tank-top-clad men to my left who were slamming back beers like there was no tomorrow. That was fine. I could continue my musings undisturbed until the lunch diners moved on. Then, I could bug Seven.

So, where exactly was I with the investigation? Given his stormy relationship with Desiree, Darrin was at the top of my suspect list. Thanks to a new promotion, King was coming on strong. Revenge was a dish best served cold, so Drunk Paul couldn't be discounted. Then there were the Farrell sisters. That was a trio I'd never want to cross. Had Desiree done something to anger them so much they took her life?

"What's it going to be, Elmo?" Seven raised an eyebrow, then looked down at my drink. The glass was empty. Even the ice was gone.

"I'll have another, please. And I need to tap that big brain of yours."

She leaned across the bar and gave me a quick peck on the cheek. The move left my cheeks burning. "You devil, you. I bet you say that to all the girls."

As a matter of fact, Seven did have a big brain. She had a master's degree in aerospace engineering, which meant she was, literally, a rocket scientist. The call of the beach and the love for the oddness of Paradise Springs had brought her home from an engineering position at the Jet Propulsion Laboratory in California. JPL's loss was our gain.

She was also a reliable source of information and could be relied upon for solid advice. And she was a notorious flirt with people she was friends with.

"Come on, Seven. I've got a girl and I'm way too old for you, anyway."

"I know." She gave me a soft punch on the chin. "It's just that you're so adorable when you blush. What's up?"

"I'm looking for info on Oliver King. I hear he gets a lot of takeout from y'all."

"Abbott's toady? Yeah, I know the guy. He used to live here back in the day. Moved before you came on the scene." She crossed her arms, the motion accentuating the muscle definition of her shoulders. "Creeps me out the door. What do you want to know?"

I got my thoughts in order while she filled an order for Skye. What did I want to know about the man? Anything she could tell me, really. No, that wasn't right. She was busy. I needed information about the here and now. His history could wait. When she returned, I was ready.

"Gretchen told me he seemed nice enough when he showed up in town with Abbott, but that changed pretty quick. Maybe right about the time Abbott hired Desiree. What's your take?"

She took a moment to wipe down the bar top. I could practically see the neurons firing inside her head.

"I agree with her. At first, he was quiet, but nice enough. Always said thank you. Then he became kind of sullen. It was like the novelty of coming to the Springs wore off. This week, he's been super on edge. He's got to be stressed out with what happened to Desiree."

"Do you think he could have anything to do with it?" I told her my idea that he might have been angry at Desiree for taking a position he thought was his. "What if that anger festered and he decided to take his revenge?"

"I don't know. Maybe? He reminds me of a house mouse. Scurrying from place to place, trying to do his work without getting himself caught in some trap."

"Fair enough." I ordered some pulled pork. If I was going to take up Seven's time, the least I could do was ring up a decent tab.

"The thing is, sometimes it's the little rodents who do the most damage. They do their work at night, behind the scenes, and before you know it, you've got a problem that can't be fixed cheap."

My jaw almost hit the bar top. She'd quoted me, practically word for word, from a visit to her house to conduct an inspection. That was three years ago.

"Might want to close your mouth, my friend. Don't want to accidentally swallow a fly."

Left to my thoughts while Seven took care of other customers, after closing my mouth first, of course, I mulled over her assessment of Oliver. It was so similar to Gretchen's, it had to be right.

After all, it was like Seven said. All too often, it was the critters we failed to notice that caused the biggest problems. The same thing could be said about people.

That's when something that had been bubbling under the surface of my thoughts bobbed to the surface. Critters—or people—we fail to notice.

I leaned across the bar and motioned Seven in close. "Do you think Gretchen could have something to do with the murder?"

She stood erect and raised an eyebrow. "Where did that idea come from?"

"Well, we were talking and she asked me about Nic. When I told Gretchen that she was in the clear, she said that was good, but she frowned. Right after that is when she mentioned Oliver acting all sketchy."

"Hold on." Seven stepped away to fill a few orders.

While she was away, I tried to wrap my head around the idea that I had just suggested my chief of operations was possibly a murderer. Boy, did I know how to pick them.

"Okay, Elmo," Seven said when she returned to her spot across from me. "I hear you. But what possible motive could Gretchen have for wanting Desiree dead?"

"To frame Nic. And with her out of the picture…" I shrugged.

Seven let out a loud laugh. "Dude, you can't be serious. I mean, you're a good guy, and I'll admit that Gretchen still carries a bit of a torch for you, but come on. Murdering someone to send someone to prison so she could have you? Really?"

"Not me. My money. She knows I'm buying the Sea Breeze. That's not public information."

"Now I get it. Gretchen found out that you're loaded. If she gets her hands on you, she gets the resort and your money." Seven grinned. "That's some diabolical thinking. If it's true."

"Do you think it could be?"

"I know some of her friends. I'll see if I can find out if she's got any feelings for you beyond friendship." When I let out a long breath, she held up her hand. "I wouldn't take her off your suspect list yet. Like they say, *Hell hath no fury like a woman scorned.*"

My shoulders sagged. "And I'm the one who broke up with her."

"That you did, my friend."

A few minutes later, Wendell arrived with my lunch order. "Elmo, my man. What are you up to this fine day?"

"Looking for info in all the right places." Out of the corner of my eye, I noticed Seven shudder. She didn't care for my attempts at humor by misquoting song lyrics. "So, what better person to see than your daughter? When she's not busy taking great care of her customers, that is."

"He said I have a big brain." Seven executed a pirouette, then pocketed a twenty that a young man had left for a tip. After not being able to take his eyes off her for a full hour. "I'm helping him evaluate murder suspects."

I recapped our discussion of Oliver, then brought up Bobby. "It's like he's disappeared into thin air. Is he hiding? Is he in mourning? His aunts say he was out of town the night Desiree was murdered, but—"

"No, he wasn't." Seven took a beer to a customer at the other end of the bar.

"They said he was in New Orleans, scouting out locations for a new Magnificent Marlin."

Wendell and Seven exchanged a look. He gave his daughter a nod.

"He was nowhere near there." She put her hand up. "Save your breath. I know because I was with him. We were at the same poker game. Bobby was still at the table when I called it a night. Up a couple grand, I'd like to add."

"That's my daughter. Brains of a Nobel laureate, beauty of the morning sunrise, and instincts of an apex predator. And knows how to use them all." Wendell was beaming as he made his way back indoors. He had every reason to. His daughter was a true force of nature.

Seven took a few minutes to fix a sunburnt man and woman in matching pink tank tops a couple of piña coladas. The tourists loved the sugary boat drinks. And the time it took her to mix them gave me a chance to home in on the key questions.

"Was Bobby up or down when you left?"

"He was down some, I think." She wagged her finger at me. "I know where you're going with this. If you want, I can put you in touch with the guy who runs the game. You need to keep it on the down-low, though. The cops wouldn't be happy if they found out what the stakes are."

She waved Skye over and whispered something in the server's ear. Then she gave me a thumbs-up and disappeared into the restaurant.

"I didn't know you had your bartender's license. Cheers to you." I lifted my glass to Skye. I appreciated how hard it could be for young people to get by these days. Making a go of it in a tourist town like Paradise Springs took a lot of hustle.

"Thanks, Mr. Elmo." They grinned and leaned across the bar. "I don't have a bartending license but Seven told me it was okay since she's doing you a favor and if anyone finds out you promised to cover any fines as payback. You're the best."

"Yeah. Happy to help." I took a big gulp of my drink as Skye danced toward a customer to take their order. Seven was only going to be gone for a few minutes. What could go wrong, right?

In the Springs, one never knew.

Lady Luck was smiling on me, though. Seven returned a short while later with a folded piece of paper in her hand. And no cops were anywhere to be seen. She slid the note to me.

"I explained the situation. You're all set. The guy who runs the game goes by the name of Don Espada." She put up her hands. "I know, it's cliché city. Don't shoot me. I'm just the messenger."

"Anything else?" I opened the note. Five digits were written on the page: 5-8-0-0-8.

"The Don will meet you at the end of the Paradise Springs Pier at 11:45 tonight. That's your code phrase. Present it when you ask for him. Go alone, unarmed, and without your phone or any kind of recording device. He was very specific with his instructions. I'd follow them to the letter."

"Seriously? I'm trying to solve a murder, not make a deal for stolen artwork."

Seven shrugged. "His game. His rules. I'll give you one piece of advice. If you do what he says, he's a super nice guy. Don't jerk him around, though. You don't want to make him mad."

"I'll consider myself duly warned." I knocked back the rest of my drink and asked for another.

Taking it upon myself to investigate a murder didn't come without danger. Someone had committed the worst of crimes and didn't want to get caught, after all. It made sense that if I was going to continue down this sleuthing path, I could find myself in peril.

But meeting a gangster, alone, at night, in a secluded location? That was the kind of peril that could give a guy heart palpitations. As I stared at the note, one conclusion was obvious.

I'd made arrangements to meet with someone who was helping me. It was probably more dangerous to back out than see it through. The last thing I needed in my life, on top of everything else, was a crime boss upset with me for standing him up.

It looked like this was a blind date I couldn't miss. Hopefully, I wouldn't regret asking Seven to set me up with Don Espada the card sharp.

CHAPTER TWENTY-ONE

O NE OF THE lessons my mom instilled in me at a young age was the importance of being prompt. From a conference call with corporate talking heads to discuss an initial public offering to meeting with a friend for lunch, it didn't matter. Punctuality was a sign of respect. That you recognized the value of the other party's time.

Standing at the head of the Paradise Springs Pier, I gazed out on the dark, open water. It was 11:42 P.M. The stars above provided the only relief from the darkness that surrounded me like a subterranean jail cell. I said a silent thank-you to my mom for the lesson on timeliness. Don Espada didn't seem the type to be patient with someone who was asking for his help.

The pier was a popular spot fishing spot for locals and tourists alike. Like a humongous rapier, it extended into the Gulf of Mexico twelve hundred feet. A bait and tackle store served as the terminal building/entryway to the concrete and wood. You could purchase all your fishing supplies there and pay the daily admission fee at the same time.

Closing time was nine o'clock. There were ways to access the pier's deck after dark, though it was a closely guarded secret. Which meant the Don and I would have the place to ourselves.

In the darkness, someone coughed. I turned. A smallish person approached. The overhead lights, which were normally on from dusk to dawn, weren't operating. It was difficult to get a good look at the individual. They stopped about ten feet from me and lit a cigar.

"Don Espada?" I took a step forward and extended my hand to shake. It was trembling. The cool breeze coming in from the ocean wasn't the cause.

"Mr. Simpson. It's a pleasure to make your acquaintance." The red tip of the stogie burned bright red as he took in a breath. It revealed a thin face with a sharp nose and prominent cheekbones. The man's hair appeared to be slicked back, like Robert De Niro's character in the gangster movie *Goodfellas*.

We shook. He barely came up to my shoulders and had the frame of a distance runner. The man had the viselike grip of world champion bodybuilder, though.

"You have something for me, I believe." Images from every gangster movie I'd seen flashed across my mind. Gifts for the Don were signs of respect and appreciation for spending his valuable time with you. In the gloom, it was impossible to tell if he was joking or not.

Here I was, with only a steel guardrail protecting me from falling into the black sea. This far out, the odds were good that if I fell, or was tossed over, I'd be swept out into the Gulf, never to be seen or heard from again.

Well, honesty was the best policy, so I decided to go with it. "I'm sorry, sir. I didn't think to bring you a gift. Is there any way you can forgive me?"

The cigar embers morphed from red to a bright yellow. Then, the man let out a long laugh mixed with nauseating cigar smoke and a fair amount of coughing. He strolled to the edge of the pier and knocked the ashes from his cigar.

"Very funny. For a minute, I thought you were serious." He took up a spot next to me. As if he hadn't a care in the world, he leaned against the rail, crossing one foot over the other. "You're a funny guy."

I had a flash of inspiration as he took another puff of the stogie. *The note with the code. Duh.* I gave it to him.

He held it close to the cigar tip. Seconds stretched into decades as he analyzed the writing. A knot began to form in my gut. What was so special about five random digits? Was he having trouble reading Seven's handwriting? It couldn't be that. She had impeccable penmanship. What if the code numbers were wrong? Maybe she misheard the man or transposed some of them.

After staring at the note for a moment, he turned it upside down. Then, he let out a long laugh. He crumpled the piece of paper into a ball, then tossed it over his shoulder into the darkness.

"Seven Banderas. That woman knows me too well. Has a wicked sense of humor, too." He waved his cigar in the air like a conductor while he chuckled again. "What do you want to know?"

The knot in my gut loosened. Maybe I wasn't going to die tonight. And if I did survive, I was going to ask for an explanation from Ms. Banderas. And then maybe request a drink with all the sweetness I could muster.

"Bobby Darrin."

The Don let out a sigh. "That is one messed-up *ragazzo*. Nothing but trouble."

"Seven told me he was at a poker game you run last Monday. The night Desiree LaFontaine was murdered."

"Indeed, he was. Lost a bundle, too."

Any fear I'd been experiencing was replaced with excitement. Finally, some answers. I clenched my fists but refrained from a show of anything more exuberant. Looking like a dork in front of this man didn't seem like a good move.

"Do you mind telling me how much?"

"Why do you want to know?" He turned to face me. With his elbow resting on the rail, he gave off a casual air, but the menace in his voice was impossible to miss. It was time to put my cards on the table.

"I'm looking into Desiree LaFontaine's murder—"

"Now, Desiree." He pointed at me with the cigar. "There was a nice young lady. Worst thing that ever happened to her was getting mixed up with that Darrin loser."

That was the kind of reaction I'd been hoping for. Even if the guy did still scare me. Probably because of the bulge in his jacket that looked like a gun holster. It was better for my emotional health not to know.

"I liked her, too." I told him about my chat with the Farrell sisters. "I don't know whether they were lying to cover for him or if they really don't know where he was. Now that I know he was in town that night, I really need to find him."

"You think he's the murderer, eh?"

I didn't want to get ahead of myself. Especially if the Don wanted to exact revenge on the murderer of someone he liked.

"He's up high on my suspect list. Thing is, if he didn't do it, I need to know that, too. Whoever did it's been on the loose for a week. That's a long time."

"I appreciate the effort you're making. Why don't you stay out of the way and let the police handle things? After all, they collared that murderer a few months ago."

"They're working as hard as they can. I guess I'm hoping to find something to speed things up. Like Bobby's whereabouts. And, I made a promise."

"Now you're talking. You seem to be the kind of man who treats a promise like a solemn vow. Something I can appreciate."

I bet you can. I kept the comment to myself as I glanced at the bulge under his jacket. Instead, I thanked him for the compliment.

"I'll tell you what." I froze as he reached into his jacket. Instead of a firearm, he withdrew his phone. After scrolling through it for a moment, he smiled. "Here it is. Your Mr. Darrin is hiding out in the Dolphin's Cove. Unit 2-A. The water and power are supposed to be off there, but he's a crafty one. Good choice for a hideout."

"No doubt."

The Dolphin's Cove was a beachside condominium development on the edge of town that never got off the ground. Only six of the planned fifty units were actually built. Five years after the first shovel of dirt was turned on the project, the developer filed for bankruptcy. The units that were built didn't stay occupied for long due to shoddy construction materials and craftsmanship. The hope among folks these days was that once the bankruptcy court finished its business, the property could be sold, the existing eyesore razed, and something new and sustainable built in its place.

"Let me ask you this. If he didn't do it, why bother hiding?"

It was a good question. I had a theory. "How much did he lose that night?"

"He brought five grand with him. When he lost it all, I gave him another grand on credit. At a reasonable interest rate, of course." He grinned. In the lurid light cast by the cigar, it had a menace to it that could rival Lucifer himself. "He lost that, too. Idiot."

It was my turn to grin. Though there was no pleasure in it.

"Here's what I think. Worst case scenario, he murdered Desiree and he's hiding until he can figure out how to get out of town. Best case scenario, he's hiding from his aunts. He was supposed to be in New Orleans. Instead, he blew it off for a poker game. And ended up in debt to you, in the process. I wouldn't want to face those three women under those circumstances."

"Good point. I wouldn't want to go toe to toe with them, either. Cheryl, maybe, if it was just her and me."

Despite the threatening situation, I snickered. I couldn't help myself. Sometimes, the best thing I could do when things looked bleak was let out a tension-releasing laugh. By the time I got myself under control, my eyes were watering.

"I'm sorry, Don. I had the exact same thought about what I'd do if I have to make another run at them. Beryl scares me to death."

"That's the idea, I think." He flicked his cigar into the ocean. "It's been a pleasure, Mr. Simpson. I hope you get the murderer. And if you could be so kind, when you catch up with Bobby, please remind him of his debt to me. Interest compounds daily."

"I'll do that." We shook. I had a handful of other questions I wanted to ask, but something told me that when the Don decided our business was concluded, it was concluded. "Thank you very much for your time and for the information."

"It has been a pleasure." He nodded and handed me a business card. "My contact information, should you find yourself in need of accounting services. Especially with your new purchase."

As if by magic the pier's overnight lights came on. The name confused me.

"Vernon Shipley, CPA." I looked at him. "I don't understand."

He put his hand on my shoulder as we began walking from the pierhead toward the tackle shop.

"That's my real name. I'm an accountant by day. The card games are my side hustle." He gestured toward the shore. "Living here isn't cheap. I started up the card game scheme after Hurricane Gustav. The extra cash has come in handy over the years."

"So, you're not really a…?"

"What? A gangster?" He laughed and slapped me on the back. "The nickname puts the fear of God into people. I've been known to get a little cross when people don't pay up as promised."

"I imagine." I let out a weak laugh. He hadn't actually answered the question. As long as I lived, I would never get a handle on all of the oddballs, outcasts, and hustlers in Paradise Springs.

We were almost at the tackle shop when he stopped.

"This is where we part ways, my friend. I trust this conversation will be kept confidential." At my nod, he gave my forearm a squeeze. "Best wishes to you. Don't forget. Corporate tax season will be here before you know it. I can give you a 10 percent new client discount. Think about it."

I managed to keep it together until I got into my truck. Then I let out a long laugh and flopped over on my side. Good golly, the place was such a magnet for weirdness. From vampires to mob bosses to witches, every way I turned, I crossed paths with someone who wasn't what they seemed to be.

On the other hand, it sure kept life interesting. As I drove home, I made plans for my showdown with Bobby. It needed to be a surprise visit. That way, he wouldn't have a chance to make a run for it. Or make up answers to my questions.

Hopefully, he wouldn't have a chance to make a surprise countermove against me, either. If he *was* the murderer, confronting him in an abandoned building without any backup wasn't my best idea. Well, I'd come up with plenty of bad ideas over the years. None of them had cost me my life. I didn't intend to end that streak anytime soon.

CHAPTER TWENTY-TWO

I WOKE UP Monday morning groggy from a restless night. It didn't help that Oscar was the one who roused me from sleep. By sitting on my chest and batting at my nose. It was a move he didn't resort to often. Only when he was really hungry and was going to stop at nothing until I refilled his food bowl.

"Okay, dude, you win. Give me a minute." I batted a paw from my face and sat up. He moved to the end of the bed, where he gave me a look that seemed to say he was minutes from dying of malnutrition. This despite the fact that on his most recent annual checkup, the vet informed me he was two pounds overweight. Which was a lot for a cat that should tip the scales at ten pounds.

He'd survive another few minutes.

The T-shirt I slept in was soaked as if I'd been wearing it while caught in a rainstorm. My head felt like it was filled with swamp water. My knees ached liked I'd run a marathon in the Gulf's soft, white sand. Whatever disturbing dreams I experienced must have involved a lot of physical exertion. Or a lot of stress. Or both.

Not an ideal way to start a day that included facing a murderer. Okay, an alleged murderer.

Oscar led me from the bedroom to the kitchen. I knew better than to try to stop at the bathroom. My feline room-mate's desire to fill his empty tummy came first. It was a matter of priorities in the Simpson household.

By the time I was showered and had food in my own tummy, I was ready to take on the day. Well, and had downed two mugs of English Breakfast tea. Or, as I called it, Rocket Fuel.

Yes, the flavor isn't for everyone. Yes, Nic had literally walked away from me when I offered to let her take a sip one time. And, yes, Sybil told me that my choice of tea over coffee would lead me to a *bitter end*. Her words, not mine. It worked for me. With a visit to a murder suspect followed by Desiree's memorial service, there were bigger things in the world to worry about than what Elmo Simpson drank to help him wake up.

With no sales calls on the docket, I assigned the day's critter removal work to Jordan. I was now free to catch a killer.

My plan for confronting Darrin was simple. Deal with him early in the day, hopefully while he was still asleep. That way, he'd be in no position to run or hide.

Well, that was the hope.

"Back soon, buddy." I picked Oscar up and gave him a hug. Normally, he started to squirm after a few seconds. This time he didn't. Maybe he was transferring some kitty karma my way. I'd take all I could get.

Fifteen minutes later, I was parked a few blocks away from Bobby's hideout. Hours spent watching crime TV suggested a quiet approach on foot would help with the element of surprise. Hey, couldn't hurt to try.

The silence surrounding the row of abandoned two-story condos was eerie. This time of year, Paradise Springs was bursting with energy at all hours of the day. Not here, though. I took a swig from a water bottle and double-timed it to the front door of the second unit.

The doorknob was corroded with sea salt. It wouldn't budge when I tried to turn it. While that was a hassle for me, I had to give Bobby credit for having the presence of mind to hide someplace where an adversary couldn't just waltz in through the front door. I looked up and down the street while I debated my next move. The answer came quickly.

The buildings were designed so that the front door of each condo faced the parking area. It made sense. That way, tourists would only have to cross a short distance when they brought things inside. On the other side of the door, there was probably a short hallway. To the left, there would be a door to the ground floor unit. A set of stairs would lead to the second-floor unit. That meant each first-floor condo had a back door that opened onto a patio facing the Gulf. The second-floor unit would have a balcony that did the same.

"2-A" sounded like a first-floor designation. It made sense. Bobby could find himself boxed in on the second floor. If my assumption was correct, my quarry would have left the patio door unlocked. It would facilitate a quick getaway if Chief Eikenberry and her team came knocking.

Or worse, if Don Espada and his goons had arrived.

I headed for the back. A peek around the corner of the

building confirmed the coast was clear. A few folks were walking on the beach, but they were headed away from me. A few steps later, I was at Bobby's patio.

Fast-food wrappers and empty energy drink cans were strewn about the cracked concrete surface. They confirmed someone had been hanging around. I took a moment to photograph the mess before sliding over to the door. Good golly, I was turning into an almost real investigator.

The screen door was intact. A French-style patio door was propped open with a rock. This time of year, conditions indoors would get unbearable if all the doors and windows remained closed. At least Bobby had the sense to allow some air movement into his hideout.

I peered in. The morning sun provided enough light to assess the situation. More trash was piled on what had once been the island between the kitchen and living area. Bobby was nowhere to be seen. He was either gone or asleep in one of the bedrooms.

The odds were low that he'd invite me in, so I gave the screen door a tug. It refused to move. He'd had the sense to lock it.

"I'll give it to you on this one, Bobby. You're not as thick as I thought you were."

There's a thing about the screen door I was facing. It was cheap. When I was in college, I lived in a house with one that was similar. The only thing keeping the mesh screen intact was the aluminum frame. That meant I could cut or punch my way through. If I pulled on the handle hard enough, I could snap the locking mechanism, too.

Not that I'd ever actually tried any of those three maneuvers late at night after a few too many drinks with friends. No, sirree. Just reporting what I'd heard from other people.

After another look over my shoulder to make sure nobody was sneaking up on me, I gave the handle a sharp pull. It held fast for a second. Then, a satisfying crack followed, and it slid open with ease. Stepping inside, I couldn't help wondering if Bobby had lubricated the door's tracks to minimize noise while coming and going from his hideout.

If so, he'd made my job easier, bless him.

In the unlikely event that he was gone and had left via the front door, I slid the screen closed. The living area looked like a hurricane had passed through. A pile of beer cans was in one corner. Crushed water bottles were strewn about the room, as if Bobby had mindlessly tossed them over his shoulder after drinking them. A half dozen empty cereal boxes looked like they'd been stepped on as soon as they'd landed on the faux hardwood floor.

I tiptoed around an accumulation of shorts and tank tops, which gave off a stench that made my eyes water. The life of a fugitive. Not exactly glamorous.

Doors on one wall indicated that the unit had one bedroom and one bathroom. Both doors were closed. I went to the one closer to the ocean.

Here goes nothing. I counted to three in my head, then pushed the door open. Bobby was asleep on an air mattress. He was shirtless, with a grungy white sheet covering him from the waist down. I said a prayer to the stars above asking them to make sure he was wearing a pair of shorts. Or at least underwear.

The thought of interrogating Bobby Darrin in the buff made me want to run away and drink myself blind. *Here goes.*

"Bobby!"

My shout bounced around the room, startling the man into wakefulness. He sat up straight and looked at me, his eyes wide with fear. In his frightened response, he'd kicked the sheet away to reveal that he was wearing a pair of gray athletic shorts.

Thank goodness for small favors.

"What?" Shaking like a maple leaf about to fall to the ground, he looked around the room for a means of escape. A window was open, but the screen was in place. He must have decided against that because he shifted his attention to me. "I didn't do anything."

"Then why are you hiding?" I swept my arm around the room. It was as disheveled as the rest of the condo. "This place is a dump."

He slipped a T-shirt over his head. "I'm, uh, practicing my survival skills. I'm going to try out for that show on TV. You know, the one where they leave you on a deserted island."

I laughed. "Really? That's the best you can do?"

"It's true. What do you want, bro?" He backed himself up against the wall but remained in a sitting position.

"Where'd you go last Monday night after you left Don Espada's poker game? Why were you in town instead of New Orleans, like you told your aunts?" I took a step toward his cowering figure. "Why have you been hiding out ever since your ex-girlfriend was murdered?"

He gave me a blank look, as if I was speaking Urdu, then he furrowed his eyebrows. "Who says I been hiding out?"

With a groan, I slapped my forehead with my palm. Bobby Darrin wasn't going to be invited to join MENSA anytime soon.

"Seems to me, all the trash around here speaks for itself. Oh, and your aunts told me they thought you were in New Orleans."

The color drained from his face. "You talked to Aunt Beryl? Is she mad at me?"

"Not yet." I kept my arms loose at my sides to grab him in case he tried to make a run for it. "The Don isn't, either. They will be, if you don't come out of hiding soon. He's expecting repayment in full, with interest, by the way."

I didn't think it was possible for the man to look any more pitiful. Then he got on his knees and begged me to help him. That was even more pathetic.

"You want my help, you answer my questions. Right here. Right now. The cops are looking for you, too. I'm your best option."

"Deal, bro. I'll do anything. Just get me out of this hellhole." He got to his feet. The stench of an adult male who hadn't washed in a week made me want to puke.

I took him by the arm and escorted him to the beach. "First things first, you smell like the unholy spawn of stale beer and rotting vegetables. Into the water with you."

"But I can't swim. That's the truth."

"Then don't go any farther than waist deep. And make sure you rinse off everywhere including your head." I pushed him toward the water. The guy would drive the pope to cursing.

A few minutes later, a drenched and defeated Bobby returned to me from his bath. His sandy brown hair fell limp over his ears. It was an improvement over the rat's nest that was there before he went in the water, though.

"What now?" He stared at the sand as water dripped from his arms and legs. His shorts hung low around his waist. Almost too low, in fact. One wrong move and his private area wouldn't be so private.

I shuddered at the thought. I mean, literally shuddered. Good golly, I needed a drink, and it wasn't even noon.

"First, you're going to hike up your shorts. Then we're going to have a little chat. What happens after that depends on how the chat goes." I pushed him in the direction of my truck. "My ride's that way."

Bobby whined and moaned more and more with every step we took. First, he was thirsty. Then he was hungry. Then he wanted shoes. When he said we needed to go back to the condo so he could get his phone, I squeezed his shoulder. Tight.

"Now is not the time to be making demands. Once you're in the truck, I'll fetch your phone for you."

Bobby agreed, unaware I had a supply of zip ties in the glove box. They came in handy making sure the cage door was fastened while I moved a critter to a safe location. Once he was in the truck, I made my move. With the speed that came from years of practice, I bound Bobby's legs together, then fastened his wrists to the steering wheel before he knew what had happened.

The string of obscenities he shouted at me as I jogged back to his hideout could probably be heard a hundred yards away. I wasn't concerned if the police showed up. He was going to end up there anyway, and in my defense, I'd left the windows open a bit so he could get fresh air.

That was Elmo Simpson, generous to a fault.

Soon enough, I was back, Bobby's phone in my hand. It was a fancy foldable model. Something told me that he didn't pay for it himself. If he did, he probably didn't get the money to pay for it in a lawful matter. More likely, he used the proceeds from the sale of Desiree's car.

Yeah, I had bad feelings about Darrin, and I hadn't even questioned him yet. Sheesh.

"Here." I freed his hands, then tossed him the phone. "Where'd you go when you left the card game?"

"I drove around town for a while. Trying to figure out what to do. The five grand was supposed to cover expenses for the NOLA trip."

"Your aunts aren't going to be happy when they find out you flushed their money down the toilet."

"I know." He moaned like a spoiled child who didn't get enough birthday presents. "That's why I had to go incognito until I could figure out how to fix things."

Incognito? I shook my head. It would be a waste of time to attempt to correct him on the misuse of the word. Besides, there were more important issues at hand.

"When did you leave the game?"

"Around midnight."

Desiree was still alive at that time. "How long did you drive around?"

"Maybe an hour. I was running low on gas."

"Did you drive by the Magnificent Marlin at any time?" When he said he couldn't remember, I started the truck's engine and pulled into traffic. I was going to take him to the police station anyway. I might as well do it in air-conditioned comfort.

"I hid the car at the junkyard. Then made my way here. That was a long walk." He went on with a meandering story about his epic adventure traversing Paradise Springs in the dead of night.

The junkyard Bobby was referring to was more formally known as Paradise Springs Reuse & Recycle. It was run by an acquaintance of mine who went by the name Big Baby. I could talk to them to verify that part of Bobby's story.

"So, you were aimlessly driving around town at the time your ex-girlfriend was murdered. You were angry at her for calling the cops when you sold her car without her permission and then dumped you. Did that anger boil over after festering for a while? Did that drive you to take her life?"

"Nah, bro. The only reason I know she was killed was because of a text I got from my aunt Cheryl. Then my phone died. You got a car charger, by the way? I need to check on some bets I placed."

"Sorry." I did, in fact, have a charger in my glove box. I wasn't going to share it, though. Bobby would probably try to swipe it from me. We were almost at the police station anyway.

He started cussing me out when I turned into the station parking lot. Then switched to begging when I called the chief and asked her to join me outside.

"Why are you dragging me from my office, Simpson?" She took advantage of me lowering the driver's-side window by leaning into the truck's cab. "And why do you have an almost naked man bound at the ankles in the passenger seat?"

She kept a straight face while she asked the second question. The woman was a credit to her profession.

"I'm surprised you don't recognize our good friend Bobby Darrin, Chief. Then again, I guess if I'd been hiding out for a week, I might be unrecognizable, too."

"Where did you…? Never mind." Susan made her way around to the other side of my truck. "Mr. Darrin, I'd like to talk to you about Desiree LaFontaine. Do you consent to questioning voluntarily?"

Bobby's jaw was trembling as he looked from the chief to me and then back to the chief. He took a long breath.

"I'm in big trouble with my aunts, aren't I?"

"You'll be in bigger trouble with the chief if you don't cooperate with her." I cut the bindings around his legs. "Then there's the fact that as a law enforcement officer, it's illegal to beat a confession out of you. Something your aunt Beryl wouldn't have to concern herself with."

It took Bobby all of two seconds to decide which scary authority figure he'd take his chances with.

"I'm all yours, Chief." He stepped from the truck and held out his hands, as if ready to be cuffed.

"You can expect a call from me, Simpson. I have questions for you now, too."

I gave her a little wave in acknowledgment of the promise. Or was it a threat? When I was dealing with Susan Eikenberry, I was never 100 percent sure.

Whatever, my good deed for the day was done. I couldn't be happier with the results, either. Bobby was in custody and safe.

Before I put the truck in gear, I overheard him ask the chief for a charging cord for his phone. And if there was someplace he could take a shower. And if she could get him something to eat since he hadn't had a decent meal in days. And if he could take a nap before they talked because he was tired.

Leaving the parking lot, I kept an eye on the rearview mirror. It wouldn't have surprised me one bit if Bobby got chucked right back out the front door in retribution for treating the chief like the concierge at a five-star hotel.

CHAPTER TWENTY-THREE

MY TIME SPENT in the grimy presence of Bobby Darrin left me literally in need of a shower. I couldn't go to Desiree's memorial service looking and feeling like a fish that had been out in the sun too long. After getting cleaned up, I consulted with my fashion advisor, Oscar. In consultation with Oscar, we decided on a sky blue guayabera shirt, white linen pants, and sandals. It was the most dressed up I'd been in months.

It was the least I could do for Desiree's memory.

I picked up Rambo on the way to the service. His outfit—a tan summer suit, white shirt, and green tie—put mine to shame. The guy had lived in the Paradise Springs area his whole life. His level of heat tolerance was miles higher than mine. Still, for an event scheduled to take place outside when the temperature was hovering in the nineties, it seemed excessive.

My friend was a huge man. The last thing I wanted was to have him overcome by the head and humidity because he was wearing a suit and tie.

"Nice threads," I said as we got moving.

"It's the least I could do." He tugged at his shirt collar. "Desiree was a good person. A good employee, too. The gators respected her."

And there it was. Waldo "Rambo" Quigley raised alligators for a living. With his massive frame, bushy beard, and unruly hair, he looked like he was straight from central casting for a movie that needed a scary mountain man. He also had a huge heart and was a bit of a sentimentalist. When you add that to the fact that Desiree had worked for him, the formal attire made complete sense.

"Are you going to speak at the service?" Two nights before, Nic had told me Desiree's parents asked her to speak. The woman's parents had hoped their daughter and her former boss would reconcile and were saddened that the opportunity never came to pass.

"Yeah. Nicola and I worked on what we're going to say last night. You figure out who killed Desiree yet? It's been a week."

The edge in Rambo's voice could have sliced right through a block of ice. While the accusatory vibe of his comment hurt, I needed to remember that he was grieving and wanted answers to the crime.

"Making progress. Dropped a suspect off at the police station earlier today, in fact." I brought him up to speed on developments since seeing him at the Riptide. Enough had happened that it took most of the drive.

Rambo stroked his beard as I navigated into a beachside parking spot. "Shipley does my taxes. I've heard stories about Don Espada. Had no idea they're the same dude."

"Do me a favor and keep that under your hat. If the Don's cover gets blown, I don't want to be the one to blame."

He let out a laugh and gave me one of his friendly slaps on the back. It was the kind that only left my teeth rattling instead of sending me flying.

The service, held on the beach adjacent to the Sea Breeze Resort, was to be a simple affair. When I heard Desiree's parents wanted to hold the event near the water, I asked Gretchen to offer them whatever they needed, with the resort's deepest condolences.

She'd done an outstanding job preparing the site. A special event tent large enough to accommodate a hundred people had been erected halfway between where the water ended and the seagrass began. The steel poles supporting the structure were covered with green and purple crepe paper. The colors were Desiree's favorites.

Underneath the tent, fifty white folding chairs were arrayed in a semicircle facing a lectern. About half were occupied when Rambo and I arrived. We were greeted by Desiree's parents and sister. Rambo exchanged hugs and a few words with them, then headed toward an empty chair in the second row, where the other folks who were speaking, including Nic, were seated.

I introduced myself to the grieving family and told them how much I had enjoyed my time spent with Desiree.

"She always had the nicest things to say about you." Her mother, Sandrine, gave me a hug. Desiree's father, Raul, and sister, Camille, followed suit. The bloodshot eyes and the puffy eyelids were proof their grief hadn't abated. I could only hope time would help heal the wounds to their hearts.

We chatted for a moment, then I stepped away to find a seat. I hadn't gone far when there was a tap on my shoulder. It was Camille.

"Nicola told me you're trying to find out who killed my sister."

"That's right." It didn't seem like a good time to overload the woman with details.

"Do you have any leads?" She dabbed at the corner of her eye with a tissue.

"Some." I told her about taking Bobby to the police. "I have a few other things that I'm looking into."

"That's good to hear." She took my hand. "The night before she was killed, Desiree told me she regretted how things went down between her and Nicola. She was going to try to make things right between them."

A lump formed in my throat. It was impossible to imagine the number of goals, hopes, and dreams Desiree had that would never be realized. How many plans had she made that would never be brought to fruition?

The utter wretchedness of the situation doubled my resolve to bring Desiree's murderer to justice.

"Have you told Nic this?"

Camille shook her head. "I've been trying to find the right time, but things have been so crazy."

I took her hand in mine. The poor woman's nails were chewed down to the quick. The service wasn't scheduled to begin for another ten minutes.

"Tell her right now. Nic told me how much she regrets the harsh words they exchanged. I'm sure she'd appreciate you sharing what Desiree told you. I'll be right back."

Less than a minute later, I returned with my bewildered girlfriend in tow. "Nic, Camille has a message from Desiree. It's important and I think you should hear it before the service starts."

With my work done, I slipped away and took a seat in the back row. Before long, Raul welcomed us to the service. He shared an anecdote involving a nine-year-old Desiree asking in a roundabout if a wild boar piglet would make a good pet. When he told her probably not, she tried slip away unnoticed so she could free one such animal that had wandered into the garage. The story had us all alternating between laughter and tears and set the stage for a sixty-minute love fest dedicated to Desiree.

Rambo made short work of his turn to speak. Uncomfortable being in the spotlight, he talked about her love for the Florida Panhandle and the uncanny connection she made with his alligator herd.

After that, Craig took to the lectern. I had to give the man credit. He was dressed every bit as nice as Rambo. Even though I didn't like the guy, I had to tip my hat to him. His suit showed respect. His words were eloquent and a testament to how easily Desiree made newcomers to the area feel like a part of the Paradise Springs family.

After a few friends and relatives spoke, Nic approached the lectern. She wiped at the corners of her eyes with her index finger, then took a deep breath.

"Desiree was the most talented seafarer I've ever met. She was an amazing work wife who loved sharing our little corner of the world with countless visitors over the years. She was also my friend. I loved her like a sister." Nic closed her eyes as her voice cracked. "I imagine y'all know about our breakup a few months ago. What you probably don't know is that the night she was taken from us, she reached out to me. We were going to get together. Patch things up. We never got the chance. I never got to say how much I loved her, so I'm going to say it now. I love you, Big D. I'll see you somewhere over the rainbow."

Then she broke down in tears.

I went to her side and kept my arm around her for the rest of the service. Camille brought the eulogy part of the service to a close by inviting us to join the family as they scattered Desiree's ashes on the water. While they did so, Rambo performed Jimmy Buffett's "A Pirate Looks at Forty" on the harmonica. He'd played the melancholy tune in his garage after a few beers dozens of times, but never before in public.

The performance was flawless and a perfect sendoff for a woman who, like Nic, loved the sea with all her heart.

At the ceremony's conclusion, a group of us gathered at the water's edge to toss water lilies into the surf. As the waves carried the symbols of rebirth out into the Gulf of Mexico, I put my arm around Nic.

"I didn't know you and Desiree talked."

"It wasn't much. Craig went to the bar to get us drinks. While he was away, she told me she was sorry for screwing me over—her words, not mine—and wanted to know if we could get together to talk."

"That must have made you feel good."

"Well, yeah. At the time, I thought it was a nice gesture, but didn't think too much more about it. I told her to text me." She let out a sigh that carried the weight of the world on it. "And then Craig came back and made his pitch and that's when I threw my drink in his face and left. I never got to have that talk with D. And now I never will."

I gave Nic a hug. I mean, what could I say to her? Words would be about as useful as an old eight-track tape. No, what mattered was action.

That evening, I sat on the patio with an Irish whiskey in one hand and a battered copy of Mark Twain's *Following the Equator* in the other. Instead of reading, I found myself reviewing the day's events. What an emotional roller coaster. From the high of turning Bobby Darrin over to the police to the low of saying goodbye to Desiree, I think I experienced every emotion possible, and my emotional well was empty.

Yet my mind was running like I'd just chugged two Red Bulls. There was something that wouldn't stop bugging me, like a mosquito bite on a part of your back you can't scratch without the aid of ruler or something like that.

Desiree had told Nic she wanted to talk. Harmless enough, right? The women had worked together for years. It was totally reasonable to assume that after a few months, Desiree had decided it was time to make amends. If that was the case, why had she told her sister that she wanted to talk to Nic without elaborating?

Why not tell Camille what she wanted to say? That's what you'd do when you were asking someone for advice, right? But Desiree didn't do that.

What did she want to talk to Nic about? I took a drink as the next questions formed in my brain. Did Desiree have a confession to make? Did someone murder her to stop the confession?

If that was the case, what was the confession about? And who wanted to make sure that the confession never saw the light of day?

CHAPTER TWENTY-FOUR

WHEN IN BUSINESS, your success will depend in large part on who you surround yourself with. I know, it's not an original thought. It's true, though. Back in my tech days, I worked with people who were smart, creative, and motivated to make a lot of money. That last played a big role in my breakdown. In the end, they cared more about getting rich than they cared about me.

That was one of the reasons why I enjoyed my single-person enterprise so much. I shared the same values with myself. It made it easy to make important decisions. Oh sure, Oscar had his opinions about issues of the day, but they were usually addressed with a kitty treat or a fresh morsel of meat.

In recent months, the demand for Elmo's Critter Removal services had skyrocketed like a ship blasting off from Cape Canaveral. A sight that's totally worth seeing in person, by the way. Just make sure to take earplugs.

Anyway, while I didn't need the extra work, I didn't want to turn business away. My personal finances were plenty healthy, but one could never tell what the future would bring. Especially when I hatched the crackpot idea to buy the Sea Breeze. The long and short of it was that the increased interest in my company made me feel good.

Even if a lot of the service requests turned out to only be people wanting to get a selfie with the guy who helped catch the murderer of Fran Cohen. There were enough real requests that I was working fourteen hours a day and barely keeping up.

It was after I let a snake get its fangs into me one evening after a long day that I faced the inevitable and admitted to Nic and Rambo that I needed help.

"I've been saying that for years, buddy." With a laugh, Rambo punched my arm with enough force that I was almost knocked to the ground.

"Not that kind of help, blockhead." Nic gave Rambo a backhand slap to the big guy's head. She was the only person I knew who could get away with that. "He needs help dealing with the critters."

"Know anyone who'd be a good fit? I mean, literally, because sometimes those crawl spaces get really cramped." I was fairly certain the mention of a crawl space was unnecessary, but my arm wasn't up to taking another punch from Rambo, even if he was just joking.

After a moment, Nic snapped her fingers. "I have the perfect candidate for you. Do you know who Jordan Selassie is?"

A few days after our initial encounter at the pier, I sat at a table in a corner of the Lah-De-Dah Café. It was a tourist favorite known for its margaritas served in mason jars and tapas-style menu. Jordan sat cross-legged in a chair across from me. The interview was more of a get-to-know-you session than anything else, so we chatted over a lunch of street tacos and a cheese plate.

I needed help and Nic recommended him. That was good enough for me. If he wanted the job, it was his for the taking. Especially after he reached behind him and caught a purse that had slipped off the shoulder of a customer who was passing by. Without looking. Before it hit the floor.

"What makes you think I'm looking for work?" he asked when I offered him the job. "I make a good living as a street performer. Thinking about taking my act to New Orleans or Key West."

"It's steady work to get you through the slow times of the year. I promise it won't interfere with your performance schedule during tourist season. With your unique flexibility, you can get into tight spots in crawl spaces and attics that are tough for me." Actually, there were a few that were down-right impossible for me, but I thought a softer approach would be better at this stage. "I need you."

"What's it pay?"

"I'll start you at twenty an hour, plus paid time off and healthcare benefits."

In the past, I wouldn't have been able to offer anywhere that much. We weren't in the past, though, and if my body didn't get a break soon, I was going to need healthcare benefits because I was going to end up in the hospital.

He scratched his chin, then took a look around the res-taurant. I had to hand it to him, the guy knew how to make someone sweat.

"Twenty-two and you teach me all the ins and outs of

the operation."

"Deal." I extended my hand to shake.

With a smile, he took my hand in his. "When do I start?"

"How about tomorrow?"

Over the ensuing months, Jordan had proven to be worth every penny I was paying him. There was something about the guy that made me feel good.

Which is why I was whistling a tune as I pulled into his driveway Tuesday morning. Normally, Jordan came to my place so he could use the truck for the daily rounds while I enjoyed my one day off. He'd return the vehicle at the end of the workday, and I'd take him home.

"What's up with the change of plans?" He raised an eyebrow when I told him to get in. "Seriously, dude. What's going on?"

"We've got an errand to run before you first appointment."

I held my tongue until we pulled into the parking lot of Honest Bob's Paradise Springs Motors, a reasonably respectable used car dealer. And one of my clients.

"These guys aren't on the schedule until next week." Jordan scanned his tablet. "Did I miss something?"

"Nope. We're here to get you a company truck. Surprise!"

I got out and pointed at a silver Ford pickup. Okay, it was more gray than silver, but my client Roberta "Bob" Goodpaster, the third generation of Honest Bob's, had promised me it was in fine working condition.

After a few moments of hesitation, Jordan made his way to the vehicle. He circled it at a deliberate pace with furrowed brows.

While my coworker was inspecting his new wheels, Bob sidled up to me, sporting her customary red, white, and blue visor, garish tropical shirt, and five-inch heels.

"What's the word, Elmo? Ready to sign on the dotted line? I recall we agreed on fifteen thousand with financing at a special friends-and-family rate."

"You know I love you like the sister I never had." I draped my arm over her shoulder. "And your dad would be proud of the effort, but…"

"But what?" She batted her lashes at me. She was a friend of Nic, so we both knew the flirting would get her nowhere. She deserved credit for the effort, though.

"But I recall we agreed on ten grand. Cash. And you're going to wash it and top off the tank before Jordan drives it off the lot."

"Uh-huh. Bossy today, aren't we?"

She called out to Jordan, then tossed him the keys. "Take it for a test drive, my man. Elmo and I have a few details to iron out."

"I'm glad I was able to refresh your memory. Shall we?"

"You take all the fun out of selling used, I mean *preowned*, cars, you know that? Next time, I won't roll over so easy."

I started walking toward a modular home Bob's father had bought for a song and repurposed as his operations center a decade ago. The three-foot gap between the ground and the trailer floor became a haven for snakes looking for some extra warmth when the winter months arrived. That's where I'd entered the picture.

"Come on, Bob. I know for a fact you only paid five for the truck and it's been on your lot less than a week. You're making a killing. Let's not spoil things by trying to get me to haggle. I have places to be."

"One day, you'll come to regret turning your nose up at the fine art of haggling." She motioned for me to enter the operations center.

Thirty minutes later, I gave Bob a fist bump. Jordan had just taken off for his first appointment in his new take-home company vehicle. As he waved goodbye to us, his smile was brighter than the sun. I smiled, too. For the moment, all was well with the world.

With the expansion of my company's fleet complete, it was time to return to my sleuthing.

Paradise Springs Reuse & Recycle center was not far from the spot where Bobby Darrin had allegedly hidden his car. While I wasn't much of a betting man, I was confident in assuming that it was still there. The guy had probably clammed up once Chief Susan tried to interrogate him. That meant the police hadn't found it yet.

The center's proprietor, Big Baby, greeted me by placing their palms together and bowing at the waist.

"Namaste, my friend. What brings the area's most esteemed amateur sleuth to my humble establishment this fine day? Are you on the hunt again, perchance?" The bald-headed giant of a person gestured for me to join them in their office.

There was no point in trying to play coy. Like the Vampire, Big Baby was a member of the Springs' Old Guard of independent businesspeople and oddballs. It was a group that I had come to respect.

"Bobby Darrin claims he was driving around town the night Desiree LaFontaine was murdered and ditched his car close by. Do you mind if I look for it?"

"How thrilling." They clapped their hands. "By all means, proceed, provided I may accompany you on your search. I believe the term used by the younger generation would be serving as your wing person."

Big Baby was easily seven feet in height and three hundred pounds or more in weight. Despite their massive size, they were quite nimble and had no trouble navigating the brush that we encountered growing along the outside of their fence. The junk dealer was truly fired up by the quest, as they kept up a constant stream of commentary during the search.

Thirty minutes into the trek, we rounded a cluster of buttonbushes. Before us, a tan canvas tarp covered something in the shape of an automobile.

"Jackpot." I quickened my pace, excitement bubbling up inside of me.

With their long stride, Big Baby got there first. They put a hand on the tarp. "May I have the honor? We are still on my property, after all."

"By all means." Hey, it was the least I could do. Big Baby had helped me enough in the past. Why spoil their moment in the amateur sleuthing sun?

They pulled back the tarp with a flourish to reveal a black Tesla. I snapped a few photos, figuring I could send them to friends asking if the vehicle belonged to Bobby. I stopped when I made my way to the rear of the vehicle and got a look at the license plate.

"It rather solves any mystery about the identity of the owner of this vehicle. No?" There was a note of triumph in Big Baby's voice. The plate read B DARE 1.

"Agreed. You want to call the cops, or do you want me to?"

"It will be my pleasure. I realize losing one's parents at a young age may lead to negative outcomes in people. It does not change the fact that I find that man to be utterly odious and his aunts manipulative and untrustworthy."

I couldn't argue with that.

While Big Baby made the call, I gave the car a close-up look. It was a long shot, but I hoped to find evidence that might prove Bobby was actually the murderer. There were no scrape marks or pieces of fabric near the trunk. Nor were there any splotches of dried blood. A lack of evidence didn't mean the guy didn't do it, though.

"Do you have any surveillance cameras around here?" I asked.

"I do, indeed." They tapped a few keystrokes into their phone. "Shall we watch a film while we wait for the authorities?"

Like a lot of the oddball denizens of Paradise Springs, Big Baby was full of surprises. In this case, the surprise was a high-tech security system that would put a bank to shame. All operated from an app on their phone.

Big Baby had a dozen security cameras distributed throughout their sprawling property. Four inside the fence were stationed in prominent locations. Eight were hidden among the trees and brush to keep an eye on things outside the fence. As they switched from camera to camera, they shared the reasoning behind the placement of each device.

"The majority of souls with whom I do business refrain from attempting to burgle me. Hence, the inside cameras function as much of a not-so-gentle reminder to conduct one's business honorably."

"Makes sense to me." Between their humongous size and mysterious business contacts, the last thing I would ever do was try to rip Big Baby off. I was pretty sure things wouldn't go well for someone who tried to steal from them.

Like being visited late at night by scary people hired to make sure the thief made amends. Fast.

"The outside cameras perform the lion's share of my surveillance work, as it were. At least once a month, often when the full moon is out, for what that's worth, a misguided soul attempts to climb the fence to abscond with their ill-gotten gains."

"Not cool."

They paused their scrolling through the videos long enough to look at me with a raised eyebrow. "Indeed."

After another couple of minutes, Big Baby smiled and turned the phone's screen toward me. "Our ne'er-do-well, Mr. Darrin, I believe."

The images were sharp, despite the late hour the recording was made. Bobby's car entered the camera's range and came to a stop right where we found it. He pulled the tarp from the trunk, covered the vehicle, and walked away. When he disappeared from the screen, his phone was in one hand and a wallet was in the other.

"This is amazing." I had to reach up to give them a pat on the back. "Can you confirm the time?"

"Arrival at 2:07. Departure at 2:18. How does that fit into your timeline?"

"After Desiree's time of death." The dull rumble of a car's engine caught my attention. The police were almost here. "I can't thank you enough for this. Is there any way I can repay you?"

"My dealings with the local constabulary may be characterized as strained. To be fair, they are as suspicious of my business dealings as I am of their motives. The relationship has improved since Madame Eikenberry took the reins. To repay me, you may make your exit now so I may be the concerned citizen to report this find. Good hunting, my friend."

That was good enough for me. We shook and I headed for a path Big Baby pointed out as a shortcut to my truck.

I slipped away without drawing the attention of the *local constabulary*, what a fabulous term.

With the main gate closed, whoever responded to the call must have figured there was no need to station an officer there. My getaway was clear. It was a good thing, too, because the gate was heavy. It took me a few moments sitting in the truck sucking air to recover from opening and then closing it again all by myself.

The scrapes from tromping through the brush and the exertion needed to deal with the gate were reminders that I probably, okay definitely, should start working out again. Nonetheless, the excursion was more successful than I could had anticipated.

I was mulling over the implications of what I'd learned when an unknown number came up on my phone. With my friendly-but-professional voice, I let the caller know they'd reached Elmo's Critter Removal and asked how I could help them.

The caller introduced himself as Julius Cronenberg, the owner of Southeast Pest Services.

"We're both busy, Mr. Simpson, so I'll cut to the chase. I want to form a strategic alliance between our companies. Your name is golden in this part of the country. My firm has a breadth of operations and resources that could be put to good use in the Paradise Springs area."

Mr. Cronenberg was no stranger. His face was on billboards throughout the region. Right next to a caricature of a rattlesnake with impossibly long fangs. Cronenberg was holding it by the throat. Its eyes had been replaced with large X's. The image was both offensive and disturbing.

I did everything I could to save animals' lives. Over the years, I'd relocated countless critters. Most handled the removal process without difficulty and went on to spend their time on Earth in the wild. Some, though, were injured when I removed them and didn't survive the transition, even when I had my vet friend provide treatment. I wept every time one of those poor, innocent souls crossed the Rainbow Bridge. Life was precious, from the tiniest gecko to the most intimidating wild boar.

The man on the phone didn't put as much value on the preservation of nonhuman life as I did. Off-the-record chats with a few of his technicians had revealed that, while the goal was to remove an animal unharmed, the critter's long-term survival wasn't a concern. Speed was. Stories like that made my blood boil.

"Strategic alliance sounds like a fancy way of saying that you want to buy my company." I rolled to a stop at an intersection and waited a couple of moments before going through. Even though there didn't appear to be any traffic, one could never be too sure. Motorists tended to speed once they got away from Spock's radar gun.

"Please, Mr. Simpson, give me a chance." He sounded as oily as the slick from the Deepwater Horizon spill in 2010. "I want to work with you. What would you think about being the face of a new venture? The two of us, working together. You out front, making customers and the community feel good. Me in the background, making sure the bottom line feels good. For the both of us."

"I appreciate your interest, but I just made a sizable capital investment in my business today." Okay, one used truck might not sound like much to Cronenberg, who had a fleet of hundreds. It meant a lot to me, though.

"Even better. That's a sure sign you're on a strong growth path. What do you say to a lunch meeting? Hear me out. All it will cost you is an hour of your time."

"I'll need to check my calendar." It was my go-to stalling tactic. I wasn't crazy about the idea. It would be foolish to reject it out of hand, though. With the Sea Breeze purchase complete, things weren't going to slow down anytime soon. A free lunch was always appealing, too. It couldn't hurt to listen.

"Let me send you some dates and times, just to get the ball rolling," he said. A little too quickly for my comfort.

Before I could respond, a thunderous boom filled my ears. The truck went into a violent spin. I fought the steering wheel but ended up cab-first in a deep drainage ditch. The air bag deployed with a *whoosh*, then all went black.

CHAPTER TWENTY-FIVE

S OMETIME LATER, I was brought back to the waking world by a bright light.

"What the...?"

"Try to stay still, Mr. Simpson." A dark-haired woman was pointing a penlight at my eyes. "You were in an accident. Are you experiencing pain anywhere?"

The inside of my head felt like it was filled with pea soup. My chest hurt, too. No doubt the result of the air bag, which was now drooping from the center of the steering wheel.

"No. I'm okay, I think." The moments leading up to the crash bubbled up in my brain, which was becoming less sludgy with each breath I took. "I was driving, talking on the phone, when...I heard something."

She slipped the light into a pocket of her light blue work shirt, then ran her fingers along the sides of my neck and the back of my skull, applying pressure from time to time. When she asked again if there was any pain, I shook my head.

"My girlfriend would tell you that there's no brain inside my noggin to injure." That got a laugh out of her. I unbuckled my seat belt and stepped out of the truck. I'd been in accidents before, so I knew what to expect from my muscles over the next couple of days.

What I didn't expect was to find a police car, with its lights revolving round and round, parked next to the ambulance.

The responding officer turned out to be Spock. In a total case of imitation being the sincerest form of flattery, he donned a pair of reflective sunglasses identical to the style his boss wore. His approach, long strides with his hand resting on his gun holster, was probably an attempt to stamp his authority on the scene.

His effort came to an inglorious end when he lost his footing on a patch of loose gravel. I managed to grab ahold of one of his pinwheeling arms to prevent him from tumbling into the ditch and taking us both down in the process.

I scowled at the paramedic, which brought a snicker to a stop. Nobody was going to laugh at him in my presence. Like I said, he may have been a dork, but he was our dork.

"Officer Nimoy, it's good to see you. I'm sorry for dragging you out today. Must have had a blowout." I massaged my temple as a headache began to form. Apparently, I'd taken a bigger pop than initially thought.

"You didn't drag me out. Can you tell me what happened?" This time, it took three attempts, but he eventually managed to open his notebook. He needed a different means for recording information.

When I finished recounting the minutes leading up to the crash, Spock looked at the paramedic.

"Same thing he told me." She slipped her stethoscope into a holder attached to her belt. "His vital signs checked out okay. No sign of concussion, so I don't think a trip to the emergency room is needed."

"Good. I prefer to limit my visits there to animal bites. Have I ever told you about the time a pelican attacked me when I got too close to its nest?" I shivered. "The stuff of nightmares."

The paramedic let out a laugh. "I saw a video of that on YouTube. I thought you looked familiar. Now I know why. You're good to go, Mr. Simpson. But if you start to feel nauseous, call 911."

I promised to do so. When we were alone, Spock removed his shades. "YouTube?"

"Yeah, not my finest hour. Especially when someone posted a version with *Keystone Cops* music added to it."

"Wow. And I thought I had it rough around here at times."

"Believe it or not, it actually led to an uptick in business. I think people figured if I was crazy enough to take on an angry pelican, I'd remove anything."

"That's Florida for you." With a roll of the eyes, he led me to the passenger side of the truck to take a look at the damaged tire.

"Okay, that's weird." I blinked a few times to make sure my vision wasn't messed up. The tire's sidewall, while worse for the wear due to the episode, looked to be intact. It hadn't separated from the rim and there was no shredding that a burst would have caused. "Thought a blowout would look a lot worse."

"That's because it wasn't a blowout." He pointed out a

spot near the tread I'd overlooked. It was circular in shape.

A hole.

"Zoinks. Somebody shot my tire out." Images of little Ralphie Parker lying in the snow after a pellet from his brand-new Daisy Red Rider ricocheted off a metal sign and broke his glasses flashed in my head.

I shook my head to get rid of the picture. Maybe I was concussed worse than initially thought.

"Maybe." Spock took a quick look at our surroundings. It was mostly marsh, with a few longleaf pines mixed in. The closest building within sight was a gas station a couple hundred yards down the road. "May have been a stray bullet from someone out hunting."

"At this time of the day? In June?" Growing up in Indiana, the highest profile hunting season took place in November, when outdoorsy folks went after whitetail deer. Beyond that, I didn't know much about hunting. I stalked my prey in the grocery aisle.

Spock held up his index finger, like a professor in a lecture hall. "Rabbits, wild hogs, raccoons, opossums, skunks, nutrias, beaver, and coyotes can be taken year-round by bow or firearm."

"So, I crashed my truck on account of someone taking a pot shot at an animal and missing?"

My truck was undrivable. My head hurt. I wanted pain reliever. Now, I was going to have to deal with my insurance company.

It was still better than finding myself face-to-face with a wild boar who was honked off because I'd just taken a shot at him. And missed.

"Could be worse. You're here talking to me instead of on a stretcher in the back of that ambulance." The medical vehicle pulled away while a tow truck approached. "What were you doing out here anyway? I figured you'd be crewing for Nicola."

Pretty much everyone in Paradise Springs knew Tuesday was my day off, so the fact that Spock was aware of that fact didn't surprise me. What caught me off guard was the assumption that I'd be helping Nic on her boat. It actually made me feel kind of good that he thought, since Nic and I were back in an on-again phase, I should be with her.

"I'm on call if she needs me. I was actually looking into a rumor about Bobby Darrin."

The conversation came to a halt so I could confer with the wrecker driver. After I fetched my phone, which had fallen from its perch and slid under the passenger seat, I gave the guy my approval to take it to the local collision center. With all the fender benders and other accidents that occurred in my town, the center's owner was one of the wealthiest people around.

When the truck departed, Spock and I resumed our conversation. I told him Bobby had ditched his car somewhere in the area and I was trying to find it. He didn't need to know the real story. I'd promised Big Baby their moment. I wasn't going back on that.

"You're in luck." Spock gave me a friendly pat on the back. "Well, I guess, not totally in luck. I mean, with your tire and all that. What I'm trying to say is that his car's been located."

"Great." I faked a smile, hoping he wouldn't notice how fake I probably looked. Nic and Rambo both had told me I'm a terrible liar. "Your investigation's making progress, I take it."

The speaker on Spock's microphone squawked. I opened an app on my phone and started submitting an insurance claim. The person on the other end of the connection sounded like the teacher from the Charlie Brown TV specials I watched as a kid. All *wah wah wah wah*. How he could make any of that out was beyond me. Maybe all cops took a class in deciphering radio conversations.

When the conversation was over, he scratched his collarbone and frowned. "That was the chief. She's on her way to give you a ride home. I'm needed on another vandalism call. That's the third this week. It's totally out of hand. Jenkins has a stack of vandalism case files a mile high. I'm helping him."

At first, people shrugged the vandalism reports off. The summer had seen the greatest influx of vacationers in the town's history. With all the additional traffic, both on land and on sea, more incidents were bound to happen. Such was the *live and let live* lifestyle in the Springs.

When case after case kept being reported, indifference turned to concern. The local electronics store couldn't keep personal surveillance cameras on its shelves. Some people were using the camera on old cell phones to keep an eye on things. With the July Fourth holiday around the corner, concern had turned to borderline panic in the mayor's office.

Which made the thought of going for a ride in the police chief's cruiser less than appealing. She was busy, so giving me a ride home wasn't a random act of kindness. There had to be an ulterior motive.

It didn't take long for me to find out what that ulterior motive was. My seat belt had just slotted into position with a sharp click when the chief handed me a water bottle and said she had news.

I waited, with my hand on the bottle cap. If it was good news, I'd take a drink. If it was bad news, I'd hold on to the water and mix it with some Irish whiskey when I got home.

"I shouldn't be telling you this, so if you breathe a word of it, I'll toss you off the pier. We got the test results back from the multitool you turned in the other day. The blood on the knife matches Desiree's. The size of the blade matches the fatal wound, too. Thanks to you and your concerned citizen friend, we've got the murder weapon."

The water in that bottle went down my throat faster than you could say *party on*. Now, I had to figure out how to put the good news to work.

CHAPTER TWENTY-SIX

THE CHIEF'S BLOND hair was normally as luxurious as spun gold. As I crushed the empty water bottle, it was impossible to miss that it had taken on the texture and dullness of straw. Both of the vehicle's drink holders were occupied with large paper cups brandishing the logo of the Springing Dolphin, the Springs' beloved local coffee shop.

It didn't take a professional investigator to figure out that she was running on empty.

Maybe I could help. Letting me know about the lab results was a kind gesture. She sure wasn't under any obligation to share case information with a civilian. Even one who was spending his free time trying to emulate Detective Inspector Humphrey Goodman from the wonderfully offbeat *Death in Paradise*.

"When's the last time you got a good night's sleep, Susan?" I used her first name on purpose. She needed to know I cared about her as a person as much as I cared about her as my town's chief law enforcement officer.

She put her hand up like a STOP sign. "Don't start, Simpson."

"I know y'all are stretched tighter than a rubber band. Spock was just telling me that the vandalism cases keep piling up. Let me give you a hand."

"But that will leave you with only one."

"What?" A couple of moments later, I chuckled. "Well played. Seriously, though."

We came to a stop at an intersection on the edge of town. Four cars were ahead of us on the two-lane road. Traffic was creeping along at fifteen miles per hour, and we were still two miles from Gulfview Drive, the town's main drag. Not a good situation for the chief, who probably needed to be ten other places at once.

The nanosecond the light turned green, some doofus laid on their horn. As if that would improve the situation in any way, shape, or form. She let out a long sigh.

"You know what, Simpson? On days like this, I wish I would've stuck to modeling. Instead of stuck in traffic, I could be somewhere insanely beautiful for a location shoot with a dedicated assistant at my beck and call."

The chief rarely talked about the years she spent as a model before turning to law enforcement. Bringing it up now was a sure sign she was near the end of her rope.

"All that luxury and glamour? That'd be boring." I stuck my finger in my open mouth and pretended to gag. "What do the models working today have that you don't have?"

"A bigger bank account."

"Well, sure." I couldn't argue with that one. "I bet there's nothing else, though." We finally made it through the intersection. Traffic managed to keep moving. Thank the stars.

"Endorsement opportunities for things like clothing and

skin care products. Do you have any idea how diligent I have to be to make sure I don't end up sunburned? I'm a lot more fair-skinned than people realize," Susan said.

"Really? I didn't know that. Someday, you'll have to ask Wendell about the events that led him to introducing me to pure aloe vera lotion." An image of me from my first summer in Paradise Springs came to mind. I couldn't help laughing.

Susan glanced at me. "How sunburned did you get?"

"Let's just say if you put me next to a cooked lobster, there was virtually no difference in color."

She put her hand over her mouth to stifle a giggle.

"In my defense, it wasn't my fault. It'd been a hard week on the job. I fell asleep in my hammock. I think even the insides of my nostrils got burned."

This got her laughing. "Please tell me you weren't just in a swimsuit. The thought of Elmo Simpson, ruby red from head to toe, scares me."

"I can report I was wearing shorts, a tank top, and shades. In my defense, I ended up having some pretty solid tan lines. The raccoon eyes weren't a great look, though."

Tears started streaming down her face as she let out a snort. "God, Simpson, you are such a dork. Thanks. I needed that."

"Wendell has pictures. He charges people ten bucks a look and donates the money to the local animal shelter."

"You're lying."

"Nope. He's raised over a thousand bucks. This past March alone, he took in a couple hundred. He said he couldn't let my sudden notoriety go to waste. After, you know…"

"I do, indeed." She slowed to take a right-hand turn. "Speaking of which, it seems to be quite the coincidence that you took a bullet to a tire not far from where Darrin's car was found. And not long after Big Baby called in the discovery."

"It is." Despite the near-polar temperature of the air blasting from the vents, my cheeks got warm. Fibbing to the police chief, a woman for whom I had the utmost respect, made me uncomfortable. "I thought you didn't believe in coincidences."

"I don't. So out with it." She poked me in the shoulder. "Darrin clammed up the minute I got him in the box. If you know something about the LaFontaine case, I need you to tell me because you getting shot at wasn't a coincidence."

"Wait a minute. Spock said it was probably just a hunter's stray bullet. A case of being in the wrong place at the wrong time."

"A logical enough conclusion." She chuckled. "One that fails to see the big picture, though. You turn in Desiree's murder weapon. You collar Darrin. You find his car. Somebody wants you to stop what you're doing and go back to corralling wild critters."

My heart started racing. I couldn't catch my breath. The implication of Susan's words crashed over me like a wave in a tropical storm. It wasn't until we were turning into my driveway that I was able to get the words out.

Words I never thought would ever apply to me. Not in a

million years.

"You're saying somebody tried to kill me."

The chief put her hand on my shoulder and gave it a re-assuring squeeze. "Face it, Simpson. You've got someone's attention. Whether they tried to kill you or just scare you off, I don't know. That's why we're going to have a serious chat right here on your patio."

Without giving me a second glance, she got out of the cruiser, marched right to the fake rock by the stoop where I keep my spare key, removed it, and entered the trailer. I was finishing the insurance claim when she returned with two tall glasses of ice water and a bowl with a scoop of ice cream. Oscar had followed her out of the house. There wasn't much mystery who the treat was for.

"My cat likes you more than he likes me." I raised my ice water to Susan.

"He's smart. Knows to respect authority." She placed the ice cream in an unoccupied chair. "Enough chitchat. Your girl Nicola didn't kill Desiree. An initial perusal of Darrin's car indicates he may be a complete lunkhead but he's not a murderer. I'm in the mood for a little brainstorming. Who else you got?"

I put the glass to my forehead. The icy cold water soothed my throbbing skull. Susan was in a pickle, so I told her everything I knew. "That leaves me with the Farrell sisters, Paul, and Oliver King."

She ran her fingers along Oscar's spine. My cat started purring loud enough to make his chair vibrate. The noise calmed me. It must have helped Susan, too, because she began to bob her head, as if she was keeping time with a song in her head. Probably Olivia Rodrigo, who was her current fave.

"Anything else?"

All of a sudden, I was back in college in my Intro to Computer Science class. The professor always asked us if there was something we wanted to add to our answers. That there was always something else to consider. It was an approach to help us to learn to think critically and with an open mind.

Here we were, decades on, and I was being given the same challenge. After some thought, I came up with an answer.

"Bobby and I didn't talk much about his relationship with Desiree. Maybe he knows something but doesn't realize its important."

She pulled a few bobby pins from her hair, which was twisted up in a bun. Then she removed a hair tie and let her hair fall down around her shoulders. "God, that feels good. Sometimes, I think I should cut my hair short like Nicola does. Sure would make life easier."

"Especially when it's hot like it is now."

During an intense heat wave a few years back, I got a buzz cut. It felt good. Until one night, mosquitos attacked my bare noggin. I stumbled into the trailer yelping like a deranged donkey. From that moment on, I wore an Indy 500 baseball cap until my hair grew back out. Nowadays, whenever the temperature gets that intense, I resort to a sweatband.

Which reminded me of something.

"Holy samolie. I was on the phone with Julius Cronenberg when I crashed. I should call him back. He's got to be wondering what happened."

"He's the one who called 911. Reported it as a crash."

I told Susan about our conversation while I shot off a text to Cronenberg to let him know I was okay.

"Tell you what. If you think you can get Darrin to talk, go for it. We've charged him for illegal entry and some other things for when he was hiding out, but his aunts got him an attorney and he's invoked his right to remain silent. Without anything more serious to hold him on, we had to release him when he made bail."

I sat up straight. This was the first time Susan had mentioned my sleuthing without begrudging tolerance at best and professional disdain at worst. Here she was, a professional law enforcement officer, setting aside her pride for the common good. I made a mental tip of the hat to her.

"Will do. The way I see it, the lamebrain owes me. If the Don or his aunts"—I grimaced—"would have gotten to him first, who knows where he would have ended up. Or in how many pieces."

The chief let out a laugh. "That is a fact."

"Is there anything else I can do?"

She raised her glass, which was down to a few melting ice cubes. "You can get me a refill while Oscar and I discuss it."

A few minutes later, I returned with two full glasses of ice water for the humans and a bowl of room temp for the feline. When I placed the bowl on the seat of a spare chair, my roommate stared at it but didn't move from Susan's lap.

"Aren't the two of you a little hot with that arrangement?" I looked at the weather icon on my phone. It read ninety-four degrees.

"Oddly, no. Your cat is a much-needed source of tranquility in turbulent times." She took the bowl from the chair and held it a few inches from Oscar's nose.

He gave it a sniff, then began *lap*, *lap*, *lapping* away like he'd never tasted water. He never did that with me. The traitor.

"So?" I raised my eyebrows. "Any other assignments?"

"Yeah. Keep this between you and me. God knows if this town finds out I'm welcoming outside help, I'll have Sybil on my doorstep faster than you can say *What's my fortune*."

"Understood." I drummed my fingers on the plastic tabletop. "You know I'm just trying to help, right?"

"I do. And I appreciate what you told the press a few months ago. You earned some latitude with me. Don't make me regret it." She scratched Oscar's ear and told him how handsome he was.

The matter was closed.

A number of people knew the role I played in figuring out who killed Fran Cohen. When asked about it by the press, I stuck to the story Susan and I came up with. The Paradise Springs Police Department cracked the case. Nic and I just happened to be in the right place at the right time to provide assistance. It was a matter of having each other's backs. Susan and the Paradise Springs police got the official credit and praise from the law enforcement and government communities. I got a boost in notoriety, and business, via the Springs Signal.

It worked out for all parties involved. The next object of my attention was Bobby Darrin. At least he'll have showered since the last time I saw him.

"Do you know where I can find him?"

The chief raised an eyebrow high enough to be visible above the frame of her shades. "As a matter of fact, I do. Be careful, though. He may be in trouble with his aunts, but they're still ultraprotective of him. I don't want to find my team investigating your sudden disappearance because you asked the wrong person the wrong question."

I didn't want that, either. Sometimes, though, what I wanted and what I needed took two wildly divergent paths.

CHAPTER TWENTY-SEVEN

B OBBY DARRIN WAS right where Susan said I'd find him. I had to pause my approach to wipe the smirk from my face. Oh, how the mighty had fallen. He was definitely reaping what he'd sown.

And then I ran out of clichés, so I resumed my walk toward him.

"Afternoon, Bobby." I tipped my cap to him. "Good to see you out and about."

He placed his elbow on the end of a push broom. The doofus was sweeping the parking lot at the Marlin. In ninety-six-degree heat. A plastic trash bag stuck out of a back pocket of his jeans. A dustpan hung from a ring attached to a belt loop.

"I thought hiding out was rough. My aunt Beryl has me doing all the grunt work around here now. After I get all the glass swept up, I have to clean the grease traps. Then I have to haul out the trash."

"That's rough." As a critter removal specialist, I'd come across too many restaurant grease traps to count that hadn't been properly maintained. That lack of care had resulted in creatures with anywhere from four to eight legs moving in. Bobby's next task wasn't going to be any fun.

It was still way better than having to deal with insects and small rodents, though.

"You don't know that half of it. Instead of letting me finish my trip to New Orleans to scout locations, now Aunt Meryl is going. I have to do all kinds of stuff until I've paid them back. With interest at 25 percent. And they're only paying me minimum wage."

To show some empathy, I coughed to cover a laugh. In truth, I had no sympathy for him, whatsoever. I mean, how stupid do you have to be to gamble away five thousand dollars you've been given for a business trip?

Which made me wonder.

"Did your aunts really give you five grand in cash?"

"Yeah." He scratched the back of his neck. "I know it looks shady. It was to help grease some wheels if I found a promising location. Pretty much all the work I do for them is off the books, if you know what I mean."

Great. The Farrell sisters entrusted their dim bulb of a nephew with a pile of cash for a trip to the Big Easy. What could possibly have gone wrong?

All of a sudden, I had no sympathy for the sisters. It was a true comedy of errors. They were probably lucky Bobby didn't make it there. He might have annoyed the wrong person, been separated from his bankroll, and dumped in Lake Pontchartrain in the dead of night.

All of which gave me an idea.

I draped my arm over him. "I know how I might be able to get you out of this mess."

He took a look over his shoulder. The Magnificent Marlin stood like a menacing *kaiju*, ready to bring its unholy wrath down upon Bobby if he took another step out of line.

"How? Whatever it is, I'm in. It's gotta be better than pushing a broom in this heat." He moved a small pile of broken glass into a larger one a few feet away. "I have to work while I talk, though. Aunt Beryl said she'll dock my pay if she catches me lollygagging."

I glanced at the sky. A bank of gray clouds foreshadowed the daily rainstorm. While it was insufferably hot and humid at the moment, the conditions would be absolutely oppressive if I found myself soaked to the gills with the humidity even higher after the rain blew through.

"I know you and Desiree split up a while back. Did you ever try to get back together with her?"

"Why?" He shoved the broom forward, tiny clouds of dust and sand forming with each stroke.

"Because if you were talking to each other, maybe she said something to you that would be relevant to the murder investigation. You do want to find her murderer, right?" My response was more akin to a blunt sledgehammer than the scalpel I wanted to use. The moron was too annoying for me to employ subtlety, though.

"Chill, bro. Of course I want to find her killer. Yeah, I was trying to win her back. I was so stoked about the New Orleans trip, I went to her place to tell her about it. You know, to show her I was being responsible."

I chose not to mention that the New Orleans trip ended up with him hiding in an abandoned condo thousands of dollars in debt. To any number of shady characters. Discretion, and all that. Instead, I asked him when this meeting took place.

He pushed the detritus that had accumulated at the end of the broom toward the larger pile.

"Couple of weeks ago." He went back to his sweeping. For a guy who said he wanted to help, he wasn't being very forthcoming.

"Okay. What did you talk about? What kind of mood was she in? Did she say anything that seemed, I don't know, odd?"

He told me about the conversation as he swept. He'd talk for a bit, then went quiet while he focused on his work. It was filled with references to Bobby's unbelievable opportunity and glorious future and Desiree's ambivalence. She seemed happy for him but lacked interest in the details.

A rumble of thunder in the distance served as a not-so-welcome reminder that Mother Nature wasn't concerned with my desires for both information and to stay dry. Then Bobby stopped and scratched his head.

"You know, come to think of it, she did say something that was weird."

When he didn't continue, I twirled my index finger in a circle to prompt him. If I wasn't careful, I was going to find myself behind bars for attempted murder of Bobby Darrin by strangulation. My defense would be loss of patience. I was pretty sure no jury would convict me.

"She told me to be careful what I wished for. That she never should have gone to work for Craig."

I looked at him. For a moment, I was unable to move

while the implications of Bobby's information sank in.

Could it really be that simple? Was Desiree murdered because she wanted to quit working for Craig? That seemed drastic. Yes, she was the man's point person here in the Springs. She'd only been with him for a few months, though. I could see some hard feelings, especially going into the Independence Day holiday. But to commit murder?

No. There had to be something else at play.

Another rumble of thunder got me moving. I told Bobby thanks and promised to put in a good word with his aunts and the cops. Then I sprinted for my e-bike before the daily deluge arrived.

I needed to think things through. In a place out of the elements. The Springing Dolphin was close. It would be an excellent place for some cogitating while I waited for the storm to pass.

The first thing I did once I was inside was call my insurance agent. Buying one truck and crashing another one, in the same day, was an accomplishment for the ages. After some good-natured razzing, my agent promised me she'd take care of everything and would let me know where I could pick up a rental.

"Bummer about your truck." My server, a brown-haired young man with tattoos covering both arms, placed a glass of water on the table. "Didn't mean to be eavesdropping. You were talking a little loud."

I told him thank you then ordered coffee and a blueberry scone. I figured it was nicer than telling him to bugger off and stop listening in on customers' conversations.

Sheets of rain started coming down the same time the server brought my order to me, followed in short order by blinding cracks of lightning and ear-splitting booms of thunder.

During weather like this, all it took was a quick look around to tell the locals from the visitors. Folks who'd been here a while glanced out the window, shrugged, and went back to their business. On the other hand, one man in an IOWA HAWKEYES tank top let out a little scream while his dining mate made a move under their table. They also looked like they'd been day drinking, so alcohol may have been the reason for their skittish behavior.

I returned to the issue at hand. A picture was beginning to come into focus. It was like Choctawhatchee Bay becoming more and more visible as the morning fog burns off. Within recent weeks, Desiree expressed regret about going to work for Craig. Then, she told her sister that she wanted to talk to Nic. After that, she asked Nic to meet with her.

The conclusion was obvious. To me, at least. Desiree realized she made a mistake and wanted to return to work with Nic. So, what was the big deal about that? I drummed my fingers on the Formica tabletop while I considered the ramifications for Craig's Cruises.

Was quitting enough of a reason for Craig to commit murder? No. It was safe to assume he wouldn't be happy. I didn't like the guy, but he was a businessperson. Word would get out if he tried to make things difficult for Desiree after she gave notice. Hiring new staff in the aftermath of an uncool move like that could prove to be difficult. That scenario didn't add up. If he was the murderer, there had to be more than a job change at play.

While Desiree's exit meant a loss for Craig, it seemed to be a win for Oliver King, though. The guy arrived on the scene as Craig's go-to person. His demeanor changed around the time Craig hired Desiree.

Coincidence? Not by a long shot.

There was a problem with that scenario, though. From what I saw the other day, Oliver wasn't up to the task of being Craig's second-in-command. Admittedly, that was my opinion, something Wendell was more than happy to remind me was worth as much as an old wad of gum stuck to the bottom side of a barstool. That typically happened after I'd had one too many drinks and was getting mouthy about my belief that John Kennedy Toole's *A Confederacy of Dunces* was the best piece of fiction in the history of the United States.

I will hold on to that position until the day I die, by the way.

Back to the subject at hand, though. Oliver may have seen Desiree as an interloper. And after a few months of daily humiliation, he may have snapped and taken the woman's life. Especially, if he found out about the meeting at the Magnificent Marlin and was angry that he wasn't included in it.

That could have been the final straw.

"Nah." As much as I wanted to go with that scenario, I wasn't sure it held water. By all accounts, Oliver seemed to be the type of person who took his ball and went home to pout when he didn't get his way. And, later on, suck up to the playground bully. Who, in this case, would be his boss.

Questions started blowing up in my mind like kernels of corn in a popcorn popper. Where was Oliver the night in question? How did he get his hands on Nic's multitool? Was he in cahoots with the murderer? Could Craig have murdered Desiree with Oliver's assistance? What was the point of stabbing Desiree with the harpoon spear? If I leaned on him hard enough, could I get information out of him? Was there someone else I needed to take a closer look at?

Like Gretchen, for instance. She knew details about the deal I hadn't shared. She also hadn't been going out with anyone for a while. Love and money were an intoxicating duo.

All the questions were making my head spin.

The rain was letting up. In a few minutes, the storm would have moved on, and the sun would be out again. Such was the nature of Florida weather in the summer.

That meant I'd be able to ride home without getting wet. Thank goodness for fenders. Especially when one was on two wheels instead of four.

A little while later, I eased back on the throttle and rolled to a stop by my front door. My shoes were a touch damp from all the rain, but overall, I was none the worse for wear. The ride had given me time to decide what my next move would be.

I needed to have a chat with Oliver. There were too many questions that only he could answer.

CHAPTER TWENTY-EIGHT

M Y WEDNESDAY STARTED off on a positive note, despite the soreness from my crash. First, as I sat down for a breakfast of scrambled eggs and an English muffin, a text message from Cronenberg arrived. It was short and to the point. He hoped I was doing okay and would still like to get together at my convenience.

"What do you think, Oscar?" My cat was lounging at my feet, having just snarfed down a breakfast of shredded chicken. "Should I sell to the guy? I mean, at least he had the sense to pretend that he cares about how I'm feeling."

My buddy flicked his ears at the sound of his name but made no other move.

"Silence, eh? I'll take that to mean you don't want to commit at this time. Good call. I'll put it on the backburner until Desiree's murderer is behind bars. Sound good?"

Oscar stretched one front leg, then the other, leaving the second one resting on my toes. There was probably nothing to be read into the move, other than maybe he wanted to warm his toe beans on my bare foot. I was secure in my insecurity to know that I wanted his approval, though, so I chose to believe the movement was his way of showing his agreement.

When you lived with a cat, you learned to take whatever attention you could get from it. And sometimes, you took that attention and told yourself that it was something more.

Hey, it worked for me. Why overthink it?

The day got better when I checked my email. My insurance agent was totally on the ball. A truck was waiting for me to pick it up at one of the local rental agencies. I let out a long, cleansing breath. My afternoon was booked solid with removal appointments. Now I didn't have to worry how I was going to make them without some major shuffling with Jordan.

I shot off a text to my partner in animal rescue to let him know all was well. We'd talked on the phone the night before, and I'd assured him that things would work out. We'd meet all of our obligations. The company's reputation would even improve when folks found out our little two-person crew hadn't missed a beat despite a crash that had left us one vehicle down.

Service above all else. That was Elmo's Critter Removal.

And now it was time to do some work in the service of the greater good.

The police had already talked to everyone close to Desiree. Family, friends, and coworkers alike sat down with the chief herself for interviews in the first days after her body was discovered. That included everyone working for Craig. The fact that nobody had been arrested yet wasn't a poor reflection on the police. It was a reflection of the slower, more methodical approach they had to take with their investigation. There were laws they had to follow, after all.

When you combined that with a dearth of evidence connecting the crime to a specific suspect, it wasn't a surprise Susan was willing to allow some out-of-the-box thinking.

Like looking the other way while I did my best impression of Jim Rockford.

From the cover of a gumbo limbo tree, I scoped out the Craig's Cruises trailer. Employees were buzzing around like bees as they got ready to provide visitors with a day of fun in the Florida sun. Two young men in matching yellow T-shirts were lugging cases of bottled water from the trailer to the company's boats. A middle-aged woman, singing "Fly Me to the Moon" so loud I found myself tapping my foot to keep in time, was washing the sales office window. Oliver popped in and out of the trailer's office, barking orders and gesturing as if he was communicating via semaphore.

The main man was nowhere to be seen. Eight in the morning was probably a little on the early side for him. His absence was a good thing. It saved me having to cook up a story justifying why I needed to speak with Oliver.

I had to sit tight for a few minutes while the office staff took care of customers. When the final customer stepped away from the window, Oliver emerged from the office yet again. This time he was carrying a white plastic trash bag. It wouldn't have caught my attention, except for the fact that he took a long look around before closing the door behind him.

When he was satisfied nobody was around to see what he was up to, he sprinted to a trash barrel behind the trailer. Lucky for me, I only had to move a few feet to my left to keep it in sight. It was a good thing, too, because before he tossed the bag in, he removed something from his pocket, then dropped it in. The trash bag followed in quick order. After another look around, as if he was the Road Runner scoping out any signs of Wile E. Coyote, he double-timed it back inside the trailer.

Curiosity killed the cat, but it didn't change the fact that I really wanted to know what Oliver tossed in the trash. So, throwing caution to the wind, I made my way to the trash can. And was happy that for once, I wasn't a cat.

My plan changed when I was twenty feet from the trailer. Oliver emerged, holding a cell phone a few inches from his ear. Whoever was on the other end of the call wasn't happy. While I couldn't make out all the words, the cursing among the shouting made the message clear enough.

He ended the call, then almost ran into me. Well, I might have noticed he wasn't paying attention to where he was going and angled my approach to facilitate contact. A point to Elmo for being sneaky.

"Hey, watch where you're going." I grabbed both of his shoulders to steady him. "Wouldn't want to walk into a wall."

"Oh." He slipped his phone into a pocket of his board shorts. "Sorry about that, Mr. Simpson."

I smiled as I flicked sand from his shoulders. "It's Elmo. Mr. Simpson's way too formal for me. Do you have a minute?"

"I'm afraid not. I've got a boat full of tourists and the crew can't get the engine to start. I need to see what's going on." He took off at a jog without giving me another look.

For a second, my heart went out to the guy. For only a second, though. His and Craig's operation had been a source of indigestion for my friends and me for months now. And, way more importantly, Desiree would still be alive if they'd never come to town.

With that in mind, I had no trouble readjusting my plans. Instead of questioning the man, I made my way to the trash barrel.

After a look around to make sure I wasn't being watched, including taking a moment to make sure nobody was hiding behind my gumbo limbo tree, I removed the trash bag. If needed, I'd rummage through it. Only if I had to, though. The thought of dealing with a half-eaten sandwich or a bunch of snot rags made me want to gag.

Another bag lay at the bottom of the receptacle. A crumpled piece of paper was on top of it. Was that what Oliver had dropped in first? My curiosity picked up as I unfolded it. After all, if the paper wasn't important, why didn't he get rid of it with the rest of the trash?

"You have got to be kidding me." My shoulders sagged as I read the crinkled sheet. It was a poem. The verses were cringeworthy, but the sentiment and subject of the work were impossible to miss.

Oliver had a crush on Seven.

The woman sure had that effect on men. I chuckled as I crumpled the page back up. Unless he was prepared to debate whether *Don Quixote* was a better read in its native Spanish or translated to English, Oliver wasn't her type. I had to give him points for good taste. His regular appearance at the Riptide made a whole lot more sense now.

His secret was safe with me. But only for now. If it turned out he was involved in Desiree's murder, even in the tiniest way, I didn't want him coming anywhere near my friend.

With that mystery solved, I removed the second bag. Couldn't be too thorough, right? After all, a glimpse at the literal bottom of the barrel was a hundred times better than landing at the bottom of a metaphorical one due to an oversight.

I was hit with a whiff of stale beer when I leaned in for a closer look. Yikes, that was gross.

The floor of the container was littered with the detritus of a typical trash can. Used paper napkins, crushed beer can, a broken rubber band, some promotional flyers, and a pen with a red cap that had been chewed to within an inch of its life.

And something I recognized.

"What do we have here?" Among the discarded items lay a device that was oh, so familiar. A wave of cool relief rushed through me. The moment was reminiscent of how I felt when Oscar reappeared on my front stoop after being gone for three days. Few things were better than seeing an old friend again.

Recovering Desiree's multitool was one of those things.

My happiness at stumbling across it faded when the implications of the find hit me. Why was Desiree's multitool in a trash can behind her workplace? How did it get there?

How long had it been there? Had anybody noticed it was missing?

And even more worrisome, did its presence at the bottom of a trash can have something to do with her murder?

CHAPTER TWENTY-NINE

I NEEDED TO talk to the chief. She'd want to know about any evidence sooner rather than later.

I banged my fist on the steering wheel when I entered the police station's parking lot. Her spot was empty. So much for being able to stroll into her office and present her with another piece of evidence like some hotshot private eye. A phone call went to her voicemail.

"Think, Elmo. Think." Susan Eikenberry was under a lot of pressure. If she was out of touch, there had to be a good reason. Like taking time to relieve stress. What did she do to relieve stress? She went to the beach. I put my truck in gear and headed that way.

A few minutes later, I was trudging across the sugar sand in an isolated section of Paradise Springs' coastline. The chief was in the midst of her favorite workout. It was a mixture of yoga and a form of martial arts that featured the use of two *katana* swords. The last time I bothered her during one of these workouts, she almost sliced my neck wide open.

Well, that was the way it had felt in the heat of the moment. Later on, Susan had confided that she'd stopped the swords with plenty of room to spare, a full quarter of an inch from my skin.

The next thing I knew, Wendell was easing me into a chair and offering me a glass of water while Susan, Seven, and Nic were sharing a laugh.

I didn't ask if they were laughing at Susan's story or my fainting spell. A guy had to have some pride, after all.

"Morning, Chief," I called from fifty feet away. A safe distance. I hoped.

She sprung up from a crouching position and spun toward me. The swords were pointed in my direction, as if she was ready to strike me down at any moment.

"This better be good, Simpson. I was just getting in the zone."

A bead of sweat trickled down the back of my neck. It wasn't from the weather, that was for sure.

"I've got new information about the LaFontaine case."

She lowered one sword until the tip scraped against the sand. "I'm listening."

I walked to within a few feet of her. A range some might call within stabbing distance. I didn't want to chance our conversation being overheard, even though there was nobody else in sight. The soreness in my neck and back were reminders you couldn't be too careful.

"I found Desiree's multitool." With a sense of accomplishment, I opened my palm and pulled back the clean paper napkin it was wrapped in.

"I didn't know it was missing." She placed both swords on her exercise mat.

Susan was a *get to the point* kind of person, so I dispensed with the details and told her where I found it.

"Interesting." She tapped an index finger on her thigh. "Humor me. Any theories about how it got there?"

"Someone stole it, used it for something illegal, and then got rid of it when word got out Desiree'd been murdered."

She took a swig from a water bottle, then squirted some of the contents on her forehead. "Okay, a little obvious, but I don't disagree with your thinking. The next question is why."

I scratched my head. After a few seconds, though, a scenario began to come together. It was a long shot, but it was something.

"What can you tell me about the vandalism cases the past few weeks? Anything that connects them?"

"Taken individually, they're all small-time stuff. Minor property damage. Probably not enough to make it worth reporting to insurance." She waited a moment, then shrugged, as if deciding what the heck. "Except for someone taking potshots at the new WELCOME TO PARADISE SPRINGS sign, the victims are people doing business in the vicinity of the marina."

"You don't think that's a coincidence."

She tapped the tip of her nose, then pointed at me. "Two beachside equipment rental shacks reported cast nets were damaged. Someone had cut the netting with a knife. There have been cases of rental Jet Skis with severed fuel lines. A radio had been smashed. Holes gouged into seat cushions. I could go on."

"What if the person who stole the multitool is the same person behind the rash of vandalism? You've got stuff that's been ripped, punctured, cut, and smashed. A multitool could do all of that."

"True." She grabbed a towel from a gym bag and wiped her face with it. "If one person's behind all the damage, why are they doing it? And don't tell me they're just out to cause trouble."

"To make Nic look bad. What if the vandalism started about the same time Nic's multitool went missing. And"—I raised my index finger for emphasis—"what if vandalism calls stop coming in now?"

"I don't know, Elmo." She shook her head. "Seem like a lot of effort just to cause your girlfriend problems."

"True. The thing is, Nic, Desiree's sister, and Bobby Darrin all told me that Desiree wanted to talk to Nic about something but never got the chance. What if she was the vandal and wanted to fess up?"

The chief pursed her lips. "Why? It was only hurting people she knew."

It was a great question. Desiree loved the Springs. She was born and raised here. There was no reason for her to hurt her friends.

Unless she was forced.

"They made her."

"What?" Susan blinked and cocked her head to one side. Apparently, my response had lost her.

"Bear with me. What if someone, say Craig or Oliver, was forcing her to commit the vandalism? From what I've heard, the victims are all people in competition with Craig in one way or another. That would be a way to drive business to your door—"

"But Abbott's outfit got hit, too. One of their Jet Skis was damaged." She tapped her teeth with her finger. "Unless they did that to throw off suspicion. They've got a bunch of them. Having one out of commission wouldn't be much of a problem. Still…"

I took a moment to think. Questions kept bouncing around in my head. From what I could tell, business had been decent for Craig from the start. Why would he feel the need to sabotage his competitors? Along with that, what could he have on Desiree to make her commit criminal acts? I voiced my concerns.

"Good questions. I had Nimoy do a routine check on Desiree's background and financials. We didn't find anything that caught our attention. The woman didn't have much, but she was debt-free. Her only bills were the normal things—utilities, phone, stuff like that."

I breathed a sigh of relief. Sometimes I could get ahead of myself. Hashing this out reinforced my hope that blaming Desiree for the vandalism didn't make sense.

Then I had another idea. One that I liked a lot more than my previous one.

"What if we're overthinking this? By all accounts, Oliver wasn't happy when Craig hired Desiree. What if he got it in his head that one way to get back in the boss's good graces was to generate extra business? He could have stolen Nic's multitool and committed all the vandalism on his own. Maybe she found out and confronted him about it. And he killed her. Then, to frame Nic, he took Desiree's multitool and replaced it with Nic's. I know it sounds crazy, but what do we know about Oliver?"

"A fair amount, actually." She gathered her things and stuffed them into her bag. Except for the swords. She slid them into leather scabbards, then handed them to me. "You can carry these to my car. Did you know that Oliver grew up in Paradise Springs?"

"Jordan mentioned it. I don't know more than that."

"Don't feel bad. He left town before you got here."

"And the past is a taboo subject here in good old Paradise Springs, Florida." I fell in beside her as we marched through the soft sand. "A bit of a double-edged sword, that. Pardon the pun."

"That it is. Except for your friends in law enforcement. Do me a solid. Take the multitool to the station and have Nimoy log it into evidence. While you're there, ask him what he knows about Oliver's time here and why he left. I'll be there after I get cleaned up. If you're still there when I arrive, this conversation didn't happen."

The request seemed odd. Living in Paradise Springs, I knew odd.

In the past, I'd asked Susan if she minded sharing the reasoning behind a decision. She responded that yes, in fact she did mind and refused to answer. Now I knew better than to ask permission.

"Will do. Why are we keeping this on the down-low?"

"Even though he hasn't said a word to me about it, I'm aware of Officer Nimoy's desire to make detective. He'll take your report and run with it. He's got initiative. I'd like to be able to reward that someday." She pointed a finger at me. "You breathe a word of that to anyone and I promise I will feed you to one of Rambo's gators. Got it?"

I gulped. The way Susan's demeanor could change at the drop of a hat was unnerving. Half of me thought she did it on purpose, to keep people off-balance. The other half of me insisted that it was best not to think about it. The other half won the argument. After all, I had no doubt she could follow through on her promise.

Or was it a threat? When Susan Eikenberry was involved, sometimes it was the same thing.

I, for one, was not going to mess around and run the risk of finding out. I was a fan of self-preservation, after all. Which meant it was time to head off for a visit with Spock.

CHAPTER THIRTY

I TOOK ADVANTAGE of modern technology by handling critter removal calls while I drove to the police station. Without ever taking my hands off the steering wheel. I loved voice-assisted technology. And wouldn't have minded being part of the team that brought that software to the market.

That was a story for another day, though.

By the time I put the truck in Park, I'd returned two phone calls, forwarded three text messages to Jordan, and added another two appointments to my schedule. While I was pleased with the productivity, I couldn't dismiss the thought that life would be simpler if I got out of the business.

If I did bow out, it would be on my terms, though, not Cronenberg's.

With the day job mischief managed for the moment, I entered the police station. Spock was at his workstation. A stack of files six inches high balanced precariously on the corner of his desk. His jet-black hair, which normally didn't have a strand out of place, was standing on end in clumps, like he'd been running his fingers through it time and again. The four empty coffee cups in his trash can might have had something to do with his current state of dishevelment. Or was it dishevelness? Disarray? Anyway.

I exchanged greetings with the desk officer. With a shake of her head, she reported the temperature might hit one hundred degrees later in the day. In normal places, extreme weather conditions often translated into a reduction in crime. When it was too hot, too cold, or too rainy, criminals tended to stay put. In the Springs, more often than not, it meant an uptick in alcohol- and controlled-substance-related disturbances.

Just like death and taxes, you could count on folks over-indulging in Paradise Springs. Especially at times when logic suggested refraining from grown-up beverages. And weed. And psychedelics. And, well, you get the idea.

I could spend an evening spinning yarns about people I know going surfing during a hurricane. Yet more stories for another time, though.

Spock looked up from a form he was working on. At first he smiled and waved. A moment later, his brows furrowed. He got out of his chair and shuffled toward me. With a slightly stooped back, he reminded me of the character Mr. Tudball from the classic *Carol Burnett Show*, which my mom loved to watch over and over again.

"I'm sorry I don't have any information about your tire getting shot. Since you're okay, your case had to go to the, uh…"

"Bottom of the pile. No worries." I gestured toward his desk. "I'm here on other business. Can I talk to you?"

"Absolutely." He straightened, perhaps no longer in fear of getting yelled at.

I handed the multitool to him. While he donned a pair of latex gloves, I told him where and how I found it. The conversation with the chief never came up. At the conclusion of my report, I shrugged. "Hope this helps with the LaFontaine investigation."

"Thank you for bringing this in. We'll look into it." His tone was clipped. Maybe giving the aspiring detective something else to do wasn't the best plan. Well, it was too late now. Some buttering up couldn't hurt.

"I heard Oliver King used to live here. Figured if anyone knew why he left, it'd be you."

He raised an eyebrow. The good old Spock had returned.

"Why do you want to know?"

"I was curious about whether Oliver and Desiree knew each other. If his decision to leave had anything to do with her."

"You know, of course, that it would be inappropriate for an officer of the law to engage in gossip." He looked around the office, then leaned toward me. "This doesn't go beyond this desk, understand?"

For not wanting to gossip, certain members of Paradise Springs' law enforcement didn't mind doing it.

"You're the boss." If he was going to give me intel, I was going to keep serving up the niceties.

"First off, Oliver's about two years older than Desiree. Back in the day, they had a bit of a rivalry."

"What about?"

"Each of them thought they were the best young sailor in town. I won't bore with the details, but when Miss

Nicola was looking to hire someone, they both applied. Desiree got the job. Oliver got super mad. He pouted for a while, then took off."

"Wow. Seems extreme. Even for this town."

"No kidding." He smoothed his wonky hair with the palm of his hand. "I didn't see it myself, but before he left town, Oliver confronted Desiree and let her have it. Called her all kinds of stuff and said she would never be the mariner that he was. Goob supposedly saw the whole thing. Talk to him if you want the deets."

So, Oliver had a long-simmering beef with Desiree. Yes, that sounded like something worth discussing with Goob. Over some chicken gumbo, perhaps.

"Y'all brought up the fight when you talked to him, I assume?"

Spock nodded. "He admitted he'd said some really stupid things to her. Blamed it on being young and drunk. He was believable, so there wasn't much more we could do."

"Does he have an alibi?"

"He said he was in his condo at the Sea Breeze. That's as solid of an alibi as anyone we've interviewed."

"And as flimsy."

"That's why we're working as hard as we can, Elmo. Whoever murdered Desiree was smart enough to cover their tracks."

I got to my feet. "Do you think, with the multitool, you've got enough to bring Oliver in?"

"I'll have to talk to the chief. Anybody could have dropped it in the trash, so it's not like we'll track him down with our firearms drawn. We'll ask Mr. Abbott if he has surveillance footage for that area."

"Thanks, man. Live long and prosper." The legendary phrase spoken by Mr. Spock in all forms of media was out of my mouth before I realized it.

"No problem, Elmo. Peace and long life." The man's thoughts were on the multitool. He was probably too busy studying it to pay any attention to what I said. Thus, the equally legendary response without any thought.

I left without hesitation, happy to dodge the bullet of Spock taking offense. Yes, he wasn't the most accomplished law enforcement officer ever. Still, insulting him was not cool. If the chief had faith in the guy, I would, too.

Especially with a killer still on the loose.

CHAPTER THIRTY-ONE

G OOB GREETED ME upon my arrival at his store with a scowl. I'd never seen the man scowl in all the years I'd known him. He was one of the friendliest and kindest souls on the planet. If he didn't like something, he didn't scowl. Instead, he closed his eyes for a few seconds. When he reopened them, he'd be smiling.

There was no smile to be seen.

"What's wrong?" I took a seat at the dining counter.

"*Diversify your holdings*, they said. *Real estate's a sure bet*, they said. What a load of horse hockey. It's a losing bet if you ask me."

It didn't matter what the problem was. Goob had welcomed me to Paradise Springs with open arms. In a way, he'd also played a role in my introduction to Nic. It made my heart ache to see the man so distressed.

"How can I help?"

He gave me a half smile while he shook his head. "This is my problem, not yours."

"Bull cookies." If he was going to borrow a phrase from Colonel Sherman Potter from *M*A*S*H*, I would, too. "You've been there for me too many times to count. I'm not letting go until you tell me what's going on. Now, out with it."

We spent a few moments in a stare down. Somebody had wounded my friend. His pride seemed to be injured the most. In my experience, it was easy to engage in self-blame when one's pride had taken a hit. Whatever had happened was not Goob's fault.

Of that, I was certain.

And I wasn't certain about a lot of things. Not after a decade in Paradise Springs, where someone who might be a vampire lived. Where a junk dealer had an awful lot of security cameras and seemed to have mysterious dealings all over the world. Where nightclub owners might be witches. And where a burned-out animal removal specialist all of a sudden was a real estate mogul.

Well, that last part might be a stretch. Whether the burned-out part or the mogul part was more accurate could be debated. Still.

Goob broke eye contact. Then he gave me a big smile. "I've got a slice of ham and pineapple pizza under the warmer. You eat that and I'll tell you what's going on."

"Bring it on." In the week since I'd first tasted the concoction, the flavor had grown on me. Not much, but enough for me to polish off the slice without the fear of dying. Besides, if it helped Goob, the effort was totally worth it. "And a Diet Coke."

"Trying to keep that slim and trim figure, I see. I'm sure Miss Nicola appreciates it." He chuckled, then stepped away before I could formulate a witty retort. He could have stayed; I had nothing.

Other than he was probably right.

Ten minutes and most of the soda pop later, the only thing left on my plate was a slightly oily sheet of wax paper and a few crumbs. Time to get some answers.

"I used to have two stores here on the marina. Twenty years ago, I closed the other location. I rented it for a while. When it started costing more to maintain than I was getting in rent, I knocked the place down."

He wiped the perspiration from his head with a purple hand towel. I kept my mouth shut. He'd get to the point in his own time.

"I wanted to sell the parcel, but people convinced me to hold on to it. Said it'd be worth a small fortune someday. So, I did what they suggested. I decided to rent out the land when a nice young man approached me over the winter. Everything was all kittens and rainbows for a while. To make a long story short, I haven't seen a payment in three months."

My blood began boiling. The thought of ripping off the patron saint of Paradise was the lowest of lows. Except for murder and a few other things. It was heinous, regardless.

"Who's ripping you off?"

"That's the thing. I don't know for sure. I can't get ahold of the young man I dealt with. I've talked to Abbott about it. He's subleasing the land. He gave me the contact info of the company where he sends his rent payments. I can't get a response from anyone there, either. I feel like such a dunce for letting this happen."

"I take it you haven't told anybody about this?"

Goob shook his head. His eyes misted up. "No. I've been

too embarrassed. After all the years I've lived here, I should have seen this coming."

"No. You're the victim. Sounds like someone's using shell companies to rip you off." I rubbed my hands together. We were on territory where I could actually help. "Give me what you've got on these entities. I'll figure out who's behind this."

He wrote the information on a page from the notepad he used to take orders. The company names were all random numbers and letters. A clever way to frustrate someone trying to figure out what the firms did. It would be fun to put my tech skills to work.

Especially since Craig Abbott's company was part of the picture. The question was how much his company, he, and Oliver, were involved.

With Goob reassured, I returned to the reason for my visit and asked him about Desiree and Oliver.

"I've seen a lot. Most things I've forgotten about. I'll never forget the way those two went at it."

Between breaks to ring up purchases and fill lunch orders, he told me the long, sordid tale. Oliver completely lost his cool when he didn't get the job and, after a few too many rounds of liquid courage, confronted Desiree.

He screamed at her and called her every name in the book. Then he knocked her off-balance and she fell into the water. Goob rushed to intervene. Once she was back on deck, a soaking-wet Desiree said she had the situation under control. She then turned to Oliver, who'd been laughing at her.

"She told him in a tone sharp enough to cut grass that he needed to leave town. She was going to make sure he never worked in Paradise Springs for as long as she lived."

"Did she really say that last part? 'For as long as she lived.'"

"Afraid so. The way she said it, like a judge handing down a sentence, made it impossible to forget. Talking about it now gives me the shivers."

Holy smokes. I almost fell off my stool. I mean, I literally had to grab the counter to steady myself. The argument sure put Oliver in a bad light.

"And the cops know about this?"

"Well, obviously, since Spock sent you here."

"Right." The man had a point. It still seemed to me that a long-simmering grudge should be a good enough reason to haul Oliver in.

Goob cleared his throat. "I heard a rumor about another confrontation they had. Earlier this year. I didn't see it myself, so I can't vouch for its accuracy, but since you're asking."

"Lay it on me. The more information the better."

The man let out a long sigh. "Keep in mind, this is thirdhand. Supposedly they got into it down by Poseidon's Trident. This time, though, Desiree gave it right back to Oliver every bit as much as she got."

This sounded bad, like *getting your roof blown off by a hurricane* bad. I had to know, though. The sooner I got the rest of the story, the sooner I could figure out my next step.

"Tell me about it."

Goob scratched his chin as he pondered. "He said screwing him over once was more than enough, and he wasn't going to let her get away with doing it again. She called him a clown and said he was stupid to come back. There was some shoving, then he took off. Before he could get far, she pushed him in the water."

"Has anyone told the police about this?"

His cheeks turned pink. Well, that answered the question. "You know this town. People get in shouting matches around here all the time. Especially when people have had a drink or four. I'm not going to bother Chief Eikenberry with a thirdhand rumor."

I looked him in the eye. Seconds ticked by on the analog clock on the wall. How could such a good man be so dismissive? It seemed so out of character.

"Really, Goob? A friend's been murdered. The killer's still out there. Don't you think the chief would prefer to decide for herself whether a rumor's worth pursuing?"

"Be careful with that tone. I won't be disrespected in my own store."

"My bad. I'm sorry." I placed my hands on the counter. "I'm frustrated."

"Apology accepted. I get where you're coming from. The thing is, over the years, I've been hurt by rumors. If you want verification, talk to Drunk Paul. I overheard him talking about it."

That gave me pause. Paul could be the cover model for the Unreliable Narrator Club. In my view, the circumstances hadn't changed, though.

Oliver had to be the murderer. How could he not be? It was like I was making a Suspect Stew and all of the ingredients pointed at him. Since Goob wasn't going to report the fight, and nobody else evidently had, I'd do it. Then, I'd do my research on the shell companies.

Figuring out who took Desiree's life and figuring out who was ripping off Goob was going to be quite the pair of achievements. Was it really going to be as straightforward as it seemed? Probably not, but one could hope.

CHAPTER THIRTY-TWO

BACK IN MY rental, I texted a recap of Goob's story to the chief. My old friend had a point. Rumors sprung up like weeds in Paradise Springs. If she thought the information was worth pursuing, she'd get back with me.

After all, she was the cop, not me.

I had a business to run. Two, to be precise. I didn't want to run two businesses. I'd gotten comfortable removing critters from spots they weren't supposed to be in. If I was going to be honest with myself, though, years of squeezing through attics, crawl spaces, and other cramped areas had left my back, shoulders, and knees aching more often than I wanted to admit.

Expectations were only going to go up at the Sea Breeze. My days of ignoring my new investment had to end.

Where did that leave me?

In control. That's where it left me. Just like I was taking the initiative in Desiree's case, I needed to take the initiative with my own life. With a nod to myself in the rearview mirror, I dialed Cronenberg.

Five minutes later, I had a meeting scheduled with the man to discuss his interest in Elmo's Critter Removal. There was no way I was going to *strategically align* with him. What

I planned on doing was sussing out how badly he wanted to get his hands on my company. Once I knew that, I'd decide how to respond.

One thing was certain. I wasn't going to leave Jordan dangling in the wind. He'd proven himself an excellent partner. He deserved better than to be caught up in a takeover where he'd be little more than an employee with some random ID number.

I was waiting my turn to exit the marina parking lot when Craig's gold SUV passed me going the other way. Had he been notified that Desiree's multitool was found on his property? More critical than that, did he know that one of his employees was looking more and more like suspect number one in the LaFontaine murder case?

There was one way to find out.

I pulled a U-turn, shouting apologies at motorists whose lengthy honks let me know they didn't appreciate my impromptu maneuver. Unlike Jim Rockford and other intrepid TV private eyes, who made amazing moves at the drop of a hat, I had to turn the truck, stop, put it in reverse, and turn again, twice before I completed the U-turn.

So much for my own starring role in *The Simpson Files*.

Lucky for me, Craig wasn't hard to find. He was parked in a spot near his ticket office. Confronting him again would get me nowhere. I was too close to a breakthrough to blow things up by getting ahead of myself. Instead, I parked close enough to keep an eye on him but not so close that he could see me. I patted the steering wheel. In a weird twist of fate, being in a rental made me less recognizable.

It only took a second for a plan to come to mind. It seemed safe and even plausible. *Safe* and *plausible*, two words that often didn't go together in the Springs. Oh well, at least I had an idea.

Craig was still in his SUV when I got out of my truck. I pretended to scroll through my phone while I waited for his door to open. The plan was to catch him right after he'd exited the vehicle and give him the news.

A bead of sweat had trickled down my forehead and reached the bridge of my nose when the man finally emerged. He was holding his phone to his ear with one hand. In the other, he was holding a suit jacket. Which was a little odd, since he was wearing a short-sleeved dress shirt.

With his attention on other things, he didn't notice me. Which was good, I suppose, because that way he wasn't able to see me grimace at his fashion choices. I was no Ralph Lauren, but I had my standards. One of which was that a suit jacket required a long-sleeved shirt, regardless of the temperature.

I had almost caught up to him when he shoved his phone into a pocket. With a growl, he shrugged into the jacket. A patch of white on his upper arm flashed in the sunlight, then was gone, covered by the linen blazer.

A few thoughts ran through my mind. Was he trying to quit smoking by wearing a nicotine patch? No, the size was wrong. Was it a bandage covering up a surgical procedure or injury? That seemed way more likely. I tabled the question as I came up alongside him.

"Hey, Craig. Did you hear the news?" I left my greeting

nebulous to see how he'd react.

"What news?" He glanced at me with furrowed eyebrows.

The response seemed genuine. Or, he was a skilled liar. I decided to give him the benefit of the doubt.

"Someone found Desiree's multitool in the trash can behind your trailer. Apparently, nobody even knew it was missing."

He didn't break his stride. The only physical response was a small shrug. "Good, I guess."

"Yeah, well, you see, it went missing about the same time the vandalism spree started. Now that it's been found, hopefully that means the vandalism problem is over. You wouldn't happen to have a surveillance camera that points in the direction of the trash can, would you?"

"I don't. The only one I have covers the customer service desk. Sorry I can't be of more help."

We were almost to the trailer. So far, the conversation had gone about as how I had predicted. It was time to set my trap.

"I know you're busy. The thing is, there are rumors going around town that Oliver's the one who left the multitool in the trash can. And that he's the one who was behind all the vandalism." I grasped him by the arm, right around where the patch or bandage or whatever it was, and gave a quick squeeze. "I thought you should know."

"Hey." He swatted my hand away from his arm and took a step back. Someone wearing a nicotine patch wouldn't react like that. It had to be something that made the area sensitive, like a rash or an injury. "Keep your hands off of me."

"Sorry. This is important, Craig. Word gets around this town faster than a dolphin can swim. If people hear your righthand man's responsible for a lot of property damage, that will blow back on you. Believe me, I know all too well the challenges of dealing with staff behavior, even when they're off the clock."

Actually, I didn't know anything about that. Jordan was an absolute joy to work with. Now, sometimes my own off-the-clock behavior could get a little cringeworthy, but that was a different matter entirely.

Craig looked from me to the trailer, now only ten yards away. He drummed the fingers of his right hand on this thigh. He probably didn't want to leave Oliver hung out to dry. If for no other reason than that would leave him more shorthanded than ever.

"Look, man, I know this has got to be tough. You brought Oliver with you from Houston. I'm sure there's a sense of loyalty between the two of you. The vandalism might be the tip of the iceberg, though."

"What do you mean?" He stepped toward me. I had his attention now.

"Evidence is pointing to Oliver as Desiree's murderer. He hated her for years. When you hired her, that was the second time he lost a job to her."

"Wait." He chewed on his lip for a moment. "Are you saying what I think you're saying?"

The man was clever. I was walking a tightrope and

wasn't going to fall into his trap by putting words into his mouth.

"All I'm saying is that there's a lot of circumstantial evidence that makes things look bad for him. It wouldn't surprise me if the police have him at the station right now. If you know something, anything, you need to tell them." I stopped for a beat, then set the hook. "I know Chief Eikenberry. She's smart and she's unrelenting. You don't want to get yourself caught up in this."

"Huh. Thanks for the heads-up, Mr. Simpson. You've given me a lot to think about." He shook my hand, then headed for his office. As he entered the building, he rubbed his arm where I'd grabbed him.

I returned to my truck. On my way, I had a light bulb moment that literally knocked me off-balance. I mean, I actually stumbled for a few steps as the epiphany took hold.

I had to get home. Finally, the pieces were, like a line of computer code, slotting into place. I was sure the research into Goob's deadbeat tenant would fill in any missing components.

CHAPTER THIRTY-THREE

I ARRIVED HOME to find Oscar on the patio. He was lounging in his favorite chair, enjoying the conditions. That wasn't a surprise. He was a Florida cat, born and bred in the semitropical environs of the Panhandle. As such, he tolerated the heat much better than me.

My closest friends knew this. When Rambo, Wendell, or Nic stopped by and I wasn't home, they'd use the hidden key to let him out. He was never lacking for food or drink inside, so it wasn't a matter of making sure he was okay. It was making sure he was happy.

My friends liked me. They loved my cat.

The surprise was the person sitting next Oscar, stroking his spine with the greatest of care.

"Paul. What brings you by my humble abode?" Between his battered bike leaning against the trailer and his affectionate treatment of Oscar, one would have thought his visit was commonplace. In fact, the man had never set foot on my property for as long as I'd lived in Paradise Springs.

"Hey, Elmo." He waved with his free hand, but kept his attention riveted on Oscar. "I like your cat. He's really nice."

Given the man's skittish nature, and the unpleasant ending to our most recent encounter, there was no way under the blazing July sun he was here simply to hang out. He wanted something. Since Oscar was outside, he must have talked to someone close to me before coming here.

Either that, or the spot where I hid my key had become a matter of common knowledge around town. Lucky me.

I put my hand on a chair but didn't pull it out. The man's flight instinct kicked into overdrive at the slightest provocation. Even though he was here of his own volition, it didn't mean he wouldn't bolt if he got the sense I was pressuring him.

"Mind if I join you two?"

"Go ahead." He slid the door key across the table toward me. "Miss Nicola said I should come talk to you. She told me where I could find the key."

Well, at least the key's location wasn't common knowledge. Yet.

"What do you want to talk about?"

"Desiree." With his free hand, he picked at his scalp. It wasn't the behavior of someone bothered by a mosquito bite. There was something deeper at play.

"Sure. We can talk about her. Would you like a glass of water?"

He nodded, then turned his attention back to Oscar.

I returned a few minutes later with a serving tray. There were two pint glasses filled with ice, a pitcher of cold water, and bowl of cashews for the humans. I also had a bowl of water and some kitty treats for Oscar.

It would be a criminal act to ask my cat to go without.

Paul drained half of his water in one go. After that, he

downed a handful of the nuts, then finished the glass. I refilled it. This troubled man had something important to say. I wasn't going to get out of him by force, though.

After a second glass of water, he leaned back in his chair and closed his eyes.

"In high school, I had a crush on Desiree. You probably know that since you're trying to find her killer."

Now that he was opening up, I didn't want to risk him getting off track. I kept my response simple. "Yeah."

"It hurt a lot, the way she turned me into a big, fat joke. It still hurts." He took another drink, using both hands to keep the glass steady. "I got counseling along with physical therapy after the accident. It helped me a lot. I made my peace with Desiree then."

"Good for you. Therapy helped me." One of the things I'd learned during my inpatient stay after my breakdown was the importance of active listening and demonstrating empathy. I could only hope I was doing it right with the man sitting across from me.

He pursed his lips as he looked at me. "I didn't know that. Something we've got in common, I guess. Anyway, I never really got over her. My counselor told me that's the way it is with your first love."

My first love was Faith Klein, a girl I met in in my high school American Literature class. We went out for a few weeks. She dumped me when a baseball player asked her out. Right after high school graduation, she ran off to Las Vegas to work with an Elvis impersonator in his magic show. The last I knew, she was working at a dolphin show in Miami and was on her third marriage.

In retrospect, I dodged a bullet when she dumped me. Big-time. I wasn't as sure as Paul was about not getting over your first love. Now wasn't the time to argue with him, though.

"I knew it was stupid, but even when I was done with therapy, I kept an eye out for Desiree. That Darrin dude's bad news and I didn't want her to get hurt."

The mention of Bobby Darrin set off alarm bells in my head. Now we were getting to heart of the action.

"I knew Desiree and her boss were meeting Nicola at the Magnificent Marlin the night she was killed. I also knew Darrin wasn't in New Orleans like he told his aunts, so I thought I'd hang around to see if he showed up there."

"Did you have anything in mind?"

He shook his head. "No. I mean, I knew all about the thing with her car. I heard stories she wasn't happy working for her new boss. Something seemed off to me. I don't know. I guess I thought if there was trouble, I could help her out."

Holy moly, had Paul actually witnessed Desiree's murder? I put my hands around the arms of my chair to keep myself from making any sudden moves.

"You saw something that night. What did you see?"

"I saw Miss Nicola leave. Then I saw her boss leave. When I didn't see Desiree leave, I went to have a drink at the Boar's Head."

I shuddered. The Boar's Head was a dive bar with a capital *D*. The clapboard structure a stone's throw from Rattlesnake Swamp was home to the roughest, meanest crowd in the county. The only vehicles allowed in the place's parking lot were motorcycles and pickup trucks. There was a flagpole in front of the joint. The lone banner that ever flew from it was the Jolly Roger. I made a mental note to ask Paul why he went to such a scary place. At another time.

"You went back to the Marlin, didn't you?"

"Yeah. On my way there, a gold SUV passed me going the other way."

Gold SUV? It had to be Craig's. "What time was this?"

"I don't know. Around closing time. I left when the bartender made last call."

In general, closing time for bars and nightclubs in Florida was no later than two A.M. During the offseason, the Paradise Springs watering holes closed earlier. This time of year, they kept the doors open as late as possible. That meant Craig was out and about in the vicinity of the crime scene.

Well within the window of Desiree's death.

"Did you tell the cops? I heard they talked to you." That was a nice way of putting things since some people, me included, had Paul on their suspect board. Had I been wrong to dismiss him? Was he here to confess?

No. That didn't make sense. At the very least, Nic wouldn't have sent him to me under those circumstances. She looked out for her fellow Paradise Springs Old Guard members with the fierceness of a mama bear protecting her cubs. She didn't tolerate criminal activity, though.

Well, 99 percent of the time she didn't. If a law was broken in the pursuit of justice, then she was a little more flexible. That's what I've heard.

Paul tossed a handful of the cashews into his mouth. His gaze darted to the left, then to the right as he chewed. He didn't get out of his chair, though. If I'd triggered an increase in his anxiety, at least he was keeping it under some degree of control.

After swallowing, and another long drink, he sniffed and looked at me. If was the first time we made eye contact.

"Yeah, Chief Eikenberry talked to me a couple of days after they found her. She was nice. Said she needed to because of my past with Desiree and since people saw me at the Marlin that night."

That sounded like Susan. She knew how to connect with people. Meet them on their terms. It built trust. It didn't change the fact she'd use her lightning-quick reflexes to put you someone the ground if needed, though.

"Did the gold SUV come up during your conversation?"

"No. I didn't think about it then. Sometimes, my memory's a little fuzzy. It's been that way ever since the accident."

I kept my expression neutral. His evasive answer worried me. Paul's failure to share this information could be a problem.

"I get it. It can be tough talking to the cops. It's easy to get nervous." I rubbed my hands together. "And then, when you're nervous, it's tough to keep things straight. When did you remember seeing the SUV?"

"Day before yesterday. I was down by the marina and saw it. That's when it came back to me."

"Have you told the chief?"

"No. I'm afraid to." He banged his fist on the tabletop hard enough to send Oscar scurrying away. "I know what people think about me. What they call me. If I go to her now, the chief will think I lied to her. I don't want to go to jail."

Tears welled up in the poor guy's eyes. I couldn't imagine the battles he fought simply get from one day to the next. This added pressure on him must have been suffocating. To his credit, though, he hadn't shut his mouth and pretended it never happened.

"Instead of going to the police, you went to Nic, right? And she told you to come see me."

"Yeah." He wiped his eyes with the hem of his tank top. "She said you'd know what to do. And I won't get in trouble."

I'd been taking the wrong path with my investigation. And I was pretty sure I knew which new direction to take. I refilled Paul's glass.

"Thank you for coming to see me. I do know what to do. And I promise that you won't get in any trouble."

The man's smile made me feel like I was ten feet tall. Of course, I still had to make good on my promise. And do it before Paul, or anyone else, found themselves in danger.

CHAPTER THIRTY-FOUR

I SENT PAUL on his way after filling a plastic grocery bag with ham and cheese sandwiches and a few other things from my pantry. It was the least I could do for the poor soul. Despite his troubles, and there were a handful of them, he wanted to do the right thing. I could totally respect that.

The rest of the day passed by in a research-fueled blur. While I searched for the identities of Goob's mystery tenant and associates, Oscar kept busy by giving himself a bath, then taking a nap.

During my tech days, I learned a lot about shell companies and how they can protect business interests. There were a lot of honest reasons for using them, including tax benefits and liability protections. Shoot, I'd had my lawyer create a shell company I could roll both the resort and the critter removal business into.

There were reasons that were not so aboveboard. Like using shell and dummy companies to launder money. And to make it darn near impossible to figure out who were the faces behind the companies that were screwing Goob over.

It was eleven o'clock when I finally struck gold. My vision was bleary. My neck ached and my tailbone was sore from working in the same position for hours on end. The sense of satisfaction that my hunch was right was *so* worth it, though.

"Oscar, I believe we have our murderer." I woke him by rubbing both of his ears. He responded to the unwanted attention by chomping down on my finger. He was an expert at keeping me grounded.

To make up for the indiscretion, I gave him a half dozen kitty treats. Then I called Rambo. To apprehend the murderer, I was going to need a little help from my friends.

"This better be good, Simpson. *Roman Holiday* just came on, and I haven't seen it in ages." Rambo's tone had the menace of a great white shark hunting in bloody water. You didn't mess with him when it came to his beloved classic movies.

"Want to help me catch Desiree's murderer?" Sometimes bold and blunt was the best way to deal with my friend.

There was an intake of breath from the other end of the connection. A moment later, the background noise from the TV stopped. I had his attention.

"What do you want me to do?" Thank goodness for friends. Especially the ones who weren't afraid of getting into a little good trouble.

"Meet me at Goob's at seven tomorrow morning." I explained my plan. Even though it was rough around the edges, he promised he was all in. He wanted to get back to his movie, though.

"You're sure you don't mind making the phone call?"

"Not since it's for Desiree. We done?"

"Don't you want to know how I figured it out?"

"Nah. I trust you. Now, I gotta go before I miss more of the movie. Audrey Hepburn's a gift to cinema."

With Rambo on hand, all would be well. Unless the murderer pulled a gun on me. Which wasn't out of the realm of possibility.

So, I called Spock.

"I heard there may be some trouble at the marina tomorrow morning. It's about the LaFontaine case. A protest or something like that. You might want to be there in case things get heated."

"Really? I haven't heard anything. Do you know more?"

I wanted to let him in on the whole thing. That wouldn't be a good idea, though. If things went sideways, and there was still a chance it might, I didn't want any blowback to fall on him.

"That's it, I'm afraid. I don't know the people who were talking about it. I thought you should know."

"No problem. I'll take care of it." Spock cleared his throat. For some reason I got the sense he was standing a little taller at the moment. "Thank you for your support of the Paradise Springs Police Department."

I had one more phone call to make. Nic deserved to know what was going on, too.

The hour was late, so I went straight to the reason for the call. Not long ago, the two of us had worked amazingly well together bringing a murderer to justice. I didn't want to do this without giving her a chance to be a part of it again.

Especially since she never got a chance to reconcile with Desiree. And had to deal with being taken to the police station for questioning. Yeah, Nic deserved to help send the murderer to jail.

"There won't be nearly as much of a chance of bodily injury or property damage this time around. I promise. You'll know when to play your part and you'll be done in plenty of time for your morning cruise."

"Count me in. You sure you can pull this off?"

"Oh, I'll pull it off. Don't worry." I ended the call. Sounding confident for my girlfriend's benefit was one thing. Having confidence in myself? That was another thing entirely. I was pretty sure I'd worked out all the details. There was always a chance that I'd missed something important.

Well, I'd find out soon enough. For better or for worse.

CHAPTER THIRTY-FIVE

U NDER A CLOUDLESS sky, with Michael Franti and Spearhead's "Brighter Day" coming from the speakers, I drove to the marina. My spirits were high and my confidence unwavering. Mostly.

Despite my worries from the night before, I'd slept like a rock. I took that as a sign I was on the right track. Now, all I needed was for the positive vibes to carry me through the next few hours.

Well, I was going to need more than positive vibes to corral a killer, but I'd take all the upbeat energy I could gather. That was why I gave Oscar some shredded beef for breakfast. It was his favorite meal. If it earned me magical kitty bonus points, I was happy to take them and cash them right back in.

Rambo was sitting on a stool at Goob's dining counter, munching on a Belgian waffle with strawberries and chatting with the proprietor when I arrived. I waved and took a spot next to Rambo.

"Waldo's been telling me your plan. Can I help?" The man placed a bowl of grits and a bottle of maple syrup in front of me.

"This is plenty helpful right here. I have one thing. First, though, I have news."

I handed the man a small stack of pages I'd printed out. Between breaks Goob needed to take to attend to other customers, I led him through the ownership maze that had been created to rip him off. Rambo let out a low growl when I was through.

Goob wiped his glasses on his apron. "What you're telling me is that the firm renting the lot from me and the so-called agency that Abbott's renting the lot from fall under the umbrella of another company."

In unison, Rambo and I nodded.

"And that the same person's in charge of all three companies."

Again, we nodded.

"And that person's Craig Abbott."

Rambo patted me on the back while I nodded yet again. "That's solid work, my man."

"Abbott's got business interests all along the Gulf Coast. He's got dozens of companies, all with different names, locations, you name it. He takes money from some of them, transfers the cash through others, and eventually ends up with all of it. From what I could find, nobody's caught up with him."

"Until now." Rambo balled one hand into a fist and smacked it into the palm of his other hand.

Goob put a hand on Rambo's fist and pushed it down until it was against the counter. "Two questions. How did you figure out where the money goes and what do I do next?"

"The less you know about the answer to the first question, the better. As for the second question, I'd like you to phone in a tip to Clarice at the *Palladium*." I gave him enough details for the call to be convincing.

Rambo let out a laugh reminiscent of a roll of thunder. "Nice touch, Elmo. Gotta give you credit. You think of everything."

I shrugged. My friend's comment was humbling. In fact, there were probably any number of things I hadn't thought of. At this point, all I could do was hope I hadn't overlooked anything critical.

At the appointed time, Rambo and I got up to leave. When I dropped a couple of twenties on the counter, Goob pushed them back in my direction.

"To show my appreciation for all of your research work. Now I'll finally be able to get my rent money."

I waved the bills away. "Let's put a pin in that for now. There's still work to be done."

When we were outside the diner, Rambo scratched his beard. "Tell me the play one more time."

"Craig should be down by his boats checking people in. Online reviews like the fact that he personally welcomes people onto the company's morning trips. I'm going to confront him there. Oliver should be at the trailer. Make sure he doesn't make a break for it."

"If he does?" Rambo gave me a predatory smile that would have made one of this gators proud.

"Stop him and bring him to me." I held up my index finger. "But don't hurt him. I don't want you getting in any trouble."

After giving me a friendly punch on the arm that would leave a bruise, he strode off. Now it was up to me. I marched toward the section of the marina where Craig's vessels were docked, confident the previous evening's research would pay off.

Upon my arrival, I allowed myself a smile. There was a line of customers ten deep. At the head of the line, Craig was scanning tickets. A look over my shoulder confirmed Spock was on the scene. I gave him a nod then looked the other way. Nic was on her boat, sitting in a camp chair, pretending to read a book. From time to time, she'd raise her head and survey the scene with a spyglass.

Showtime.

I got in the queue. Only a few more minutes now.

"Ticket, please?" Craig didn't look up until I clamped my hand around his injured arm. He gritted his teeth. "Hey, what do you think you're doing?"

"I want to get a look under that bandage on your arm. I think it's connected to Desiree LaFontaine's murder."

A bead of sweat trickled down the side of his face as he yanked his arm free. "We've talked about this, Mr. Simpson. I don't know who killed her. Now, please step aside."

"If you've got nothing to hide, let me see your arm." I took a look around. People were gathering around us, eager to find out what the fuss was all about.

"You're crazy. Move along or I'll have you removed."

"I don't think so. You've been hiding that injury since the night you murdered her." A murmur ran through the crowd. "Desiree learned about the schemes you're running. Your move to buy out Nicola Beecham's company was the final straw. That night, after the meeting with Nic, she told you she was going to go public with what she knew, the money laundering, the vandalism, everything."

He shook his head. There was fear in his eyes, though.

"You convinced her to take the conversation outside. She agreed. When you couldn't convince her to come around to your side, things escalated. She feared for her safety, so she drew her multitool's knife on you. When you stabbed her, she cut your arm defending herself."

"This is insane. You have absolutely no proof."

The crowd's attention was focused on the two of us. Nobody was in a rush to board the craft. Spock had drawn within twenty feet.

"I do, too." It was a childish response, but it felt so good to say it. "Everyone who works here on the marina has their own multitool. You stabbed Desiree with yours, then dumped it in a trash can later, thinking the garbage collector would pick it up and it would never turn up again."

"But, but..." Sweat was pouring down his face now. "She was stabbed with a harpoon."

"You did that, once you realized what you'd done. The stab wound to her chest wasn't fatal. The one to her arm was. You cut an artery. The axillary, I think it's called. I'll give you credit, swiping the harpoon right off the barroom's wall was a gutsy move. By the time you drove it into her heart, she was already a goner."

He backed away from me. If he was looking for an escape

route, his options were limited. Water was to one side, the boat was behind him, the crowd continued to grow. Some folks had their phones out, no doubt livestreaming the whole thing.

Paradise Springs did love a spectacle. Accusing someone of murder in the middle of a crowd on a Friday morning checked pretty much every box in the definition of *spectacle*.

"You're upset over your friend. I understand that. Maybe what you're saying is true. You've got no proof I was involved in any way, though. I'm a businessperson, not a murderer."

Craig was right. It was all circumstantial. When you put enough circumstantial evidence together, though, the picture was pretty damning.

"I have to disagree. You see, I have an eyewitness who saw your SUV leaving the area around the time Desiree was murdered. It was spotted not far from where the murder weapon was found." I shook my head. "That gold ride of yours is impossible to miss, even at two in the morning."

"Move aside, people. Coming through." A gruff voice quieted a portion of the crowd. Not surprising since it belonged to Rambo. He was pushing his way through the crowd.

And using Oliver King as his battering ram.

"Hey, Elmo." Rambo gave me a nod. One of Oliver's arms was pinned behind his back, held in place by my friend's massive right hand. "Look what I caught. He was trying to sneak away when word reached the trailer about your little conversation going on here."

Oliver tried wriggling out of Rambo's grasp. The attempt was futile. My friend was the strongest person I'd ever seen.

In the split second my attention was diverted from him, Craig knocked me to the ground with a roundhouse punch. By the time I got to my feet, he'd bulled his way through the crowd and had taken off at a full sprint.

I started after him, anger and adrenaline fueling my pursuit. Getting slugged in the jaw was one of the possibilities I hadn't thought of.

As I skirted a light pole, Nic came into view. Without breaking stride, I pointed toward the crowd. "Take over. Get the customers on their boats."

She responded with a thumbs-up and headed back toward the water. Her acknowledgment gave me more fuel for the pursuit.

We were nearing the end of the marina when Craig looked over his shoulder. I'd cut his lead down from fifty yards down to twenty. My thighs started to burn when, at the same moment, the wails of police sirens filled the air.

Remembering the training for my race against the chief, I dug deep. The gap narrowed until he was almost within my reach. I extended my arm and readied myself to make a tackle. Before I could make my move, he cut to the left, abandoning the level ground of the marina's parking area for the sand of the adjoining beach.

Craig's change in direction cost me a few steps. Then, the fundamentals from weeks spent running on the beach came back to me. I shortened my stride and focused on landing on my forefeet. In no time, I had my quarry back within my grasp.

Up ahead, the Magnificent Marlin loomed large on the right. Craig angled toward it.

"Gotcha," I yelled as I lunged for him. The sugar boost from breakfast propelled me through the air like a cat leaping to capture a bird.

My shoulder rammed into his back. I wrapped my arms around him. We crashed to the beach with a *thud*. My back took the blunt of the blow and knocked the wind out of me.

Stunned for the moment, I lost my grip. Craig pushed himself off of me, throwing a handful of sand in my face in the process. I got up on one knee, desperate to see which way he'd gone. I didn't need to look far, though.

A mere fifteen feet from me, Craig lay facedown on the sand. A woman in red was towering over him. She had planted a red shoe with a five-inch heel firmly in the center of his back. Another woman, this one dressed in green, had a scarf in her hands and was bending down to tie his legs together. A third woman, sporting a dark blue sundress, had her cell phone to her ear.

I stood. Sand covered me from head to toe and had wormed its way into my nose, my ears, and other orifices I didn't want to think about. Didn't matter. Desiree's murderer wasn't going anywhere.

Cheryl gave me a wave after giving her knot a final pull. "Good morning, Elmo. My sisters and I just happened to be out for our morning stroll on the beach when we saw you tackling Mr. Abbott." She winked at me. "What a coincidence, eh?"

"Um, yeah. Coincidence." The odds of these mysterious women just happening to be in the right place at the right time were astronomical. Maybe even mystical. Especially taking Beryl's outfit into account. I mean, who goes for a walk on the beach in high heels? "Thanks for your help."

"You murdered that poor girl, didn't you?" Beryl pressed her heel into his injured arm. Her lip curled in a way that sent a shiver down my spine when he let out a yelp. She stepped away from him, only to bend down and flick him on the ear.

"Are you women insane?" He spit out a mouthful of sand. "I'll sue you for unlawful imprisonment."

Meryl put her phone in a pocket of her blazer. "Do yourself a favor. Confess to this nice man right now. It will save you a lot of trouble later on."

Craig looked at me. The panic in his eyes was unmistakable. He licked his lips, then spat out some sand.

I got out my phone and started recording. "You killed Desiree. You tried to frame Nic. You tried to kill me when you shot at my truck."

The corner of his lip curled up. He spit at me in a final act of defiance. Then, the act of bravado collapsed and a tear ran down his cheek.

"I didn't mean to. Things got out of hand. Desiree wouldn't play ball. I had no choice. When she took out her knife, I got mine out. At first, it felt like a game. I made a few threats and started poking at her. She tried to knock my knife away and stabbed me in the arm. I slashed at her. The next thing I knew, she'd collapsed and was bleeding all over the place. Why wouldn't she play ball?"

When it became clear that was all he was going to say, Cheryl took my hand in hers and brushed sand from it. "Think of this as us returning a favor. For all you did for our dear Bobby. I think it's time we moved on, sisters."

I was too winded to ask what exactly I'd done for their nephew. Instead, I shrugged and waved as they walked away. It seemed like the safest move. Who knew? Maybe they really were witches. I couldn't count out the possibility. Not in Paradise Springs.

A moment later, Spock came scrambling down the sandy embankment. In his haste to reach us, he fell to his knees and was covered in almost as much sand as me when he reached us.

"Don't move. You're under arrest." He pulled out his service revolver and pointed it at Craig.

"Um." I looked at the man, who was still facedown on the sand with his legs bound. "I don't think he's going anywhere, Officer Nimoy."

"Right." His Adam's apple bobbed up and down, then he looked over his shoulder, as if unsure what he should do next. "Um."

"I bet the chief would be happy to find out the suspect has been read his rights and handcuffed by the time she arrives. I've got his confession on my phone."

I took a step back and blew out a deep, cleansing breath. The sun was shining. The ocean waters were calm. My work was done. Thanks to a lot of help from my friends, some-how, I'd done it again.

Getting things done with friends. Not a bad way to go through life.

CHAPTER THIRTY-SIX

"HEY, ELMO. TOSS me a beer, I'm parched." Rambo was standing over the grill at the aft end of Nic's personal boat. The spatula he was holding in one of his giant hands looked like a toy. At least his KISS THE COOK apron fit. The frills on it were a little much, though.

With a chuckle, I dug through a cooler until I found one of my friend's favorites, an ice-cold bottle of Abita Brewery's Purple Haze beer. "Isn't this your third already? No offense, but you're not the best at drunk grilling."

"Got a hot date later, so I'm sticking to water. I can take over." Jordan tried to hip check Rambo out of the way, only to lose his balance and end up on his backside.

"Or not." I suppressed a laugh while I helped him back to his feet. He would have had more success forcing an elephant aside.

Rambo patted his belly. "No offense, kid. I've been serving as Miss Nicola's Fourth of July grill master for years now. Besides, I've got a teeny bit more mass to absorb the alcohol than the common man, like your boss here."

"Common man?" I raised my voice in fake outrage. "I caught Desiree's murderer. And cracked the case of the Great Vandalism Spree of 2024. Or have you all forgotten the service I provided to our community?"

"Oh, good golly, here we go," Seven said. She went to Jordan's side and slipped her arm around his waist.

"I know, right?" He leaned against her. "It's been *I caught Desiree's murderer* this. And *I cracked the vandalism ring* that. And *I blah blah blah* nonstop for the last week. My ears are getting worn out."

"Have you tried turning those ears of yours inside out? With all the other tricks you can do with that freakish body of yours, you should try that," Goob said, then took a sip from his mason jar. It was filled with a sprig of mint, ice, and a clear liquid he refused to identify. All he would say about it was that it was a secret family recipe.

We all laughed at the suggestion, even Jordan. I'd been so pleased when he accepted my invitation to join us on Nic's boat for a cookout and to watch the fireworks.

"Wait a minute." Rambo turned over a half dozen chicken fillets, then turned to Jordan. "Is your date tonight with Seven?"

"Yeah, man. Who did you think it was with?" Jordan sat up a little straighter and smiled. The fact that he had plans with the most sought-after bachelorette in Paradise Springs had been a major boost to his self-image. A well-deserved one, too. I couldn't be happier for the guy.

"Well, *I* didn't know." Rambo stuck his lower lip out. "Nobody tells me anything around here."

"Don't feel bad, big guy." Seven gave our chef a peck on the cheek. "Outside the people on this boat, the only other person who knows is my pops. It's not like we're boyfriend and girlfriend. We're just friends."

The answer, and more likely the kiss, seemed to satisfy the big guy. He gave her a quick hug, then turned his attention back to the grill so he could turn the asparagus and flip the tuna steaks.

"Speaking of girlfriends, where is your lovely better half, Elmo?" Goob grabbed himself a handful of peanuts from a table laden with snacks.

"She's in her cabin. Another interview." I sipped my Irish whiskey on the rocks. Part of me felt bad about the role I played in making Nic busier than ever. The other part was happy that the size of her fleet had increased exponentially in the matter of hours.

Goob shook his head. "I still can't believe she actually marched down to the marina and basically took control of Craig's business."

"Neither can I." Nic emerged from below deck. She was smiling. "Those steaks ready yet, Rambo? I just hired an operations manager and am finally ready to kick back."

"Yes, ma'am. And I made sure to put those abominations Elmo brought on the other side of the grill so they wouldn't cross-contaminate." He handed her a plate with a tuna steak and hearty helping of asparagus.

"Chicken fillets are not abominations." I took my place at the end of line to be served. "Y'all know how I feel about seafood."

"Yeah, we do. Wrong." Nic put some hush puppies Seven had brought onto her plate. "Especially on a boat."

Everyone laughed, even me. It was like the old saying

went, when you laughed at yourself, the world laughed with you. Or, in my case, your friends laughed with you.

We settled down to partake in a wonderful feast to celebrate America's Independence Day holiday. While we ate, Nic gave everyone an update on her takeover of Craig's business. She'd faced choppy waters for the first day or so. Once it was clear Craig and Oliver weren't returning to duty, the situation smoothed out.

She got an assist from the folks at the *Palladium*. Clarice wrote a glowing piece about the lengths Nic went to make sure all scheduled tours were held, and nobody lost their job. I couldn't help wondering if part of the reason Nic was the subject of such a friendly article was because Clarice had been on the scene to witness firsthand how Nic stepped in to calm the confused and upset tourists.

Goob had completed his assignment perfectly.

While I was getting my second sandwich, Jordan cleared his throat.

"I'm still confused. Craig murdered Desiree because she was going to spill the beans about all the shady stuff he had going on. Is that right?"

Rambo, Nic, Goob, and I nodded.

"Then what was Oliver's role? He seemed pretty harmless when he came into the restaurant," Seven said. "Good tipper, too."

I took a sip of my whiskey. Truth be told, I felt kind of bad for Oliver. In his desire to prove himself a Man of the Sea, he got himself mixed up in a criminal enterprise he couldn't get out of. My sympathy didn't go far, though. He was an adult, after all.

"First off, Spock told me this in confidence, so don't tell anyone else."

Nic let out a little huff. "Some secret keeper you are."

"Ignore her," Seven said. "Well, don't ignore her. She's your girlfriend, after all. You know what I mean. Proceed, please." She stuck her tongue out at Nic, who returned the gesture with a raised glass.

"Oliver had been working for Craig at the company's headquarters in Galveston. When Craig announced plans to expand, Oliver suggested Paradise Springs and tossed his hat in the ring to be the chief of operations. Apparently, he thought he could put his old contacts to good use."

"Not that he had any." Nic popped a hush puppy in her mouth and shook her head.

"And that proved to be his problem. Without the promised contacts, Craig lost patience with him fast. Turns out, Craig was banking on Paradise Springs being a cash cow right out of the gate."

"So, that's why he hired Desiree," Goob said. "Is it true he was paying her twice what Miss Nicola was?"

"Spock didn't get that specific but bringing her on added overhead costs that put Craig in an even tighter bind when demand didn't meet the numbers Oliver promised."

Rambo raised his hand to speak and waited until I was finished. It was something his grandfather, the toughest person within three counties, taught him as a youngster. You didn't forget the lessons that Rambo's grandfather taught.

"I think I'm getting it now. Oliver didn't come through

on his promises. Business wasn't good enough. Hiring Desiree didn't help. Craig decided to take extraordinary measures. And made Oliver help him."

Jordan looked at Nic. "Did Oliver really steal your multitool and use it to do all that vandalism?"

"Most of it. Susan told me that herself. Since it's still an ongoing investigation, I couldn't get her to tell me anything else, though."

"How did it end up in Desiree's hand?" Goob adjusted his Tilley hat to protect his pink nose from the setting sun.

"That's where it gets complicated." I took another drink. "According to Spock, Oliver went to Craig with this harebrained idea where he'd steal Nic's multitool and use it in the vandalism scheme. He paid some college kid who was here on vacation to swipe it during a cruise. When they'd created enough havoc, they'd leave it someplace to implicate her."

"What a sweetheart." Nic pounded her fist into her palm.

I swallowed. I cared for my girlfriend more than anyone other than my mom. Still, sometimes she scared me.

"According to Spock, Oliver got cold feet when Craig gave him his final vandalism assignment, so Craig took the multitool. He had it on him that night and after Desiree died, he put in her hand. Then, he took Desiree's multitool. He gave it to Oliver and told him to get rid of it."

"That's complete idiocy." Seven went to the grill to get herself more asparagus. "Anyone with half a brain knows Nicola would never do something like that."

"Not to Desiree. Elmo, maybe. Depending on my level of aggravation." Nic glanced at me, then raised her eyebrows. I chuckled at the joke. At least, I thought it was a joke.

"It was a way to mislead the cops into investigating Nic," I said. "The bad publicity would make things even tougher on Nic. They didn't count on her taking the boat into the Gulf that night."

"Which proves they don't know you, my friend." Rambo served Nic a bowl of ice cream. Those who did know her were well aware that when she was really upset about something, she escaped to the water.

"Thank the stars above for small favors," Nic said.

After the group voiced their agreement, Jordan asked about the harpoon. "What was up with that?"

I shook my head. "All Spock would tell me was that someone took it from the beach bar's wall that night. Craig's not talking, but I think it was a way to make sure she was dead. He probably didn't realize the stab wound to her chest wasn't the fatal one."

The group sat in silence, picking at their plates as they absorbed the information. It was a scheme that got crazier as things spun out of control.

The money-laundering plot to rip off Goob was the tip of the iceberg, as other people had been victimized in the same fashion. Evidently, in an effort to save his own skin, Oliver had admitted to more vandalism than had been even reported to the police.

There were also rumblings of theft charges being added as companies that had sold Craig the boats and Jet Skis hadn't been paid.

It was a mess of Florida proportions. With all the moving parts and multiple parties involved, the police had been fairly tight-lipped about the case. My friends deserved to know what had really happened, though. They'd helped, after all.

"Gotta admit, I'm surprised Spock's been flapping his jaws about the case. It's not like him," Rambo said.

"That's because, as far as everyone who's not on this boat knows, Spock's the one who cracked the case. Officially, I was just doing him a solid by chasing down Craig for him." I dabbed some sunscreen on my nose. "Word is, he's up for a commendation."

"I can't believe the chief's going along with that." Jordan shook his head. "Come on, man. You figured it out. You deserve the credit. You're a hero, man."

The rest of the group nodded in agreement. While I appreciated the support, I was more than happy to let the authorities take the credit. It made Susan look good, which made me happy. It couldn't have been easy for her to confide in me. Letting her and her team bask in the glory once again was a good way to return the favor.

Besides, I'd achieved my goals. I'd helped prove Nic's innocence and found her multitool. Watching her break into a big smile when I told her about Craig's confession had been enough of a payment for me.

"Have they figured out who shot your truck?" Seven took a drink from her water bottle. "It can't be a coincidence that it happened while you were out being Mister Private Eye."

"It wasn't. They tested Craig's rifle after taking him into custody. The bullets that shot up the Paradise Springs sign match the bullet they found in my tire."

"So much for a boar hunter with bad aim, huh?" With a laugh, Rambo gave me a punch on the arm. Even though it was a friendly gesture, it would leave a bruise. Now, I'd have a matching pair.

"Yeah." I rubbed my chin. The stubble was a reminder that I hadn't bothered shaving in a few days. Too much going on in the aftermath of catching Craig. "It's kind of funny. The fact that a murderer tried to take me out made my mom feel better. She said it was a relief I wasn't the victim of a random act of violence that would never get solved."

"Speaking of which, how is life with your dear mother in town?" Nic leaned forward, and grinned. She'd been on the receiving end of my whining since Mom and her boyfriend arrived. They'd been sharing their vacation with me. Or, oversharing really, given the constant stream of text messages and social media posts on which I'd been tagged.

"Having the time of their lives. I got them settled at the Sea Breeze and they've been constantly on the go. With all the stuff they've been wanting to do, Gretchen's practically serving as their personal concierge making all the arrangements. Thank the stars above for that woman."

I didn't mention the guilt I was feeling about having Gretchen on my suspect list. I was going to keep that secret to myself until the day I died. At least I'd figured the case out before looking into her more extensively than I had. That would have made for some awkward moments.

"Speaking of stars." Goob pointed toward the darkening sky. "Fireworks will be going off soon."

Taking our cue from our old friend, we got busy clearing the remains of our feast from the deck.

Before long, we were seated in a semicircle, looking toward the Sea Breeze. The waves added a gentle rocking motion that was as soothing as a glass of Irish whiskey on a hot day. The resort, my resort, rose above the rest of my hometown like a protective big brother, looking out over everyone and everything else in the area.

Rambo played his harmonica for us while we waited for the show to start. The music was magical. The fireworks show began with a boom, painting the night sky in every color of the rainbow. I put my hands behind my head and relaxed for the first time in days.

I was among friends. All was well again. Shoot, even Bobby Darrin was out of trouble. Somehow, he'd managed to come up with the cash to pay his debt to Don Espada. My guess, it was the result of some behind-the-scenes maneuvering by his aunts. Whatever. The flake wasn't my problem anymore.

Though I still couldn't figure out how they made such a quick exit from the beach after helping me corral Craig. Beryl was in heels, for crying out load. In all honesty, it was probably a topic best left unexplored and instead left with the most obvious answer.

It was simply Paradise Springs, in all its wonderful weirdness, being Paradise Springs.

When the grand finale concluded, we all got to our feet and applauded. Nic headed to the bridge so she could pilot us back to town. Seven went along with her. Goob and Rambo looked at photos of the fireworks they'd taken with their phones. It made me happy to see them ooh and aah at each other's pics.

I sidled up to Jordan. He was staring out to sea.

"Crazy couple of weeks, huh, boss," he said.

"Truer words were never spoken. I can't thank you enough for all your hard work covering for me. And for your help with the case, too."

"We're a team, dude." He bumped my arm with his elbow. Lucky for me it wasn't in the spot Rambo had punched. "I'm glad I was there to help. Have you decided what you want to do about the Cronenberg dude?"

"As a matter of fact, I have." Jordan and I had discussed the topic at length over dinner and beers at the Riptide a few days prior. We came to the conclusion that I couldn't be a hands-on boss of Elmo's Critter Removal and run the Sea Breeze at the same time. Something was going to have to give.

"I hate to see a good thing come to an end. My gut tells me agreeing to his quote, strategic alignment, unquote, idea won't end well for you. I don't want that."

Jordan scratched a spot on his lower back. Without the aid of a back scratcher. "Thanks for looking out for me. What do you want to do?"

Paradise Springs was my town. It had been the source of more happiness than I could have ever imagined. I'd started a small business here. I'd bought a big one. I was helping Nic purchase Craig's inventory here in town, too.

Like they said in New Orleans, *laissez les bons temps rouler*. Let the good times roll. I draped an arm around Jordan's shoulder and pointed toward the stars with the other.

"I want to go big. Want to come along for the ride?"

The End

If you enjoyed *Murder Under the Marquee*,
you'll love the other books in the...

Elmo Simpson Mysteries series

Book 1: *Panic in the Panhandle*

Book 2: *Murder Under the Marquee*

Available now at your favorite online retailer!

Acknowledgements

Big time props go to my literary agent and friend, C.H. Armstrong, who's come along for this wacky Florida mystery ride with me. I also want to thank the amazing team at Tule Publishing, especially my editors Meghan Farrell, Cyndi Parent, Kelly Hunter, Nan Reinhardt, and Beth Attwood, for their amazing ability to take my somewhat coherent words and turn them into something I hope you enjoy. And of course, the wonderfully creative and talented folks in Tule's art department who have given me another fabulous cover.

I want to thank my wife, Nancy, for sticking by me all these years. A final shout out goes to my kids and their significant others. Shea, Echo, Aidan, and Lorianne – I hope your lives are filled with as much joy when you get to be my age as I am fortunate to experience. Love you all!

About the Author

J.C. Kenney is the bestselling author of The Allie Cobb Mysteries, The Darcy Gaughan Mysteries, and The Elmo Simpson Mysteries. He's also the co-host of The Bookish Hour webcast. When he's not writing, you can find him following IndyCar racing or listening to music. He has two grown children and lives in Indianapolis with his wife and a cat.

Thank you for reading

Murder Under the Marquee

If you enjoyed this book, you can find more from all our great authors at TulePublishing.com, or from your favorite online retailer.

TULE

www.ingramcontent.com/pod-product-compliance
Lightning Source LLC
Chambersburg PA
CBHW030643020726
47493CB00006B/1845